The 60s Reader

I like a little rebellion now and then. The spirit of resistance to government is so valuable on occasion that I wish it to be always kept alive. It will often be exercised when wrong, but better so than not to be exercised at all.

—THOMAS JEFFERSON

THE 60s READER

BY JAMES HASKINS
AND
KATHLEEN BENSON

VIKING KESTREL

VIKING KESTREL
Published by the Penguin Group
Viking Penguin Inc., 40 West 23rd Street, New York, New York 10010, U.S.A.
Penguin Books Ltd, 27 Wrights Lane, London W8 5TZ England
Penguin Books Australia Ltd, Ringwood, Victoria, Australia
Penguin Books Canada Ltd, 2801 John Street, Markham, Ontario, Canada L3R 1B4
Penguin Books (N.Z.) Ltd, 182–190 Wairau Road, Auckland 10, New Zealand

Penguin Books Ltd, Registered Offices: Harmondsworth, Middlesex, England

First published in 1988 by Viking Penguin Inc.
Published simultaneously in Canada

Printed in the United States of America
by Arcata Graphics, Fairfield, Pennsylvania
Set in Aster
Book design by Virginia I. Norey
1 2 3 4 5 92 91 90 89 88

Photograph credits:
Page 79: Copyright 1970, Valley Daily News, Tarentum, PA, John Filo.
All other photographs are courtesy of AP/Wide World Photos.
Pages v–vi constitute an extension of this copyright page.

Library of Congress Cataloging in Publication Data
Haskins, James, 1941–
The sixties reader.

1. United States—History—1961–1969—Sources.
2. United States—Social conditions—1960– —
Sources. I. Benson, Kathleen. II. Title.
E838.3.H37 1987 973.92 85-40886
ISBN 0-670-80674-9

PERMISSIONS

Grateful acknowledgment is made to the following for permission to reprint copyrighted material:

Andrews, McMeel & Parker: excerpts from the introduction to *The Black Messiah* by Albert B. Cleage. Copyright 1968, Sheed and Ward, Inc. Reprinted with permission of Andrews, McMeel & Parker. All rights reserved.

James Forman: excerpt from *The Making of Black Revolutionaries* by James Forman. Copyright by James Forman, 1972; published by Open Hand Publishing, Inc., 210 Seventh St. S.E., Washington, D.C. 20003.

Harper & Row, Publishers, Inc., and Joan Daves: abridgement of "Letter from Birmingham Jail, April 16, 1963" from *Why We Can't Wait* by Martin Luther King, Jr. Copyright © 1963 by Martin Luther King, Jr. Reprinted by permission of Harper & Row, Publishers, Inc.

Henry Holt and Company, Inc.: introduction to *Prison Journals of a Priest Revolutionary* by Philip Berrigan.
Compiled and edited by Vincent McGee. Introduction by Daniel Berrigan. Copyright © 1967, 1968, 1969, 1970 by Philip Berrigan. Reprinted by permission of Henry Holt and Company, Inc.

Kenyon College Public Affairs Conference Center: excerpt from "The New Jacobins and Full Emancipation" by James Farmer.

Timothy Leary: excerpt from "You are a God, act like one" from *Changing My Mind, Among Others* by Timothy Leary.

The New Yorker Magazine, Inc.: excerpt from "Non-Violent Soldier," copyright © 1967 The New Yorker Magazine, Inc. Reprinted by permission.

The New York Times Company: excerpts from "National Teach-In, May 15, 1965" *The New York Times*, issue of May 17, 1965. Copyright © 1965 by the New York Times Company. Reprinted by permission.

Robert Oates, Jr.: "The State of Enlightenment" from *Celebrating the Dawn: Maharishi Mahesh Yogi and the TM Technique* (G. P. Putnam), copyright © Robert M. Oates, Jr., 1976.

Mark Rudd: "Columbia: Notes on the Spring Rebellion" by Mark Rudd.

Mario Savio: "The University Has Become a Factory, "an interview with Mario Savio edited by J. Fincher from *Life* magazine, February 26, 1965.

Schroder Music Company (ASCAP): lyrics from "Little Boxes," words and music by Malvina Reynolds. © Copyright 1962 Schroder Music Co. (ASCAP). Used by permission. All rights reserved.

Simon & Schuster, Inc.: excerpt from *Do It!* by Jerry Rubin, copyright © 1970 by the Social Education Foundation. Reprinted by permission of Simon & Schuster, Inc.

Warner Bros. Music: excerpts from the lyrics to "The Times They Are A-changin' " by Bob Dylan, copyright © 1963 Warner Bros. Inc. All rights Reserved. Used by permission.

Andrew Wylie Agency: excerpts from "Academy 23: A Deconditioning" by William S. Burroughs, copyright © 1984 William S. Burroughs. Reprinted by permission of Andrew Wylie Agency.

CONTENTS

INTRODUCTION

It has been called the Killer Decade, and it has been blamed for everything from the soaring divorce rate and the general breakdown of the family to the spread of the herpes epidemic; from the collapse of the educational system to the graffiti scourge; from the movement away from a sensible American foreign policy to the rise of the national deficit. It has also been called the era of the last Children's Crusade, and the high noon of the Age of Aquarius, according to the lyrics of a song from the sixties Broadway musical *Hair*. It was both.

It was a time of excess—an excess of love and an excess of alienation. It was a time of division—children divided from their parents, people divided from their country. It was a period of moral and political enlightenment, and a period of moral and political confusion. Above all, it was a time of incredibly high energy and of wave after wave of political and social movements. As television personality Linda Ellerbee commented on the fifteenth anniversary of the Woodstock Festival: "In the sixties, there were no time-outs."

Like any other ten-year span in the history of the United States, the sixties are difficult to put into a neat capsule. But from the perspective of twenty years later, it is possible to draw some general conclusions about what made the decade unique in American history.

One such conclusion is that the sixties were more than just a decade—they were a state of mind, and it was embodied in the young, educated, affluent group that came of age during that period. The Baby Boom generation, those fifty million new Americans born between 1945 and 1955 after the soldiers came home from World War II, were reaching adolescence. By 1960 more than half the U.S. population was under the age of thirty; and since it is usually in the teenage years that people have the strongest desire to change the adult world they are about to enter—and the strongest belief that they can succeed in changing it—it would have been surprising if a great social upheaval had *not* taken place in the sixties.

In addition to their numbers, this generation of young people was the most prosperous youthful generation in U.S. history. Their parents had lived through the Great Depression in the 1930s and World War II in the 1940s. And so, when the country began to prosper in the 1950s, they were eager to buy for themselves and for their children all the things they could now afford. A large number of young people who reached high school and college age in the 1960s grew up in houses that their parents owned, had every toy and item of clothing they wanted (some even got cars for their sixteenth birthdays), and took it for granted that they would go to college after they graduated from high school. They also took it for granted that they would get good jobs and make good money.

Even before they entered college, the young people of this generation were beginning to feel the power of their sheer numbers in ways that they probably could not themselves express, or were not even really aware of. They were the first generation to grow up with television, a fixture in most middle-class homes by the late 1950s. Television depends on advertising revenues, and since young people had a great deal of time to watch television, much of the advertising was aimed at them. Manufacturers targeted their products on the potentially strong market of the huge "younger generation" and the advertisers pitched everything from cosmetics and clothes to records, radios, and cars.

The younger generation responded with both acceptance and rebellion to all this affluence and advertising influence. On the one hand, they accepted the idea that they ought to have whatever they wanted. On the other hand, some of them turned against the consumerism and materialism of American society and asked if there wasn't more to life than what money could buy. They looked at television and wondered if they, too, were somehow being "programmed."

Some people then, and now, suggest that the sixties generation was simply spoiled. Others suggest that as a generation accustomed to having things, they had more time to think about issues, about what they wanted to do with their lives and what kind of society they wanted to live in.

And then there are those people who suggest that the sixties would have been a decade of great social change even without the Baby Boom generation or television. Historian Arthur M. Schlesinger, Jr., believes that there are "cycles" in American history and that every thirty years or so the mood of the country shifts between two poles: from materialism and private purpose at home and a willingness to intervene in world affairs, to a sense of selflessness and public purpose at home and an unwillingness to intervene directly in the affairs of other countries. Thus as the sixties dawned it was time for the inevitable swing from conservatism to liberalism.

It may yet be too soon to look back on the sixties and try to understand what that decade meant to the history of the United States, not to mention to the history of the world. But in some ways it may already be too late. There are young people today who see the name Malcolm X and read it as "Malcolm 10," who buy Paul McCartney records and do not realize he was once a Beatle, who cannot imagine that there were ever such things as "Colored" and "White" drinking fountains in the South, and who do not understand what it is like to face the possibility of being drafted to fight in a distant war. Yet, if historians such as Arthur Schlesinger, Jr., are to be believed, we are about to enter, in the 1990s, a period when some of the same political views that marked the 1960s will reemerge. America will once again become more liberal and reformist, more drawn to public purpose on the home front and more willing to coexist with the rest of the world. If he is correct, then the people who are teenagers today may enter the next decade feeling many of the same stirrings that their parents felt thirty years earlier. And if this is the case, then the more today's teenagers understand about what happened in the 1960s, the more likely they will be to build on the triumphs of the decade and the less likely they will be to repeat its mistakes.

CHAPTER ONE

THE EARLY SIXTIES

In the year 1960 the United States elected the youngest president in its history, John F. Kennedy, which seemed appropriate for a country whose population was more young than old. The new president seemed to speak directly to that huge population of young Americans when he called for a New Frontier, urging people to "Ask not what your country can do for you, ask what you can do for your country." As part of his New Frontier, he created programs aimed at young Americans, such as the Peace Corps, in which volunteers enlisted to go abroad and help people in underdeveloped nations.

Aided, or perhaps spurred, by his beautiful wife, Jacqueline, the young president made the White House a center for the arts and intellectual thought, often inviting musicians and artists to official functions. There was an atmosphere of openness and a welcoming of new ideas in the Kennedy administration.

The sixties were indeed a "new frontier," a frontier that had already begun to open before the decade dawned. In October

1957 the Soviet Union had launched *Sputnik I,* the first artificial satellite to go into space. The United States, caught unawares, launched its own drive to educate its children so as to catch up with and surpass Russian technology. President Kennedy's use of the term "New Frontier" related, in part, to his desire for the United States to explore and conquer the new frontier that was outer space. While the emphasis on education was in math and the sciences, education in general was now a national priority.

Meanwhile, science proceeded in areas that had little to do with space. Birth control pills were first introduced in 1960, paving the way for the later sexual revolution, which some parents probably felt had already begun in the 1950s with the introducton of rock 'n' roll and the sexually suggestive performances of Bo Diddley and Elvis Presley.

Also in 1960, Chubby Checker introduced a new song and dance called "The Twist," and by 1962 the dance had become a national craze. Partners danced without touching, but somehow their suggestive movements were more sexy than in almost any kind of contact dancing that had existed before—so sexy that some communities even banned the Twist.

Pop Art first appeared in 1961. The Pop artists, who were mostly young, took everyday objects like soup cans and hamburgers and painted their images on huge canvases. Andy Warhol, a young commercial artist who made a good living drawing shoes for newspaper ads, became famous when he started painting Campbell's Soup cans. Another young artist named Roy Lichtenstein painted huge comic strips. Their aim was to poke fun at the shallow, commercial culture that dominated the lives of Americans. They set up studios in abandoned garages and threw parties and started an "underground art scene" that did not depend on the approval of older established critics and art dealers.

These underground artists and their followers often traveled in the same circles as the Beats, or Beatniks, a small group that had arisen in the 1950s in defiance of middle-class standards.

The philosophy of the Beats was "do your own thing," and they disdained middle-class trappings such as steady jobs and permanent addresses. They used drugs before this practice became acceptable among otherwise well-brought-up young people. They wrote poetry and considered themselves more aware of the life around them than ordinary people. They prided themselves in living a hand-to-mouth existence; their hero was Jack Kerouac, a writer whose any-place-I-hang-my-hat-is-home way of living seemed highly romantic. Their bible was Kerouac's 1957 book *On the Road,* which continues to find a large audience today.

In literature, particularly in fiction, there was also a lot of fun-poking at the prevailing culture. Ken Kesey's *One Flew Over the Cuckoo's Nest,* published in 1962, questioned just who was sane and who was insane. In 1961 Joseph Heller's *Catch-22* caused a stir. Heller's hero, Yossarian, is a World War II pilot who is afraid he will be killed before he completes the required twenty-two missions, and so he wants to be discharged. But to be discharged, he must be judged insane; and by requesting discharge he proves he wants to survive, and is thus sane. "Catch-22" became a catchphrase to describe a no-win situation.

There was also more overtly serious fiction. *Fail-Safe* by Eugene Burdick and J. H. Wheeler, published in 1962, speculates on how easy it might be for America to become involved in nuclear war—a serious concern for Americans, even though at the time the country was not actively involved in a war. Back in the 1950s, battlefield-type war had been replaced by the "Cold War" between the capitalist West and the Communist USSR. A large number of Americans were convinced that the Soviet Union was intent on taking over the world, either by infiltrating American society with Communist doctrines or, if that didn't work, by bombing its enemies. Across the country a vast civil defense network had sprung up; families built bomb shelters and schoolchildren took part in regular air raid drills. People, especially those in government and the arts, who were suspected of sympathy with Communism or with any beliefs regarded as "anti-American" were spied on, called to testify before congressional committees, and blacklisted—refused jobs.

In nonfiction, three extremely important books were published in the first half of the decade. Rachel Carson's *Silent Spring,* published in 1962, exposed the dangers of pesticides being used by farmers who grew the nation's food, and spawned a new awareness of what industry was doing to the environment. Betty Friedan's *The Feminine Mystique,* published in 1963, criticized the second-class citizenship of women and led to the formation the following year of NOW, the National Organization for Women. Ralph Nader's *Unsafe at Any Speed,* published in 1965, exposed the many dangerous features of cars being manufactured in the United States and started what came to be called the Consumer Movement. While the Ecology Movement, the Women's Movement, and the Consumer Movement all got their start in the 1960s, it was not until the 1970s that they really gained momentum. Still, the publication of these books in the 1960s shows just how far-ranging were the questions that Americans were asking about their society.

In the movie industry, Hollywood came out with some thought-provoking films about the nuclear threat with the film version of *Fail-Safe* and with *On the Beach,* based on a novel by Nevil Shute about life after a nuclear war. More entertaining, but still to the point, was *Dr. Strangelove, or How I Learned to Stop Worrying and Love the Bomb,* Stanley Kubrick's 1964 satirical look at the military and politicians. America's continuing interest in Cold War spies and conspiracies was reflected in such films as *The Manchurian Candidate* and the first film in the James Bond series, *Dr. No,* both released in 1962. Racial injustice was explored in *To Kill a Mockingbird,* released in 1963, based on Harper Lee's novel about a lynch mob in the South.

Television did not deal with such serious subjects. The small screen was the most conservative mass medium, for its primary reason for being was then—and still is—to sell products through advertising. It was television, however, that brought the assassination of President John F. Kennedy in November 1963 into the living rooms of Americans, replaying the tape of his shooting in Dallas, Texas, over and over. The impact of that event on the sixties generation is difficult to measure, but everyone old enough to understand what had happened remembers to this day exactly where they were and what they were doing when they first heard the news. There are some who suggest that the assassination of the young and vital president did more than anything else to turn the nation's young people against "the system" and the culture of their elders. Certainly, it dashed the hopes that many had placed in Kennedy and his New Frontier.

Television, being the first truly mass medium, also brought the members of the sixties generation into closer contact with one another, for it showed those in one part of the nation what other people were doing around the country. It contributed greatly to the quick popularization of new cultural phenomena, from the Hula Hoop to the latest fashions. It was television that brought the Beatles into the homes of Americans for the first time, in 1964, and it was Beatlemania that led to one of the most talked-about countercultural moves on the part of young people—the style of long hair.

The Beatles all sported mops that included bangs and hair below their ears, and it wasn't long before young male Americans began to adopt that style, as well as their style of clothing—tight "Beatle boots" and carefully tailored "mod" suits. The word *mod,* meaning hip and modern, was another import from the British music scene, and young Americans who had never been abroad posted CARNABY STREET street signs in their rooms in honor of the street in London's Soho section that became famous as a center for music, fashion, and pop culture.

Girls also began to favor long hair, and not just long but straight, like that of folksingers Mary Travers—of the group Peter, Paul, and Mary—and Joan Baez. Some had to actually iron their long, wavy tresses to achieve the effect.

In 1964, Mary Quant, another British trendsetter, introduced the miniskirt, which caused parents and school officials nearly as much consternation as did long hair on boys.

Such was the new-felt power on the part of young people that not a few of them took their parents or schools to court to win the legal right to dress or wear their hair as they wished—and many of them won their cases.

Cases concerning hair and dress codes were not the only instances of litigation between individuals and schools. In the early 1960s a long-standing argument over the constitutionally guaranteed separation between Church and State was decided when in 1963 the U.S. Supreme Court outlawed prayer in the public schools.

Important as such cases were to the people involved, the majority of court cases about rights in the sixties were concerned with even more fundamental questions—especially the question of rights for a group of Americans who were not allowed even the most basic freedoms outlined in the Constitution. This struggle for civil rights for black people was the first major movement of the 1960s.

CHAPTER TWO

THE DIRECT ACTION CIVIL RIGHTS MOVEMENT

Of the many movements that marked the 1960s, the one that established the pattern for protest was the movement for racial equality, which employed nonviolent protest techniques to achieve its goal. Because these nonviolent tactics worked so well, the Direct Action Civil Rights Movement influenced all other movements of the decade, particularly the Revolution on the Campus and the Peace Movement.

The movement for civil rights for black people began long before 1960. In fact, there have always been people, black *and* white, working against the terrible conditions under which blacks were forced to live since being brought to the New World as slaves. Despite their efforts, blatant discrimination and segregation were present throughout the United States as recently as the 1950s.

The worst discrimination was in the South, where the Direct Action Civil Rights Movement primarily took place. There, schools were rigidly segregated. White students rode buses, sometimes

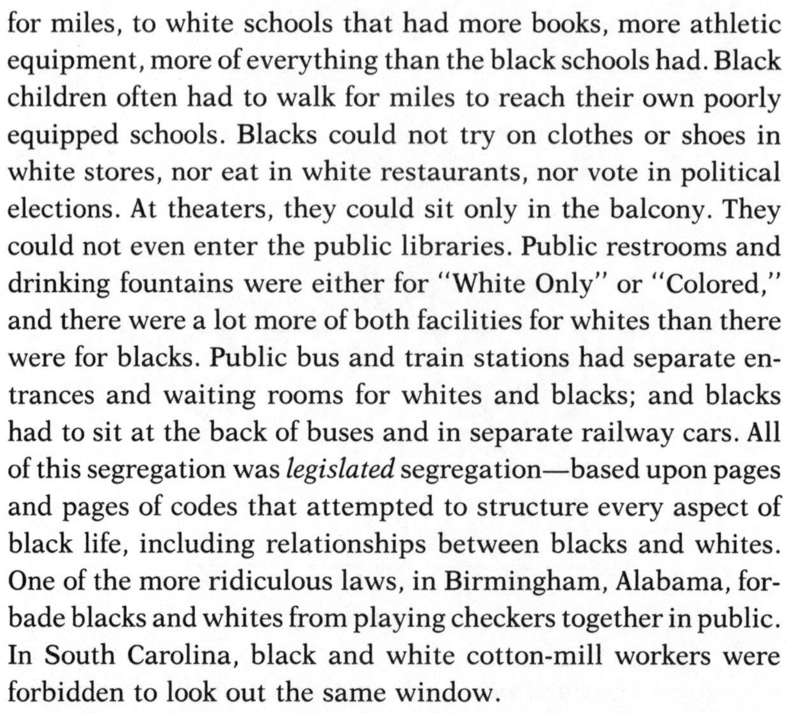

for miles, to white schools that had more books, more athletic equipment, more of everything than the black schools had. Black children often had to walk for miles to reach their own poorly equipped schools. Blacks could not try on clothes or shoes in white stores, nor eat in white restaurants, nor vote in political elections. At theaters, they could sit only in the balcony. They could not even enter the public libraries. Public restrooms and drinking fountains were either for "White Only" or "Colored," and there were a lot more of both facilities for whites than there were for blacks. Public bus and train stations had separate entrances and waiting rooms for whites and blacks; and blacks had to sit at the back of buses and in separate railway cars. All of this segregation was *legislated* segregation—based upon pages and pages of codes that attempted to structure every aspect of black life, including relationships between blacks and whites. One of the more ridiculous laws, in Birmingham, Alabama, forbade blacks and whites from playing checkers together in public. In South Carolina, black and white cotton-mill workers were forbidden to look out the same window.

Black people never willingly bowed to these conditions in the South, but they did not feel they had the power to do anything about them. Most southern whites wanted to maintain a segregated society, and they had their laws and their sheriffs, not to mention self-appointed keepers of the status quo such as the Ku Klux Klan, to ensure that nothing would be changed. They treated blacks as second-class citizens who did not deserve the same civil rights as white people.

Conditions for blacks were better in the North. There were no signs that said WHITES ONLY or COLORED. Blacks could ride in the same railway cars as whites, and sit wherever they wanted to on buses. There were hotels and restaurants that would not admit blacks—these tended to be expensive ones that most blacks could not afford anyway. Blacks tended to live in black neighborhoods and thus the schools they attended were also mostly black. But the discrimination in the North was economic more than legal. It was *de facto*–in fact, though not in law.

The national attitude toward blacks began to change during World War II. In that war, many black Americans distinguished themselves in the armed services, and back home many white Americans saw the irony of blacks fighting for the freedom of people abroad when they did not enjoy the full rights of citizenship in their own country.

In 1948, the federal government actually took the first steps to abolish segregation when President Harry S. Truman ordered the armed services to integrate. Organizations such as the National Association for the Advancement of Colored People (NAACP) took advantage of this change of attitude and stepped up their efforts to have the laws that upheld segregation declared unconstitutional. Choosing the federal courts as their battleground, these organizations went all the way to the U.S. Supreme Court with their charge that black students in southern segregated schools were not receiving an education equal to that of whites.

The legal basis for segregated schools, as well as for most other segregated facilities, was the 1896 Supreme Court decision in the case of *Plessy* v. *Ferguson,* which held that separating the races was legal as long as the facilities provided to both were equal. While everyone knew that facilities for backs were nowhere near equal to similar facilities for whites, this "separate but equal" doctrine had been the law of the land for a long time. It was necessary for the NAACP lawyers to go back to the U.S. Supreme Court to overturn it.

In 1954, these lawyers, among them Thurgood Marshall, who later became the first black to be appointed a justice of the U.S. Supreme Court, won a landmark decision in the case *Brown* v. *Board of Education* in Topeka, Kansas. The Supreme Court declared the doctrine of "separate but equal" unconstitutional. The Court did not order immediate school integration, however, saying only that *de*segregation should be brought about "with all deliberate speed." Still, this decision was a major watershed in the struggle for black equality, and it gave many black people hope. *Brown* v. *Board of Education* must have been on the minds of the black people of Montgomery, Alabama, the following year, when they decided to boycott that city's buses.

The Montgomery city buses were segregated in the same way as the buses of other southern cities. Black people had to pay at the front of the bus, then go around and enter the bus at the rear. They could sit only in the back of the bus, and if the front seats filled up with white riders, they had to give up their own seats to accommodate the white overflow. On December 1, 1955, Mrs. Rosa Parks, a black seamstress who had long been active in civil rights organizations, refused to give up her seat to a white man and was arrested. She was not the first black to challenge the laws and go to jail for it. This time, however, the leaders of Montgomery's black community decided to boycott the buses in protest.

These leaders chose as their spokesman a young Baptist minister who was not only an excellent organizer but also a student of the principles of nonviolent social protest. He had read the philosophy of Henry David Thoreau, a nineteenth-century American who had practiced civil disobedience against laws he believed were unjust. The young minister had also studied the life of Mohandas K. Gandhi, whose followers called him the Mahatma, or "Great Soul," and who had helped bring about India's independence from Britain through nonviolent social protest. Martin Luther King, Jr., had yet another important quality—the ability to inspire people to follow him.

Led by King, and by other black ministers, the blacks of Montgomery refused to ride the city's buses for more than a year—381 days, to be exact. They returned to the buses only after they had won assurances that black riders would be treated no differently than white riders and that the city would hire black bus drivers. Their victory came at great expense—blacks were beaten and the door of King's home was shattered by a shotgun blast. But at King's urging, they had not fought back. They had met white violence with the singing of freedom songs, such as "We

Shall Overcome," and with a stubborn refusal to be intimidated. The city bus company gave in primarily for economic reasons: It needed the fares paid by black riders, who represented the majority of the ridership (for most whites had cars). But a few whites in Montgomery gained a new respect for black Montgomeryites after they saw their refusal to return the violence they had suffered at the hands of whites during the boycott.

It occurred to Martin Luther King, Jr., and some of his fellow clergymen that they might be able to use the same nonviolent tactics to bring about other changes in the South. In January 1957 they formed the Southern Christian Leadership Conference (SCLC) to promote a movement for black equality in the South. King was elected its president.

At first, the SCLC did not live up to its early promise. Its members were ministers with families, ties to their communities, and reputations to uphold. After much discussion and reflection they concluded that the bus boycott in Montgomery had arisen out of circumstances that could not be duplicated elsewhere. They decided to bring about change in a more traditional way—with the vote. The SCLC's first major action was a May 1957 prayer pilgrimage to Washington, D.C., where King stood on the steps of the Lincoln Memorial and delivered a call for voting rights.

The aim of the prayer pilgrimage was to encourage Congress and the president to pass the 1957 Civil Rights Act, which empowered the federal government to act against the obstruction or deprivation of voting rights and which created a Civil Rights Commission and a Civil Rights Division in the Department of Justice. Congress did pass the law, and President Dwight D. Eisenhower signed it, making it the first civil rights legislation since the Reconstruction period after the Civil War. Unfortunately, it was not a very strong law—the only way to get it passed over the objections of southern legislators was to take out the enforcement measures necessary to make it effective. Its critics charged that the law had "no teeth." Still, a law of some kind had been passed, and civil rights workers considered it a mark of progress. Real progress, however, did not take place until the 1960s.

THE STUDENT MOVEMENT AND THE FOUNDING OF SNCC

What accelerated the civil rights struggle into high gear was the student protest movement, which, like the Montgomery bus boycott, began spontaneously. In Greensboro, North Carolina, one evening in January 1960, four students from North Carolina Agricultural and Technical College decided to try to integrate the local Woolworth's luncheonette. Joseph McNeil, Izell Blair, Franklin McCain, and David Richmond deliberately challenged the rule that they could shop at Woolworth's but not eat there—they could buy toothpaste but not a hamburger. They went to the local Woolworth's, bought a few items, and then sat down at the lunch counter. After being refused service, they continued to sit there, leaving an hour later when the store closed. The next morning they returned and sat for two hours.

Local newspapers ran the story and it was picked up by the national news wire services. The following day, more black students from North Carolina A & T and three white students from nearby Greensboro College joined them. A group of white youths gathered to curse and threaten the protesters, and that resulted in more press coverage. The mayor of Greensboro asked for time to work out a "just and honorable resolution" to the problem, and the students agreed not to engage in any more sit-ins for two weeks.

By then, however, black students elsewhere had caught sit-in fever. During the two weeks when the students in Greensboro did not engage in sit-ins, students in Winston-Salem, Durham, Charlotte, Fayette, High Point, Elizabeth City, and Concord, North Carolina, did. By the end of February, black students in seven other southern states had staged sit-ins, and sit-in fever was catching on in the North. In New York City, students from Co-

As a state trooper looks on, Dr. Martin Luther King, Jr. (RIGHT, in sunglasses) leads a civil rights march in Philadelphia, Mississippi. BELOW, young black men wait in vain for service at Woolworth's segregated lunch counter in Greensboro, North Carolina. It was here that the student sit-in movement began.

lumbia University organized sit-ins at the local Woolworth's to demonstrate their support of the black student sit-ins in the South. As the geographical area affected by sit-in fever increased, so did the violence. On February 23, 1960, in Chattanooga, Tennessee, over a thousand people were involved in two days of rioting, and more than thirty persons, mostly white, were arrested.

It was entirely a grass-roots movement. Few of the students who participated in sit-ins belonged to political or civil rights organizations such as the NAACP or SCLC. Ella Baker, executive director of the SCLC, decided that the students needed to be organized on a larger scale. The leaders of the various student sit-ins met in Raleigh, North Carolina, in May, and formed the Student Nonviolent Coordinating Committee (SNCC). Martin Luther King, Jr., spoke to the students, and the statement of purpose that they adopted reflected his influence.

STUDENT NONVIOLENT COORDINATING COMMITTEE STATEMENT OF PURPOSE

We affirm the philosophical or religious ideals of nonviolence as the foundation of our purpose, the presupposition of our faith, and the manner of our action. Nonviolence as it grows from Judaic-Christian traditions seeks a social order of justice permeated by love. Integration of human endeavor represents the crucial first step towards such a society.

Through nonviolence, courage displaces fear; love transforms hate. Acceptance dissipates prejudice; hope ends despair. Peace dominates war; faith reconciles doubt. Mutual regard cancels enmity. Justice for all overthrows injustice. The redemptive community supersedes systems of gross social immorality.

Love is the central motif of nonviolence. Love is the force by which God binds man to Himself and man to man. Such love goes to the extreme; it remains loving and forgiving even in the midst of hostility. It matches the capacity of evil to inflict suffering with an even more enduring capacity to absorb evil, all the while persisting in love.

By appealing to conscience and standing on the moral nature of human existence, nonviolence nurtures the atmosphere in which reconciliation and justice become actual possibilities.

It is clear from this statement that the founders of SNCC were not radical firebrands. It is *not* clear just what they wanted to do; their statement contained no plan, no list of goals that they wished to achieve. In fact, the leaders at SNCC were not at all certain what their next action would be.

Ironically, the organizing of the student sit-in leaders became the culmination of the student sit-in movement. The sit-ins had been a spontaneous display of dissatisfaction with segregation. Considering how conservative black colleges were at that time, it is amazing that the students had dared to take the independent action they had. Black colleges depended for their support on white legislatures and rich white benefactors, and the last thing their administrations wanted was student political activity. At many black colleges, the students involved in civil rights protests were suspended or expelled.

For a time, SNCC was a new organization with nothing to do. The students wanted to end segregation, but they were unsure how to go about it. The SCLC wasn't engaging in any direct-action protests, and so did not take advantage of the students' energy and commitment. SNCC soon turned for direction to the Congress of Racial Equality (CORE).

CORE was a well-established civil rights organizaton that had pioneered such tactics as the sit-in back in the 1940s. In the late 1950s, it had watched the SCLC take the lead in direct-action civil rights activity and wanted to reestablish its position at the forefront of the fight for civil rights. When in 1960 the Interstate Commerce Commission ordered the desegregation of buses and station facilities on interstate lines, CORE's leaders saw their chance.

In 1961, CORE launched a program of Freedom Rides aimed at testing this Interstate Commerce Commission order, and invited SNCC to join in. Racially-mixed groups would board interstate buses in the North and then try to ride through the South, sitting where they wanted to, using the "integrated" stations along the way. SNCC's leaders, eager for a cause, joined the program. This would prove to be their "baptism by fire."

A bus was stoned and burned in Anniston, Alabama. Freedom Riders were attacked by mobs in Birmingham and Montgomery, Alabama, and were arrested in Jackson, Mississippi. The media people covering the story fared no better. Reporters were beaten, their cameras smashed. Southern white racists blamed the media for encouraging the Civil Rights Movement, and with some reason: Without the unblinking eye of the media, especially that of television, the movement might not have succeeded, for the rest of the nation, and much of the world, would not have seen in action the violent racism practiced by southern whites.

While they supported these courageous young people, blacks who saw the violence the Freedom Riders met with were understandably unwilling to try to protect them. Even the most idealistic, committed young SNCC worker could not reasonably be expected to board a bus bound for certain tragedy. The Freedom Rides themselves did not last long, but they did have a lasting effect on black southerners who admired the courage of the young pioneers. Thereafter, these black southerners referred to all civil rights workers as Freedom Riders.

The Freedom Rides taught both SNCC and CORE that there was safety in numbers, and that it was better to get a *community* involved in a protest than to send in strangers, to whom the community owed no loyalty. It also taught the older leaders of CORE that if they were going to come up with ideas such as the

Freedom Rides, they had to be prepared to take part in them personally. James Farmer, executive director of CORE, recalled later that a turning point in his thinking occurred when he went to see off a group of Freedom Riders and was confronted by the frightened face of a young female student who begged, "You're coming with us, aren't you, Jim?" His explanation that he had work to attend to at the national office of CORE sounded like a cowardly excuse even to his own ears.

Martin Luther King, Jr., was also coming to this realization. How could he expect his organization, the SCLC, to lead the civil rights movement if it did not take strong action? And how could he expect black people to risk their lives in the struggle for civil rights if he did not put his own life on the line? By the early 1960s, King had concluded that the time had come for more aggressive action, though aggression was against all he had been raised to believe in.

MARTIN LUTHER KING, JR.

Martin Luther King, Jr., was born January 15, 1929, in Atlanta, Georgia. His father, a Baptist minister, was a man who managed to maintain his dignity in the face of southern racism, and young Martin wanted to be like him. He too studied for the ministry. At Crozer Theological Seminary in Chester, Pennsylvania, he discovered the writings of Gandhi and read extensively about this frail man who had helped bring about India's independence from Britain by uniting the people of that country's rigidly class-separated society by means of nonviolent social protest. King later attended Boston University and it was there he met Coretta Scott, a music student from Marion, Alabama. They were married in 1953, and the following year they settled in Montgomery, Alabama, where King had accepted the pastorship of the Dexter Avenue Baptist Church, a stone's throw away from the gleaming white state capitol building as well as from the home of Jefferson Davis, who had been president of the Confederate States of America.

King had intended to devote his life to helping his parishioners, but he had no idea how deeply involved he would become in the struggle for their civil rights, and his. Less than two years after beginning his pastorship, he was asked to lead the Montgomery bus boycott of 1956, and the following year his picture was on the cover of *Time* magazine. He helped organize and accepted the presidency of the SCLC, led that organization in the 1957 prayer pilgrimage to Washington, D.C., and served as an adviser to SNCC.

The student sit-ins and the Freedom Rides signaled to King and the SCLC that they must step up their own direct-action civil rights activity. In the summer of 1962, they pushed for desegregation of all public facilities in Albany, Georgia, but their efforts failed. Although several other organizations cooperated with the SCLC in the Albany campaign, there was too much division among the leaders of the various groups and not enough initial planning. By 1963, King and his organization had a much better idea of how to coordinate a successful movement against a segregated city, and the city they chose next would prove to be a true test of the lessons they had learned.

Few cities were as deeply racist as Birmingham, Alabama, where rigid segregation and police brutality were facts of everyday black life. City officials went to great lengths to avoid integration. After passage of another federal Civil Rights Act in 1960, for example, they closed the city's parks rather than let blacks use them. When the touring company of New York's Metropolitan Opera adopted a policy of performing only before integrated audiences, Birmingham removed itself from the Met's annual circuit. Between 1957 and 1963, seventeen black churches were bombed in Birmingham—warnings that the Civil Rights Movement would get nowhere there. Black southerners, who managed to find a rueful humor in even the worst situations, began to call the city "Bombingham." It was the obvious place for King and the SCLC to take their stand, and they announced

The nonviolent civil rights protesters often met with violent resistance. In Birmingham, Alabama, police set dogs on the demonstrators. BELOW, Birmingham firemen, having subdued one group, turn their hoses across the street to disperse another crowd.

plans for a series of marches and protests in April 1963.

A local judge issued an injunction against King and the SCLC, and other individuals and organizations, including CORE and SNCC, who planned to participate. In January, a group of eight white Alabama clergymen issued an "Appeal for Law and Order" that called for meetings among prominent blacks and whites and stressed that obedience to the rulings of federal and local courts would solve Birmingham's racial problems. It also called the actions planned by King and the SCLC "unwise and untimely."

Ignoring the court injunction, King and his assistants went to Birmingham and began organizing demonstrations. They had decided that perhaps their arrests would cause more black people in Birmingham to get involved in the demonstrations. As expected, they were soon arrested, and at Birmingham city jail, King was placed in solitary confinement.

In an isolated cell for eight days, King finally had the time to respond to the criticism of his ideas and work that was contained in the "Appeal for Law and Order." He started his response on the margins of a newspaper, continued it on scraps of paper supplied by a black prison trusty, and completed it on a notepad provided by his attorney. More than nineteen pages when it was transcribed from King's spidery script, the letter is excerpted below.

LETTER FROM BIRMINGHAM JAIL

April 16, 1963

My Dear Fellow Clergymen:

While confined here in the Birmingham city jail, I came across your recent statements calling my present activities "unwise and untimely." Seldom do I pause to answer criticism of my work and ideas. If I sought to answer all the criticisms that cross my desk, my secretaries would have little time for anything other than such correspondence in the course of the day, and I would have no time for constructive work. But since I feel that you are men of genuine good will and that your criticisms are sincerely set forth, I want to try to answer your statements in what I hope will be patient and reasonable terms.

I think I should indicate why I am here in Birmingham, since you have been influenced by the view which argues against "outsiders coming in." I have the honor of serving as president of the Southern Christian Leadership Conference, an organization operating in every southern state, with headquarters in Atlanta, Georgia. . . . Several months ago the affiliate here in Birmingham asked us to be on call to engage in a nonviolent direct-action program if such were deemed necessary. We readily consented, and when the hour came we lived up to our promise. So I, along with several members of my staff, am here because I was invited here. I am here because I have organizational ties here.

But more basically, I am in Birmingham because injustice is here . . .

You may well ask: "Why direct action? Why sit-ins, marches and so forth? Isn't negotiation a better path?" You are quite right in calling for negotiation. Indeed, this is the very purpose of direct action. Nonviolent direct action seeks to create such a crisis and foster such a tension that a community which has constantly refused to negotiate is forced to confront the issue. It seeks so to dramatize the issue that it can no longer be ignored. My citing the creation of tension as part of the work of the nonviolent-register may sound rather shocking. But I confess that I am not afraid of the word "tension." I have earnestly opposed violent tension, but there is a type of constructive, nonviolent tension which is necessary for growth. Just as Socrates [an ancient Greek philosopher] felt that it was necessary to create a tension in the mind so that individuals could rise from the bondage of myths and half-truths to the unfettered realm of creative analysis and objective appraisal, so must we see the need for nonviolent gadflies to create the kind of tension in society that will help men rise from the dark depths of prejudice and racism to the majestic heights of understanding and brotherhood.

The purpose of our direct-action program is to create a situation so crisis-packed that it will inevitably open the door to negotiation. I therefore concur with you in your call for negotiation. Too long has our beloved Southland been bogged down in a tragic effort to live in monologue rather than dialogue . . .

We know through painful experience that freedom is never voluntarily given by the oppressor; it must be demanded by the oppressed. Frankly, I have yet to engage in a direct-action campaign that was "well timed" in the view of those who have not suffered unduly from the disease of segregation. For years now I have heard the word "Wait!" It rings in the ear of every Negro with piercing familiarity. This "Wait" has almost always meant "Never." We must come to see, with one of our distinguished jurists, that "justice too long delayed is justice denied."

We have waited for more than 340 years for our constitutional and God-given rights. The nations of Asia and Africa are moving with jet-like speed toward gaining political independence, but we still creep at horse-and-buggy pace toward gaining a cup of coffee at a lunch counter. Perhaps it is easy for those who have never felt the stinging darts of segregation to say, "Wait." But when you have seen vicious mobs lynch your mothers and fathers at will and drown your sisters and brothers at whim; when you have seen hate-filled policemen curse, kick and even kill your black brothers and sisters; when you see the vast majority of your twenty million Negro brothers smothering in an airtight cage of poverty in the midst of an affluent society; when you suddenly find your tongue twisted and your speech stammering as you seek to explain to your six-year-old daughter why she can't go to the public amusement park that has just been advertised on television, and see tears welling up in her eyes when she is told that Funtown is closed to colored children, and see ominous clouds of inferiority beginning to form in her little mental sky, and see her beginning to distort her personality by developing an unconscious bitterness toward white people; when you have to concoct an answer for a five-year-old son who is asking: "Daddy, why do white people treat colored people so mean?"; when you take a cross-country drive and find it necessary to sleep night after night in the uncomfortable corners of your automobile because no motel will accept you; when you are humiliated day in and day out by nagging signs reading "white" and "colored"; when your first name becomes "nigger," your middle name becomes "boy" (however old you are) and your last name becomes "John"; and your wife and mother are never given the respected title "Mrs."; when you are harried by day and haunted by night by the fact that you are a Negro, living constantly at tiptoe stance, never quite knowing what to expect next, and are plagued with inner fears and outer resentments; when you are forever fighting a degenerating sense of "nobodiness"—then you will understand why we find it difficult to wait. There comes a time when the cup of endurance runs over, and men are no longer willing to be plunged into the abyss of despair. I hope, sirs, you can understand our legitimate and unavoidable impatience.

You express a great deal of anxiety over our willingness to break laws. This is certainly a legitimate concern. Since we so diligently urge people to obey the Supreme Court's decision of 1954 outlawing segregation in public schools, at first glance it may seem rather paradoxical for us to consciously break laws. One may well ask: "How can you advocate breaking some laws and obeying others?" The answer lies in the fact that there are two types of laws: just and unjust. I would be the first to advocate obeying just laws. One has not only a legal but a moral responsibility to obey just laws. Conversely, one has a moral responsibility to disobey unjust laws. I would agree with St.

Augustine that "an unjust law is no law at all."

We should never forget that everything Adolf Hitler did in Germany was "legal" and everything the Hungarian freedom fighters did in Hungary was "illegal." It was "illegal" to aid and comfort a Jew in Hitler's Germany. Even so, I am sure that, had I lived in Germany at the time, I would have aided and comforted my Jewish brothers. If today I lived in a Communist country where certain principles dear to the Christian faith are suppressed, I would openly advocate disobeying that country's antireligious laws.

I must make two honest confessions to you, my Christian and Jewish brothers. First, I must confess that over the past few years I have been gravely disappointed with the white moderate. I have almost reached the regrettable conclusion that the Negro's great stumbling block in his stride toward freedom is not the White Citizens' Counciler or the Ku Klux Klanner, but the white moderate, who is more devoted to "order" than to justice; who prefers a negative peace which is the absence of tension to positive peace which is the presence of justice; who constantly says: "I agree with you in the goal you seek, but I cannot agree with your methods of direct action"; who paternalistically believes he can set the timetable for another man's freedom; who lives by a mythical concept of time and who constantly advises the Negro to wait for a "more convenient season." Shallow understanding from people of good will is more frustrating than absolute misunderstanding from people of ill will. Lukewarm acceptance is much more bewildering than outright rejection . . .

I had also hoped that the white moderate would reject the myth concerning time in relation to the struggle for freedom. I have just received a letter from a white brother in Texas. He writes: "All Christians know that the colored people will receive equal rights eventually, but it is possible that you are in too great a religious hurry. It has taken Christianity almost two thousand years to accomplish what it has. The teachings of Christ take a long time to come to earth." Such an attitude stems from a tragic misconception of time, from the strangely irrational notion that there is something in the very flow of time that will inevitably cure all ills. Actually, time itself is neutral; it can be used either destructively or constructively. More and more I feel that the people of ill will have used time much more effectively than have the people of good will. We will have to repent in this generation not merely for the hateful words and actions of the bad people but the appalling silence of the good people. Human progress never rolls in on wheels of inevitability; it comes through the tireless efforts of men willing to be co-workers with God, and without this hard work, time itself becomes an ally of the forces of social stagnation. We must use time creatively, in the knowledge that the time is always ripe to do right. Now is the time to make real the promise of democracy and transform our pending national elegy into a creative psalm of brotherhood. Now is the time to lift our national policy from the quicksand of racial injustice to the solid rock of human dignity . . .

Before closing I feel impelled to mention one other point in your statement that has troubled me profoundly. You warmly commended the Birmingham police force for keeping "order" and "preventing violence." I doubt that you would have so warmly commended the police force if you had seen its police dogs sinking their teeth into unarmed, nonviolent Negroes. I doubt that you would so quickly commend the policemen if you were to observe their ugly and inhumane treatment of Negroes here in the city jail; if you were to watch them push and curse old Negro women and young Negro girls; if you were to see them slap and kick old Negro men and young boys; if you were to observe them, as they did on two occasions, refuse to give us food because we wanted to sing our grace together. I cannot join you in your praise of the Birmingham police department.

It is true that the police have exercised a degree of discipline in handling the demonstrators. In this sense they have conducted themselves rather "nonviolently" in public. But for what purpose? To preserve the evil system of segregation. Over the past few years I have consistently preached that nonviolence demands that the means we use must be as pure as the ends we seek. I have tried to make clear that it is wrong to use immoral means to attain moral ends. But now I must affirm that it is just as wrong, or perhaps even more so, to use moral means to preserve immoral ends. Perhaps Mr. Connor [Birmingham's sheriff] and his policemen have been rather nonviolent in public, as was Chief Pritchett in Albany, Georgia, but they have used the moral means of nonviolence to maintain the immoral end of racial injustice. As T. S. Eliot has said: "The last temptation is the greatest treason: To do the right deed for the wrong reason."

I wish you had commended the Negro sit-inners and demonstrators of Birmingham for their sublime courage, their willingness to suffer and their amazing discipline in the midst of great provocation. One day the South will recognize its real heroes. They will be the James Merediths [in 1962, escorted by Federal troops, Meredith was the first black to gain admittance to the University of Mississippi], with the noble sense of purpose that enables them to face jeering and hostile mobs and with the agonizing loneliness that characterizes the life of the pioneer. They will be old, oppressed, battered Negro women, symbolized in the seventy-two-year-old woman in Montgomery, Alabama, who rose up with a sense of dignity and with her people decided not to ride segregated buses, and who responded with ungrammatical profundity to one who inquired about her weariness: "My feets is tired, but my soul is at rest." They will be the young high school and college students, the young ministers of the gospel and a host of their elders, courageously and nonviolently sitting in at lunch counters and willingly going to jail for conscience's sake. One day the South will know that when these disinherited children of God sat down at lunch counters, they were in reality standing up for what is best in the American dream and for the most sacred values in our Judaeo-Christian heritage, thereby bringing our nation back to those great wells of democracy which were dug deep by the founding fathers in their formulation of the Constitution and the Declaration of Independence.

Never before have I written such a long letter. I'm afraid it is much too long to take your precious time. I can assure you that it would have been much shorter if I had been writing from a comfortable desk, but what else can one do when he is alone in a narrow jail cell, other than write long letters, think long thoughts and pray long prayers?

If I have said anything in this letter that overstates the truth and indicates an unreasonable impatience, I beg you to forgive me. If I have said anything that understates the truth and indicates my having a patience that allows me to settle for anything less than brotherhood, I beg God to forgive me. . .

Yours for the cause of Peace and Brotherhood,
Martin Luther King, Jr.

Eloquent as King's letter was, it had little direct effect on the struggle for black equality in Birmingham. It was the children of that city who eventually brought about the civil rights victory. In a plan intended to galvanize the community, the leaders of the Birmingham campaign organized the children to attempt the desegregation of libraries and public parks. Sheriff "Bull" Connor's policemen set upon the children with snarling, snapping dogs. City firemen went after them with powerful fire hoses, sending them flying helter-skelter like autumn leaves in a rainstorm. Birmingham's black adults quickly responded to these acts of brutality. Within days there were so many marches and demonstrations in progress that even the SCLC coordinators couldn't keep track of them. Soon the white leaders of the city had had enough. On May 10, King and other SCLC leaders met with a group of white Birmingham businessmen and negotiated an agreement to desegregate stores, to provide more jobs for blacks, and to set up biracial committees to look into grievances and to solve future problems.

Unfortunately, this agreement did not end the violence. On September 15, the city lived up to its tragic nickname again when the black Sixteenth Street Baptist Church was bombed, killing four black girls aged eleven to fourteen, and injuring many other children.

King's reputation for eloquence, as well as his growing renown as a leader in the Civil Rights Movement, was furthered by a speech he delivered on the steps of the Lincoln Memorial in Washington, D.C., in August 1963. The occasion was a march upon the nation's capital in support of President John F. Kennedy's proposed civil rights bill and was also intended to dramatize the need for a minimum-wage bill and fair employment legislation. The "I Have a Dream" speech that King delivered on that day has become even more famous than his Birmingham letter. Of the 250,000 marchers who heard King speak, it was estimated that between 60,000 and 95,000 were white. By this time the Civil Rights Movement had become truly multiracial.

King's articulate and passionate pleas for racial justice, and his work on behalf of that cause, earned him the Nobel Peace Prize in 1964; at age thirty-five, he was the youngest man ever to receive that honor.

Around 1965, King shifted his attention to the plight of blacks outside the South. In response to riots in Watts, a black section of Los Angeles, and in several northern cities, he attempted to organize marches and other demonstrations against the de facto segregation that operated in so many areas outside the South. He was for the most part unsuccessful. As he wrote in his book *Where Do We Go from Here?*, "Jobs are harder and costlier to create than voting rolls. The eradication of slums housing millions is complex far beyond integrating buses and lunch counters."

By 1966, the United States was becoming increasingly involved in the war in Vietnam. King spoke out against this involvement, partly because he felt that the United States was morally wrong to interfere in another country's civil war, partly because the majority of men being sent to fight and risk their lives in Vietnam were poor, and a disproportionate number were black. His outspoken antiwar stand was considered a mistake by many whites *and* blacks, and he lost some powerful supporters as a result.

On April 4, 1968, while in Memphis, Tennessee, to help the cause of striking sanitation workers, King was assassinated by James Earl Ray, a white man. Ray was caught and convicted, and insisted that he had acted alone; but some people believe he was hired to kill King as part of a conspiracy. Some people even charge that the FBI may have had something to do with King's death, for FBI director J. Edgar Hoover hated King and had long used the agency to try to discredit him. None of these suspicions and charges has ever been proven, but they remain disturbing allegations to this day.

King was only thirty-nine years old when he was killed, and the tragedy of his death—and at such a young age—was compounded by the tragedy of his loss to the Civil Rights Movement. The movement never recovered its strength, or produced a leader of King's caliber to take his place.

King's memory remains powerful, however. In 1984, Congress passed and President Ronald Reagan signed into law a bill providing for a national holiday in honor of King's birthday. He thus became the first non-president, indeed the first black, in American history to be so honored. That he has been honored in this way is a testament both to King, the man, and to the black political power that he helped to win.

Had King not been assassinated, there is some question as to how effective he might have continued to be in the nonviolent Direct Action Civil Rights Movement. It is clear that he was not very successful in taking that movement to the North. Even in the South, after Birmingham, the movement seemed to take on a life of its own and certainly was not a movement that could be controlled by one man or one organization. While King was the premier civil rights leader—and certainly the most influential—after Birmingham, as James Farmer points out in the following essay, the Direct Action Civil Rights Movement entered a new stage.

JAMES FARMER

The Birmingham campaign really united the black community for the first time. Not just the preachers and the idealists, but people who previously had had no real commitment to nonviolence became involved. There had long been tensions within the Civil Rights Movement: between the philosophy of nonviolence and the desire to fight back, between young and old, between poor and privileged, between those who wanted to work with whites and those who wanted to work independently of whites. As the movement grew, and these various factions met within it, the possibility of serious tensions loomed large. James Farmer, founder and leader of the Congress of Racial Equality, understood these tensions and thought long and hard about how to prevent them from destroying the movement.

Born in Marshall, Texas, in 1920, the son of a college professor who was the nation's first black to earn a Ph.D., Farmer was an early activist in the struggle for racial equality. He founded CORE in 1942 and pioneered the sit-in in Chicago in 1943. By the early 1960s, when black college sudents began taking more radical steps toward desegregation in the South, Farmer was in his forties and seemed likely to be classified among the old, conservative guard of black leaders. Yet it was Farmer and CORE who instituted the radical and risky Freedom Rides in 1961. Farmer was an ordained minister and was committed to the philosophy of nonviolence. He was also accustomed to working with whites and believed that the Civil Rights Movement could not succeed without their support. Yet he sometimes felt like responding to violence with violence, and in the course of his own career in the civil rights struggle he had sometimes worried that the movement was too dependent on white support. Thus he understood the feelings of the "young Turks" of the movement who were less patient than their elders and less willing to compromise. Still, he realized that their impatience represented a danger to the movement.

He also saw beyond the Direct Action Civil Rights Movement. He knew that it would end someday and that even if it succeeded in achieving legal equality for blacks, blacks still would not be *really* equal, for most blacks did not have enough education and job skills to take advantage of the new opportunities. To truly achieve equality, he planned for a second stage in the civil rights struggle, when blacks would demand that the federal government provide programs for education and training. As he states below, "When a society has crippled some of its people, it has an obligation to provide the requisite crutches."

In the 1964 article that is excerpted here, Farmer likens the civil rights workers to the Jacobins, the political club that brought about the French Revolution in the 1790s. It was composed of people of different classes, regions, religions, and political persuasions who united against the French royalty. But once they had toppled the monarchy the group split into factions because they could not agree on several important matters. Thus divided, they never again enjoyed the power they'd had when able to put aside their differences.

THE NEW JACOBINS AND FULL EMANCIPATION

It remained for Birmingham and, before that, its dress rehearsal, Albany, Georgia, to learn from the Freedom Riders' mistakes, and launch massive demonstrations and jail-ins, wholly involving thousands, not hundreds, of Negroes—local citizens, not transients—and mobilizing the respective Negro communities in toto. A score of Birminghams followed the first. Birmingham thus set the stage for a full-scale revolt against segregation in this nation. Such a mass movement was possible because of the magic name of Martin Luther King, Jr. It was possible, in a more basic sense, because of an historical merger of two social forces.

What happened after World War II, or really after Montgomery, was a kind of wedding of two forces, both bred by the war: the means-oriented idealists of pacifistic turn of mind, for whom nonviolence was a total philosophy, a way of life, and the ends-oriented militants, the postwar angry young men who saw in direct action a weapon and viewed nonviolence as a tactic.

Without such a fusion, no revolutionary mass movement could have emerged. Without the young Turks, the movement never could have grown to mass proportions, and without the idealists it could not have developed revolutionary dimensions. The anger of one without the disciplined idealism of the other could have produced only nihilism. Without the indigenous anger of the Negro masses, the idealists, for all their zeal, would have remained largely irrelevant, socially speaking, and would have gone on talking to themselves and whispering through an occasional keyhole to another human heart . . .

The idealists warn that the ends do not justify the means, and the militants assert with equal validity that means are worthless which do not achieve desired and verifiable ends. Each tempers the other, and out of the creative tension between the two has come a third position which, I believe, more accurately reflects the movement. Nonviolence is neither a mere tactic, which may be dropped on any occasion, nor an inviolable spiritual commitment. It is somewhere between the two—not a philosophy, not a tactic, but a strategy involving both philosophical and tactical elements, in a massive and widening direct action campaign to redeem the American promise of full freedom for the Negro.

This does not mean that all of the hundreds of thousands of Negroes involved in the street campaigns for equality accept nonviolence as strategy or tactic or anything else. . . . The masses have no commitment to nonviolence, or to any other specific response to abuse. . . . Obviously, the urge to conformity is not enough, in and of itself, to maintain nonviolence through the stresses of a mass direct action movement. And that, precisely, is the chief tactical dilemma of today's Freedom Movement.

The nonviolent militants, seeking to mount a revolutionary force capable of toppling manifest racism, need those folk who are not yet wedded to nonviolence, who are wedded, indeed, only to their own fierce indignation. They need them from the pool halls and taverns as well as from the churches, from the unemployed and alienated and the rootless. The entire Negro community wants now, more than ever before, to become directly involved in the "revolution." Either they will be involved or they will, by their separation from it, brand the movement as counterfeit and ultimately destroy it.

The problem, of course, is to see that they do not destroy it by their involvement. Small, disciplined groups are easy to control. Untrained masses are difficult. Violence used against us by our opponents is a problem only in so far as it may provoke counterviolence from our ranks. Thus far, sporadic incidents of violence, where they have occurred in the movement, have been contained and have not become a contagion. We have been lucky, but we cannot afford any longer to leave such a vital matter to chance. Widespread violence by the freedom fighters would sever from the struggle all but a few of our allies. It would also provoke and, to many, justify, such repressive measures as would stymie the movement. More than that, many of our own nonviolent activists would be shorn away by disenchantment. None would profit from such developments except the defenders of segregation and perhaps the more bellicose of the black nationalist groups . . .

What is possible, as well as desirable, is an expeditious and thorough program of discipline—both internal and external. Internally, the need is for rapid expansion of training for nonviolence in the ranks—classes, institutes, workshops—in every city where the struggle is in process or in preparation. The external requirement calls for a specially trained cadre of monitors for every mass demonstration, to spot trouble before it occurs and either resolve it or isolate it. With a sensitivity to any potential break in the ranks, the monitors must have specialized skills in dealing with the untrained who may join the ranks during the action . . .

The second problem in the new militants' struggle for full emancipation is more functional than tactical. There has occurred in the past few years a proliferation, though not yet a splintering, of direct action organizations of a nonviolent character. In addition to CORE, there is the Southern Christian Leadership Conference of Dr. King, the Student Nonviolent Coordinating Committee, and various unaffiliated local groups, jealous of their autonomy. Such established organizations as the NAACP are also engaging increasingly in direct action. Church groups, too, and professional associations which previously had confined their actions to pronouncements are now "taking to the streets."

All of this strengthens the movement immeasurably. But it also poses a problem. What coordination exists between the groups is largely accidental rather than the product of systematic planning. Nor is there sufficient coordination of programs within each organization.

What we have, in essence, is a series of guerrilla strikes. . . . An effective war cannot be waged in such a manner, nor can a revolution likely be won thus. Guerrilla warfare must have its place, but as part of an over-all plan.

An urgent need at this stage of the struggle, therefore, is for coordinated planning for a full-scale war against color caste. A revolution which, like Topsy, "just grew" must now submit itself to the rigors of systemization. Spontaneity, the trademark of the

1960 sit-ins, has served its purpose . . .

What we do in the South and in the North, for example, should be part of a whole, for though its dimensions and contours may vary from place to place, the institution of segregation has no separate existence anywhere. Without subsidies from both the federal government and northern capital, it could not persist in the South. And were not the South an open sore, pouring northward its stream of deprived human beings, the North could never rationalize and maintain its fool's defense—the de facto pattern of segregation. The tentacles of the beast are everywhere but none of them should be mistaken for the octopus itself.

This essential unity of the problem is beginning to take form in action with a growing clarity. If a lunch counter segregates in Atlanta or a retail store in Oklahoma City fails to hire Negroes in nontraditional jobs, while heretofore they were attacked in isolation, they are now coming to be dealt with in more realistic terms: as parts of chains if such they are. The economic boycott is a far more potent weapon when regional or national leverage can be used.

Action on any incident of discrimination should take its shape from the shape of the power structure of the machinery which controls, influences, or sustains the objectionable practice. Maximum effectiveness cannot be achieved otherwise. When, for instance, southern school bonds are floated to build and maintain segregated schools, they are marketed not in the South, but by brokers in New York, New Jersey, Massachusetts, Pennsylvania, Illinois and California. Wittingly or unwittingly, northern investors thus provide the fuel to keep southern segregation going. Income from such investments is tax exempt. So, despite the Supreme Court's 1954 decision, the federal government is providing in this manner a subsidy just as supportive of caste as are its outright grants to schools, hospitals, and services which are segregated. No campaign against segregation which fails to confront the source of funds can even approach adequacy . . .

. . . The realization is growing among the new militants that even when the walls are down, and segregation is ended, the task of full emancipation will not be finished. Because of a hundred years of discrimination, the Negro is a built-in "low man on the totem pole." Even after job discrimination is gone, under normally accepted employment procedures the Negro will most often be starting at the bottom while others are already at the middle or the top. And, due to past educational inequities, even after school segregation is over, he cannot compete on an equal footing in this generation or the next.

The responsibility of accelerating the Negro's march to equality does not rest with the Negro alone. This cannot be a sheer bootstrap operation [the reference is to the idea that blacks ought to pull themselves up by their own bootstraps and not wait for whites to do it for them]. When a society has crippled some of its people, it has an obligation to provide requisite crutches. Industry has an obligation not merely to employ the best qualified person who happens to apply, but to seek qualified Negroes for nontraditional jobs, and if none can be found, to help train them. If two or more applicants with substantially equal qualifications should present themselves, and one of them is a Negro, then he should be given a measure of preference to compensate for the discrimination of centuries.

Beyond that, a remedial education and training program of massive proportions must be launched. . . . The only source of funds for such amount [as is needed] is the federal government.

Perhaps a portion of the money saved by virtue of the nuclear test ban should thus be used to reclaim a people and a nation. But whether or not the federal government acts, the New Jacobins will continue their revolutionary thrust. To paraphrase a beaten white Freedom Rider: "We'll take beating. We'll take kicking. We'll take even death. And we'll keep coming till we can ride, work, live, study, and play anywhere in this country—without anyone saying anything, but just as American citizens."

The younger, more militant and separatist factions in the Civil Rights Movement and in Farmer's own organization, CORE, did not see the tensions within the movement as creative or healthy. Their experiences working in the South to register black voters in 1964 had been so brutal that they had begun to disdain the tactic of nonviolence. They sought to rid the movement of those who were willing to compromise or to work with whites. By 1966 these separatist factions had gained ascendance in CORE, and Farmer resigned as leader of the organization, although he retained ties with the group. He was replaced by Floyd McKissick, who stressed separate black economic development.

Two years later, in 1968, Farmer ran for Congress from Brooklyn as a Republican; he was defeated by New York State assemblywoman Shirley Chisholm, a black Democrat. President Richard Nixon appointed Farmer assistant secretary of Health, Education and Welfare in 1969, an appointment that caused much controversy among Farmer's old colleagues, who felt it inappropriate for him to serve in an administration that was regarded as hostile to the civil rights cause. Farmer hoped he would have the opportunity to establish programs to educate and train blacks so they could take advantage of their new opportunities. Earlier, he had urged President Johnson to provide such programs, and it had been during a conversation with Farmer that Johnson had coined the phrase "affirmative action." He found, however, that he had no power to do anything substantial in the job, and he resigned after a short time. Remaining based in Washington, D.C., he gave lectures at various colleges and headed a "think tank," analyzing events and government policies, at Howard University, a leading black institution.

In 1968, Roy Innis replaced Floyd McKissick as national director of CORE. Innis was even more militant and separatist than McKissick, but Farmer continued to be associated with CORE. Not until 1976, when Innis attempted to recruit black Vietnam veterans as mercenaries in Angola's civil war, did Farmer break all ties with the organization that he had founded.

In 1977, Farmer became executive director of the coalition of American Public Employees in Washington, D.C. In 1980, he led a group of former members of CORE in an attempt to oust Roy Innis from his position as leader of the organization. The move failed, as did Farmer's efforts to form a new, racially mixed civil rights organization. In 1985 he published his autobiography, a thoughtful and moving story of his life and that of the Civil Rights Movement titled *Lay Bare the Heart*. At this writing, he is visiting professor at Mary Washington College in Fredericksburg, Virginia, and as one of the "grand old men" of the Civil Rights Movement, speaks often before college and civic groups.

JAMES FORMAN

James Forman was one of the "young Turks" of the Civil Rights Movement, if not in age then in political orientation. Born in Chicago in 1929, he taught school there until he joined the movement. He was one of the early leaders of SNCC and was its executive secretary from 1961 to 1969. During those years he began to turn away from the concept of nonviolence and to consider seriously the idea of armed struggle and separatism. This change in attitude developed slowly, but in 1964 the Mississippi Freedom Summer project and the Democratic presidential convention in Atlantic City, New Jersey, solidified his new militancy.

By 1964, the Direct Action Civil Rights Movement had achieved some remarkable goals. That year Congress passed, and President Lyndon B. Johnson signed into law, the 1964 Civil Rights Act, the most far-reaching civil rights legislation since the post–Civil War Reconstruction period. It contained provisions that helped to guarantee blacks the right to vote as well as access to public accommodations such as hotels and motels, restaurants and places of amusement. It also authorized the federal government to sue in order to desegregate public facilities and schools, among other provisions. Of course, the South was in no hurry to obey this new law, and various civil rights organizations made plans to test it in the South. SNCC launched the Mississippi Freedom Summer, organizing hundreds of student volunteers to register black voters in that state.

The project had barely begun when, in June, two young white men from Yale University, Andrew Goodman and Michael Schwerner, and a young black man from Meridian, Mississippi, James Chaney, were murdered by white racists. In 1967, an all-white jury would convict seven men on charges of conspiracy to murder, the first time that anyone was convicted for civil rights slayings in that state; but that was three years after Freedom Summer. Swifter justice would have been necessary to prevent young black civil rights workers from feeling that the nonviolent philosophy was foolish. In fact, as Forman states below, the Mississippi Summer Project was almost *calculated* to produce violent confrontation. The following excerpts from Forman's book *The Making of Black Revolutionaries,* published in 1972, give a sense of what he and other blacks in SNCC were feeling.

INSIDE THE MISSISSIPPI SUMMER PROJECT

We felt that it was high time for the United States as a whole, a white-dominated country, to feel the consequences of its own racism. White people should know the meaning of the work we were doing—they should feel some of the suffering and terror and deprivation that black people endured. We could not bring all of white America to Mississippi. But by bringing some of its children as volunteer workers a new consciousness would feed back into the homes of thousands of white Americans as they worried about their sons and daughters confronting "the jungle of Mississippi," the bigoted sheriffs, the Klan, the vicious White Citizens' Councils. We recognized that the result might be great pain and sorrow, but we were not asking the whites to do any more than we had done. And our goal was not personal or vengeful: Any havoc that might be brought into the homes of white America would be acted out in the nation's political arena. As it was. Uppermost in the thoughts of some of us was the long-range implication for social change in the United States by exposing ever greater numbers to active struggle with poor people.

But there was intense resistance to the project by many staff members of SNCC and COFO [Council of Federated Organizations, an umbrella group created to receive and distribute grant monies for use in civil rights activities]. It centered around the consequences of having a huge number of white students in Mississippi. Great concern was expressed over the security problem that would be created: Whites in black neighorhoods would draw tremendous attention, intensify our visibility, make it harder for us to be absorbed in, and thus protected by, the black community. In addition to the security problem, staff members worried about the effects—especially psychological effects—of having many whites enter into work with black people that had up to then been primarily carried out by other black people . . .

The original thinking behind the Mississippi Summer Project included the idea that the heated atmosphere caused by the presence of many volunteers, especially whites, would force the federal government to intervene—possibly with the use of troops. But this idea changed through discussion and analysis. It was realized that the federal government, the Johnson administration, was unlikely to send troops into Mississippi during the summer of 1964. And even if it did send troops, they would constitute no more than a housekeeping operation . . .

Given this fact of life, we saw the local, long-range function of the summer volunteers as helping to break the pattern of white racism and helping to build viable institutions of, by, and for black people. This turned out to be a tricky proposition. The presence of so many white college students had a negative effect on SNCC workers and local people. One of our project directors, for example, began to feel ashamed of the fact that he had completed only the sixth grade in school and told people that he had graduated from college. In other areas, local black people who had been in the process of learning how to handle office work and administrative matters got shunted aside as the whites came in with their already developed "skills" . . .

The role of whites in the project was closely related to the issue of violence and, therefore, to the question of self-defense. A few days before the orientation sessions for volunteers were to begin at Oxford, Ohio, a meeting took place at which these interwoven problems assumed major proportions and were hotly debated—especially the question of self-defense. Up to that time, SNCC had never discouraged the use of arms for self-defense by the Southern blacks with whom we worked, but we did have a policy of not allowing staff members to carry weapons. At that meeting, the lines of debate were complex and intermingled, but generally speaking there was one contingent arguing that SNCC should publicly proclaim its belief in self-defense while others, including myself, argued that self-defense was something people should just do and not proclaim—for the announcement alerted the opposition. There were some actions that had to be carried out in a clandestine fashion and arming oneself stood high on the list . . .

Perhaps we ourselves, in SNCC, were not completely ready for violence. We had not exhausted the legal means of protest and hence we were not emotionally prepared to articulate and teach other forms of struggle. In my own case, I knew our struggle would eventually take a violent form, and I was ready for the transition whenever it occurred. There was never any doubt that I was psychologically prepared to kill my oppressor by whatever means I had. But I didn't feel the time was ripe.

Among the legal means of securing their goals that Forman

and SNCC had not yet exhausted was using blacks' newly won voting strength to effect change within the Democratic Party. Having established the Mississippi Freedom Democratic Party (MFDP) and registered many black Mississippians to vote, SNCC prepared to send an alternate slate of Democratic delegates to that party's presidential convention in Atlantic City, New Jersey, at the end of the summer. Sixty-eight delegates from the MFDP, all but one of them black, demanded that *they* be seated instead of the "racist regulars from Mississippi."

The Democratic Party Credentials Committee offered a compromise: the MFDP delegation would be allowed to attend the convention as "guests," and two of the sixty-eight MFDP delegates would be seated as at-large delegates. The MFDP traveled to Atlantic City, but ultimately they rejected the compromise and refused to seat any of their delegates. They had lost all belief in the ability of the Democratic Party to seriously address the issue of racism in the southern delegations.

They understood, but had no sympathy for, the fact that the Democrats were worried about the upcoming election, not just for the presidency, but also for seats in Congress. The passage of the 1964 Civil Rights Act had infuriated white racists, who had stepped up their violent acts against civil rights workers in the South. Even the leaders of several older civil rights organizations had called for the ending of mass marches, picketing, or other demonstrations until after the elections in November. They were afraid that the white backlash might contribute to the defeat of President Johnson.

Johnson won the election over the Republican candidate, Senator Barry Goldwater, and early 1965 saw a new round of civil rights activity, concentrated primarily on black voting rights. Even though provisions of the 1964 Civil Rights Act were supposed to guarantee these rights, southern blacks in large numbers were still denied the vote. In March, after two earlier attempts had dissolved in violent confrontations with police and state troopers, Martin Luther King, Jr., led a march for voting rights from Selma, Alabama, to the state capitol building in Montgomery. This march, too, was the scene of violent confrontations, and resulted in the passage of a Voting Rights Act, which President Johnson signed into law in August 1965. For Forman and others in SNCC, however, this legislation came too late to dissolve their bitterness against whites and against the government. The violence and killings had only confirmed in their minds that white racism was not going to be overcome either by nonviolence or by legislation. SNCC moved increasingly toward black separatism and militancy, and in 1966 issued a call for "Black Power."

In the course of a power struggle with Stokely Carmichael, chairman of SNCC, Forman lost all real influence in the organization, although he remained as its executive secretary until 1969. In 1968, he also served as minister of education in the newly formed Black Panther Party, which in the beginning worked very closely with SNCC. When in 1969 the two organizations split, Forman resigned from both.

That same year, as acting chairman of the newly formed Black Economic Development Conference (BEDC), Forman wrote and presented a "Black Manifesto" to white churches, demanding reparations, or payment, for black suffering. He wasn't singling out the church as the only institution guilty of racism and oppression, but as a symbol of the nation as a whole, explaining, "We have learned through experience that we have taken on the total government by taking on the church. . . . The church is the jugular vein of the country because wrapped up in the church is the vital system which keeps perpetuating the kind of exploitation of blacks which goes on." While the BEDC did not receive any "reparations" directly as a result of Forman's manifesto, the Interreligious Foundation for Community Organization, which had been founded in 1966 and which had sponsored the BEDC from its beginnings, did receive funds and acted as a channel for those funds to the BEDC. Both organizations eventually dissolved.

During the 1970s, Forman became an officer in the League of Black Revolutionary Workers, formed by dissident members of the United Auto Workers union in Detroit, Michigan. He continued to write and, after settling in Washington, D.C., he founded his own press, Open Hand Publishing Company.

There were no major civil rights marches or other kinds of demonstrations in the South after the Voting Rights Act of 1965 went into effect. There was still severe discrimination and segregation in the region—in rural areas the COLORED and WHITES ONLY signs didn't come down until about 1970. But with the enactment of so much federal civil rights legislation the Direct Action Civil Rights Movement had achieved its goals, at least on paper, and consequently it lost its momentum. Martin Luther King, Jr., began to concentrate on improving conditions for blacks in the North. Many of the young whites who had supported the movement began to direct their attention to the anti–Vietnam War crusade. Many of those whites who would have been willing to continue to work for black equality no longer felt wanted in the struggle, for by the mid-1960s the most vocal blacks were rejecting integration and racial cooperation in favor of black separatism and black nationalism. More on this Black Power Movement will be described in Chapter 5.

CHAPTER THREE

REVOLUTION ON THE CAMPUS

While the 1960s are remembered as a time of student movements and student revolt, it should be pointed out that student revolts are not a phenomenon that first arose in the sixties. There have been student movements almost as long as there have been universities. When students leave home and connect with their peers, they often begin to encounter new ideas that cause them to question what their parents have taught them. When they find college administrations trying to act like their parents at a time when they want to be independent, the seeds of revolt are planted. And when they feel that they have the power to change things, those seeds of revolt are likely to take root and grow.

In the United States, student movements have a long history, going back to colonial times; student movements played a part in the American Revolution. After the Revolution, there wasn't much organized student political activity until the late 1800s, when the ideas of socialism and Communism then being advanced in Europe began to take hold. Student organizations played active roles in the American Labor Movement, and by 1905 there were many student movements dedicated to the ideals of socialism. During and after World War I, most student movements subsided, only to reappear during the Great Depression. With World War II, there was another quiet period on the campuses, and it lasted through most of the 1950s. Thus, the student movements of the 1960s were, in one way, simply the reappearance of an age-old phenomenon. The difference was in the issues being raised, and in the size and intensity of the response.

We have already seen how the Baby Boom had created a huge young population, and how postwar prosperity in the 1950s had allowed many of these Baby Boomers to grow up in a world of financial security. It was these secure Baby Boomers who began to enter college in the early 1960s, more than doubling the U.S. college population between 1960 and 1964. They felt the power of their numbers, and they felt also that they should have more say in the issues that affected their lives on campus. In the early 1960s, the students didn't think much of the idea that colleges acted *in loco parentis,* or in place of parents. They believed that the colleges and universities, which they (or their parents) were paying to educate them, should be more responsive to their wants and needs. Instead, the colleges and universities seemed to want to control them entirely. It is not surprising that writer Norman Mailer's article "The Student as Nigger" was a widely read tract.

In addition, there was a feeling among students that there was a lot about the world, and American society in particular, that needed changing. They comprised the first generation that was exposed, through television, to the evils of the world at large: racial segregation in the South, the Korean conflict overseas, strife and war all around the globe. They were also the first generation that grew up with the knowledge that the world could be destroyed by the atomic bomb. Some of these young people believed that unless they did something to try to change the world, they wouldn't be able to live out their natural life spans. At college, such students had the opportunity to meet others who shared their feelings and to form organizations dedicated to espousing the causes in which they believed. That is how a group of students came to form Students for a Democratic Society (SDS).

SDS was an outgrowth of a socialist organization known as the Student League for Industrial Democracy, which operated from 1905 to 1948. About ten years after its breakup, a new generation of students sought to revive its principles under a new name, Students for a Democratic Society. It was started at the University of Michigan by a group of students that included a young man named Tom Hayden. Its constitution described SDS as "an association of young people on the left." It did not issue a clear statement of policy until 1962, when a meeting at Port Huron, Michigan, resulted in a basic agreement on policies, if not offering any concrete program. Known as the Port Huron Statement, it read in part:

> *We are people of this generation, bred in at least modern comfort, housed in universities, looking uncomfortably to the world we inherit. Our work is guided by the sense that we may be the last generation in the experiment with living. . . . We ourselves are imbued with urgency, yet the message of our society is that there is no viable alternative to the present . . .*
>
> *Feeling the press of complexity upon the emptiness of life, people are fearful of the thought that at any moment things might be thrust out of control. They fear change itself, since change might smash whatever invisible frame holds back chaos for them now. For most Americans, all crusades are suspect, threatening . . .*
>
> *If student movements for change are rarities still on the campus scene, what is commonplace there? The real cam-*

> *pus, the familiar campus, is a place of private people, engaged in their notorious "inner emigration" [wrapped up in themselves]. It is a place of mass affirmation of the Twist, but mass reluctance toward the controversial public stance. Rules are accepted as "inevitable," bureaucracy as "just circumstances," irrelevance as "scholarship," selflessness as "martyrdom."*

The vagueness of the Port Huron Statement notwithstanding, chapters of SDS began to spring up on a variety of campuses. Similar groups were formed on other campuses, all reflecting the growing desire among students to make a difference in the world—though, like SDS, few had a real plan of action. Some of these groups joined the Civil Rights Movement in the South; others worked with the poor in their own areas. Still others spent their time simply meeting and talking. Common to them all was a sense that they were somehow being *used*—not educated to think independently but trained to conform. The phrase "military-industrial complex" was often heard at student meetings. This phrase referred to the students' suspicion that government and industry were somehow conspiring to channel the intelligence and the energies of the nation's young into money-making and war-making schemes. This suspicion had its roots in the fact that many universities were engaged in research that was paid for by government agencies and private industry—research to develop new military and industrial products and methods. The students questioned if that was a proper kind of activity for centers of higher learning to be involved in.

None of these organizations was able to mount a major student movement until the confrontation at Berkeley in 1964 over the issue of student "free speech." That confrontation, often described as the most important single event in the history of American higher education, had long-ranging effects that are still being felt today.

MARIO SAVIO AND THE BERKELEY FREE SPEECH MOVEMENT

Long before the sixties, the University of California at Berkeley was known as a center of activism, even though the university itself had rules that rigidly controlled political activities on campus. Just outside the main entrance was a sidewalk area that all the student organizations used for speech-making and for distributing literature on everything from banning the bomb to voting for homecoming queen. Everyone assumed that the area was city property and thus outside the university's jurisdiction. That stretch of sidewalk was like an "escape valve," and as such it benefited the students and the university alike. The students had a place to do their politicking and the university did not feel responsible for it.

That is, until September 1964, when the university learned that it owned that piece of sidewalk. All student organizations were immediately notified that they could no longer use the area for political activities. For their part, the student organizations immediately charged that the university was trying to stifle student dissent.

At first the students believed they could work out some sort of compromise. But when the university refused to give the students any leeway, a full-scale student rebellion swiftly broke out. The student organizations, happily combative with one another up till then, united in the face of the threat to their collective "freedom of speech." Borrowing tactics from the Direct Action Civil Rights Movement, they organized a sit-in at the administration building and sponsored a rally that attracted thousands of students. Early the next day, more than a thousand students staged another sit-in, and when they refused to cease their demonstration by nightfall, California's governor, Edmund G. Brown, ordered police onto the campus to arrest them. More than eight hundred undergraduate students were taken into po-

Student protest virtually closed down the University of California at Berkeley. ABOVE, a protest outside the building where the university regents are meeting is broken up by police. BELOW, National Guardsmen, called onto the campus after a bloody riot, keep a watchful eye on the students.

lice custody. This action caused many graduate students and faculty members to enter the controversy, picketing campus buildings and protesting the governor's decision to call in the police—a decision that they regarded as an unforgivable violation of the sanctity of the university.

By that time Mario Savio, intense and eloquent, had emerged as the spokesman for the Student Free Speech Movement. The twenty-two-year-old native of New York, a philosophy major at Berkeley, considered himself nonpolitical. He also considered himself law-abiding and went so far as to take his shoes off before he mounted a university police car to give his speech, so as not to damage university property. He later said, "I don't know what made me get up and give that first speech. I only know I had to." For Savio, the issue of free speech was just the tip of the iceberg, the most obvious problem between the university and its students. What he talked about in that first speech was the whole relationship between university and students. He believed that the students, who paid the university to educate them, should have the power to influence decisions concerning their university lives. He felt it was wrong for the university to have all the power. What he said so inspired his fellow students, and their faculty supporters, that he suddenly found himself speaking at all the rallies and demonstrations. The national press covering the rebellion at Berkeley sought him out as the spokesman for the movement. In 1965 he spoke to an interviewer for *Life* magazine about how the Free Speech Movement had arisen and about its tactics. Excerpts from that interview follow.

THE UNIVERSITY HAS BECOME A FACTORY

The Roots of the Problem

. . . Those who should give orders—the faculty and students—

take orders, and those who should tend to keeping the sidewalks clean, to seeing that we have enough classrooms—the administration—give orders. . . . As [social critic] Paul Goodman says, students are the exploited class in America, subjected to all the techniques of factory methods: tight scheduling, speedups, rules of conduct they're expected to obey with little or no say-so. At Cal you're little more than an IBM card. For efficiency's sake, education is organized along quantifiable lines. One hundred and twenty units make a bachelor's degree . . .

The university is a vast public utility which turns out future workers in today's vineyard, the military-industrial complex. They've got to be processed in the most efficient way to see to it that they have the fewest dissenting opinions, that they have just those characteristics which are wholly incompatible with being an intellectual. . . . People have to suppress the very questions which reading books raises . . .

On the Administration

[University president] Clark Kerr is the ideologist for a kind of "brave new world" conception of educaton. He replaces the word "university" with "multiversity." The multiversity serves many publics at once, he says. But Kerr's publics . . . [are] the corporate establishment of California, plus a lot of national firms, the government, especially the Pentagon [headquarters of the U.S. military in Washington, D.C.]. It's no longer a question of a community of students and scholars, of independent, objective research but rather of contracted research. . . . The business of the university is teaching and learning. Only people engaged in it—the students and teachers—are competent to decide how it should be done.

On Being an American Student

America may be the most poverty-stricken country in the world. Not materially. But intellectually it is bankrupt. And morally it's poverty-stricken. But in such a way that it's not clear to you that you're poor. It's very hard to know you're poor if you're eating well.

In the Berkeley ghetto—which is, let's say, the campus and the surrounding five or six blocks—you bear certain stigmas. They're not the color of your skin, for the most part, but the fact that you're an intellectual, and perhaps a moral nonconformist. You question the mores and morals and institutions of society seriously. This creates a feeling of mutuality, of real community. Students are excited about political ideas. They're not yet inured to the apolitical society they're going to enter. But being interested in ideas means you have no use in American society . . . unless they are ideas which are useful to the military-industrial complex. That means there's no connection between what you're doing and the world you're about to enter.

There's a lot of aimlessness in the ghetto, a lot of restlessness. Some people are 40 years old and they're still members. They're student mentalities who never grew up; they're people who were active in radical politics, let's say, in the Thirties, people who have never connected with the world, have not been able to make it in America. You can see the similarity between this and the Harlem situation [he was referring to the largest black ghetto in the nation, most of whose poor, uneducated residents also could not "connect with the world" or "make it in America"].

On the Student Protests

At first we didn't understand what the issues were. But as discussions went on, they became clear. The university wanted to regulate the content of our speech. . . . The Free Speech Movement has always had an ideology of its own. Call it essentially anti-liberal. By that I mean it is anti a certain style of politics prevalent in the United States: politics by compromise—which succeeds if you don't state any issues. You don't state issues, so you can't be attacked from any side. . . . By contrast our ideology is issue-oriented. We thought the administration was doing bad things and we said so. Some people on the faculty repeatedly told us we couldn't say or do things too provocative or we'd turn people off—alienate the faculty. Yet, with every provocative thing we did, more faculty members came to our aid. And when the apocalypse came, over 800 of them were with us.

On Civil Disobedience

If you accept that societies can be run by rules, as I do, then you necessarily accept as a consequence that you can't disobey the rules every time you disapprove. That would be saying that the rules are valid only when they coincide with your conscience. . . . However, when you're considering something that constitutes an extreme abridgement of your rights, conscience is the court of last resort. Then you've got to decide whether this is one of the things which, although you disagree, you can live with. . . . Hopefully, in a good society this kind of decision wouldn't have to be made very often, if at all. But we don't have a good society. . . . We have a society which has many social evils, not the least of which is the fantastic presumption in a lot of people's minds that naturally decisions which are in accord with the rules must be right—an assumption which is not founded on any legitimate philosophical principle. In our society, precisely because of the great distortions and injustices which exist, I would hope that civil disobedience becomes more prevalent than it is.

Eventually, the administration of the University of California at Berkeley backed down and allowed the students to have their area for politicking. With the students' victory, the furor over the Free Speech Movement subsided, and so did public interest in Mario Savio. That was fine with him. Over the next two decades he shunned publicity; but the media never completely forgot him. In the spring of 1984, newspapers reported that he had graduated from San Francisco State University at the age of forty with a bachelor of science degree. Ironically, he himself had become one of the forty-year-old students about whom he had spoken to the interviewer for *Life* magazine. At age twenty-three, he was certain that anyone who was still in college at age forty wasn't prepared to deal with the real world. Older and wiser, married and the father of two children, he understood that sometimes other responsibilities get in the way. In October 1984, leaders of the Free Speech Movement returned to the Berkeley campus to celebrate the twentieth anniversary of the movement. Mario Savio was among them. Speaking of the movement, he said, "It has remained for me a brilliant moment when, as a friend put it, we were both moral and successful."

The Berkeley Free Speech Movement was successful not just in regaining the sidewalk area for politicking. It showed that students, if they could put their differences aside, could unite and win. It set the stage for many other campus protest movements across the United States, giving birth to the campus sit-in as a protest tactic and becoming a model for the more widespread movement against the Vietnam War later in the decade.

Across the country, college campuses were engulfed in a wave of student political activity. At one point, more than seven hundred and fifty colleges and universities either closed temporarily or seriously considered doing so. The reasons for the student protests varied widely, although in all cases students were trying to gain greater control. Sometimes they simply demonstrated for a greater voice in university rules. The 1960s saw a relaxation of the university's role as a parental substitute, with fewer rules about how late students could stay out or whether or not they could have visitors of the opposite sex in their rooms. Sometimes the students fought for a greater voice in academic matters, and across the nation they lobbied for pass-fail courses, the elimination of required courses, and more seats on university- or college-wide governing boards. But the two largest issues over which students protested were black studies and the membership of colleges and universities in the military-industrial complex.

THE BLACK STUDIES MOVEMENT: RON KARENGA AND THE KAWAIDA CONCEPT

The Black Studies Movement was a logical outgrowth of the Black Power Movement that emerged in 1966 (and which will be treated more fully in Chapter 5). If blacks were to have power, they had to have pride. If they were to have pride, they had to have a knowledge of their own history and culture. Until the mid-1960s American publishers issued very few books by or about blacks, not to mention other minorities and women. School history books barely mentioned black Americans except when talking about slavery. In elementary school readers, Dick and Jane were white. The proponents of black studies argued that black history and culture should be taught as a separate discipline, and in the course of the mid to late 1960s numerous demonstrations on behalf of black studies programs succeeded in winning such programs at a large number of colleges and universities.

One of the most vigorous and outspoken proponents of black studies was Ron Karenga. He was also one of the chief spokesmen for the concept of black cultural nationalism; he urged black Americans to stop trying to adapt to white values and to embrace their own distinct Afro-American culture. Karenga was born Ronald Everett, the son of a Baptist minister, in Maryland on July 14, 1941. Little else is known about his early life. He attended California Junior College and was the first black to be elected student body president. He received a master's degree in political science from the University of California at Los Angeles, then enrolled in the doctoral program in linguistics.

The riots in the Watts ghetto in the summer of 1965 were a turning point in Karenga's life. He realized that the majority of black people had been untouched by the gains of the Direct Action Civil Rights Movement in the South. The poor black people in Watts needed dignity, pride, and the basic necessities of life more than they needed integration. He felt that they needed a sense of history, and a culture that was their own. He believed that if there could be a cultural revolution to win the minds of black people, then the political revolution would follow as a matter of course.

In the 1960s, black Africa could be a source of history and culture and pride for black Americans. Until then Africa had been a group of European colonies—hardly a source of inspiration for black Americans. Beginning in the late 1950s, a few African colonies started winning their independence. The year 1960 was a watershed year for African independence; in that one year, Zaire, Somali, Dahomey, Ivory Coast, Chad, Congo Brazzaville, Gabon, Senegal, Mali, and Nigeria all gained their independence. By 1964, Tanganyika, Sierra Leone, Algeria, Burundi, Rwanda, Uganda, Kenya, Zanzibar, Malawi, and Zambia were independent as well. It was an exciting time not only for the newly independent black Africans but for black Americans who closely followed what was happening on the continent from which their ancestors had come. It was a time to be proud of Africa and of one's African roots. To instill pride in black heritage and to develop a separate Afro-American culture, Karenga founded an organization called simply US, meaning "us" (blacks) as opposed to "them" (whites). He took a new last name from the African language Swahili: Karenga, meaning "Nationalist"or "keeper of tradition." He adopted a new style of dress and appearance: He shaved his head, grew a mandarin-type mustache (very thin and drooping), and wore African-style shirts and an African tiki figure on a thong around his neck. His followers called him the Maulana, which in Swahili means "master teacher."

Although US never attracted a large membership, Karenga held a position of considerable influence among black activists and intellectuals. In 1967, he helped to form the Black Congress, an umbrella organization of moderate and militant black groups in Los Angeles. The following year he organized a "Black Power" conference. What attracted many people was not just his ability to organize but his creation of a very detailed new "culture" for Afro-Americans that included holidays such as Kwanzaa as an alternative to Christmas (named for the Swahili word meaning "first," it celebrates the first fruits of the harvest) and Africanized greetings like "Habari Gani" ("What's happening?"). These were all part of his idea of Kawaida (African traditionalism). They were also his own inventions. Speaking about Kwanzaa at Howard University in 1978, Karenga said, "People think it's African but it's not. I wanted to give black people a holiday of their own, so I came up with Kwanzaa. I said it was African because you know black people in this country wouldn't celebrate it if they knew it was American. Also, I put it around Christmas [December 26 to January 1] because I knew that's when a lot of people would be partying."

Inspired by Karenga, many supporters of black studies began to call the discipline Afro-American studies and to demand courses in African languages, African customs, and the arts of Africa. Karenga's followers put together a collection of his statements, and *The Quotable Karenga,* published in 1967, was indeed used by some to support their demands for separate Afro-American studies programs. Following are some of Karenga's statements about education.

NOTES FROM *THE QUOTABLE KARENGA*

Cultural background transcends education. Having a scope is different from having a content.

We're not for isolation but for interdependence—but we can't become interdependent unless we have something to offer.

Blacks must develop their own heroic images. To the white boy, Garvey [Marcus Garvey, a black nationalist of the early twentieth century who built a substantial following before his deportation] was a failure—to us he was perfect for his time and context. To the white boy Malcolm X [black nationalist of the 1960s who was assassinated in 1965] was a hate teacher—to us he was the highest form of Black Manhood in his generation.

Education without dignity is invalid.

You have to make distinctions between history writers and historians. History writers write what the power structure dictates. Historians create concrete images. Therefore, Blacks must write their own history and develop their own heroic images and heroic deeds.

The revolution being fought now is a revolution to win the minds of our people. If we fail to win this we cannot wage the violent one.

We must believe in our cause and be willing to die for it and we should stop reading other peoples [sic] literature and write our own and stop pretending revolution and make it.

We must make warriors out of our poets and writers. For if all our writers would speak as warriors our battle would be half won. Literature conditions the mind and the battle for the mind is half of the struggle.

All education and creation is invalid unless it can benefit the maximum amount of Blacks.

By the time Karenga organized US, the Black Power Movement had begun, and there was soon no clear line between his activities on college campuses and his activities off them. While black studies, or Afro-American studies, were a major issue, he was deeply involved in off-campus black community activities as well. At the same time, some of the new, community-based Black Power organizations tried to become involved in the black studies programs. In 1968, Karenga and the newly formed Black Panther Party, a community-based Black Power organization, came into conflict over the new black studies program at the University of California at Los Angeles. Both US and the Black Panther Party wanted control of the program. On January 23, 1969, two Panthers were shot dead in the UCLA student cafeteria where a meeting of black faculty was about to be held. That fall, three members of US were tried and convicted of the killings.

Even with their new openness to student and community concerns, neither college administrations nor the majority of their faculties and students wanted their campuses to become armed battlefields. The Black Studies Movement continued with marked success, but without Ron Karenga.

In 1971, Karenga was arrested and charged with assaulting a female member of US. Found guilty and sentenced to a six-month-to-ten-year prison term, he was in prison until May 1975. He charged that he received such a harsh sentence, and served five times the minimum sentence for the crime despite recommendations for his parole, not for any crime but rather for his political views. While in prison he wrote many articles on Pan-Africanism, but without him his US movement failed to grow. He admitted that he had not worked hard enough to develop a solid community base.

At this writing, Karenga is associate professor of Black Studies at California State University, Long Beach, and director of his own Kawaida Institute of Pan-African Studies. In 1982, he self-published a book titled *Introduction to Black Studies,* described as the first single-author text on the subject. US no longer exists, but the ideas of cultural nationalism that Karenga wanted US to foster still do. Cornrow hairstyles, Swahili names, and African-style holidays and greetings exist to show that black Americans are proud of their unique heritage. Black studies or Afro-American studies programs at colleges and universities throughout the country still teach some of the subjects for which Karenga fought.

AGAINST THE MILITARY-INDUSTRIAL COMPLEX: MARK RUDD OF SDS AND THE COLUMBIA STUDENT REBELLION

Student protests against the close relationship between American higher education and the military began in the late 1950s. At that time, most colleges and universities had courses that trained young men to be officers in the armed forces, part of a program called the Reserve Officers Training Corps (ROTC). Usually, all male students had to enroll in ROTC. In 1959 and 1960, students at the University of California demonstrated successfully against mandatory ROTC, leading students at other colleges and universities to undertake similar campaigns.

By the mid-1960s, with the escalation of American involvement in the conflict between North and South Vietnam, students had begun to protest their schools' association with industries that made products for use in war. Their chief target was Dow Chemical. In addition to many products made for use in the home, Dow Chemical made napalm, a chemical substance used by U.S. military forces to defoliate the dense forest areas in Vietnam where North Vietnamese troops and their South Vietnamese sympathizers might be hiding. Defoliation, or stripping trees of their leaves, was accomplished by dropping small "bombs" of napalm from planes into forested areas. The trouble was, sometimes there were people in the forests. Napalm acts on people's skin in the same way as it does on the leaves of trees. Photographs of victims displayed on television and in newspapers showed the horrible results.

SDS (Students for a Democratic Society) was a growing, active organization with branches on many campuses by then. It was in the forefront of demonstrations against companies such as Dow as well as against the government contracts with universities to engage in research in chemical and psychological warfare (how to get information from war prisoners, how to make the enemy fearful and discouraged by other than military means). One of the most active SDS chapters was at Columbia

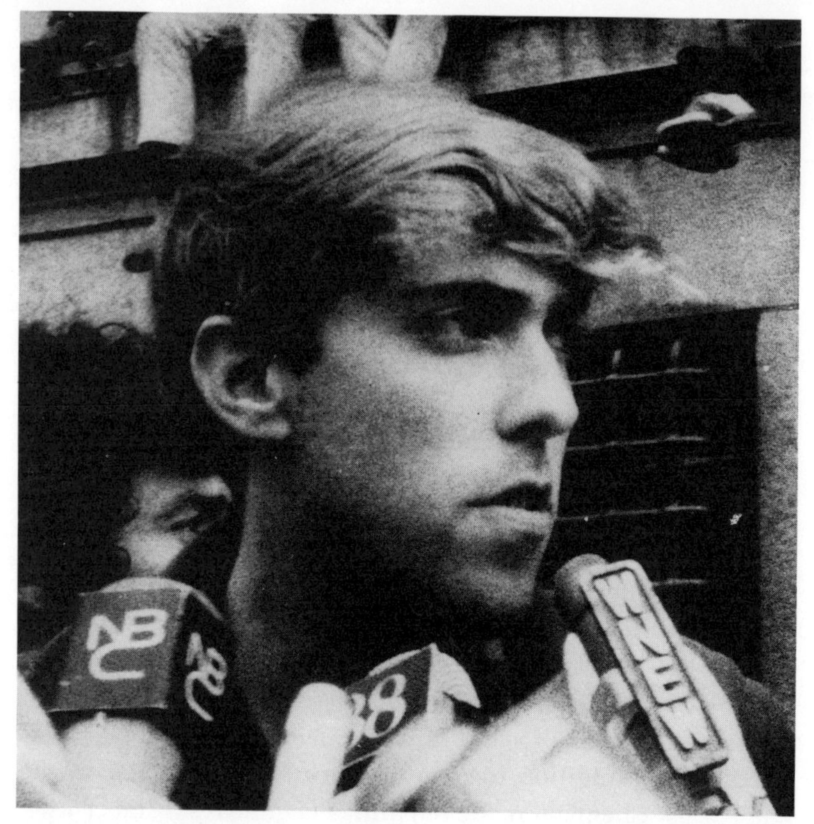

The spring of 1968 saw a wave of protest sweep Columbia University. ABOVE, Mark Rudd, president of the SDS chapter at Columbia, gives a speech before the students. BELOW, radical students fend off an attempt to enter the barricaded mathematics building at Columbia.

University in New York City, where militant students had a variety of grievances against the administration. The two most serious were Columbia's close ties with the Institute for Defense Analysis (IDA) and the university's unsympathetic treatment of the black community that surrounded it. What set off the spring 1968 rebellion was the university's plan to construct a gymnasium in Morningside Park, the black neighborhood's only recreation area. At first, only Columbia's black students actively opposed the plan, but as Mark Rudd explains, the issue brought radical students of all races together.

Rudd was born in 1947 in suburban New Jersey. Blond, handsome, and solidly middle class, he epitomized the young white radical of the sixties. He felt guilty about how easy his life had been and was idealistic and romantic enough to believe that he could change the world. He was president of the SDS chapter at Columbia when the militant black student organization, SAS (Students' Afro-American Society), took over Hamilton Hall to protest the building of the gym in Morningside Park, and he led SDS into the fray in support of them. SDS, like many revolutionary/militant organizations, lost force because it tried to reflect too many different philosophies. Writing from the perspective of several months later, Rudd recalled how SDS got involved and what he and his organization learned from the experience.

COLUMBIA: NOTES ON THE SPRING REBELLION

. . . At Columbia, we had a four-year history of agitation and education involving forms of activity from seminars and open forums on IDA to militant confrontation over NROTC (Naval Reserve Officers Training Corps) and military recruiting. All went into developing the mass consciousness that was responsible for the Columbia rebellion. The point I wish to emphasize, however, is that we had to develop the willingness to take action, minority action, before the tremendous potential of the "base" could be released. In addition, the vanguard action also acted as education for many people not yet convinced. The radical analysis never got such a hearing, and a sympathetic one, as during the rebellion . . .

[A] sit-in against the CIA [Central Intelligence Agency] . . . took place at Columbia in February, 1967, involving only eighteen people (led by the Progressive Labor Party, before it had turned right). This seemingly isolated action (even the SDS chapter did not participate) helped ready people for the direct action to come one year later by making a first penetration into students' minds that direct action is both possible and desirable . . .

We had no way of knowing whether the base was ready at Columbia: in fact, neither SDS nor the masses of students actually were ready; we were spurred on by a tremendous push from history, embodied in the militant black students at Columbia.

The Role of Blacks

Before April 23, the Students' Afro-American Society and Columbia SDS had never joined together in a joint action or even had much cross-group communication. SAS had been mostly a cultural or social organization, in part reflecting the class background of its members (SDS's position on campus likewise reflected its members' middle-class background—the tendency toward over-verbalization instead of action, the reliance on militant, pure, revolutionary rhetoric instead of linking up with the people). It was only with the death of Martin Luther King that SAS began to make political demands—though still mostly about the situation of black students at Columbia. Another important factor in the growing militancy of SAS was the struggle of the Harlem community against Columbia's gym in the form of demonstrations, rallies, and a statement by H. Rap Brown [chairman of SNCC, who changed the "N" in the organization's name from "Nonviolent" to "National"] that the gym should be burnt down if it was somehow built.

The push to the whites and Columbia SDS I spoke of came in its first form from the assassination of Martin Luther King, Jr., which spurred SDS to greater militancy. Second, and more immediate, was the speech at the sundial at noon, April 23, by Cicero Wilson, the chairman of SAS, at which we were honky-baited [called "Whitey" and challenged to act] but also at which people developed the anger and the will to engage in direct action—i.e., tearing down the fence at the gym site. This one symbolic act opened the floodgate of anger and strength and resolve against the racism and prowar policies of the university, and set the stage for the occupation of Hamilton Hall which followed.

The pivotal event of the strike, however, was the black students' decision to barricade Hamilton the night after the joint occupation began. In this decision, the blacks defined themselves politically as members of the Harlem community and the black nation who would fight Columbia's racism to the end. It was also this action that gave the whites a model for militancy and, on a broader scale, forced the whites to wake up to the real world outside themselves (i.e., become radicals).

At the time the black students in Hamilton Hall announced they were going to barricade the building, SDS's goal was the same as it has always been—to radicalize and politicize the mass of white students at Columbia and to create a radical political force of students. This self-definition, however, led to the conclusion that we did not want to risk alienating the mass of other white students by confronting them, say, from behind a barricade. Part of our decision not to barricade must also be seen as a remnant of the earlier timid and nonstruggle attitudes so common in the chapter.

The blacks, for their part, had decided that they would make a stand alone, as a self-conscious black group. This decision was also prompted undoubtedly by the lack of militancy on the part of the whites in Hamilton and especially our lack of discipline and organization.

After leaving Hamilton, a change came over the mass of white students, in and out of SDS. People stayed in Low Library "because we can't abandon the blacks." Not only did people see the model for militancy in the black occupation of Hamilton, but they also began to perceive reality—a world outside themselves—and the necessity to fight, to struggle for liberation, because of the situation in that world.

The essence of liberalism is individualism and subjectivity—"if I'm unhappy, it's my own fault; if I can get ahead in the world, everyone can make it," etc., etc. At the point that people begin to perceive that the real world transcends the individual, that people are affected as classes, and that they can join together to fight back as classes, then the first barrier toward radicalization is broken. It was the action of the black students at Columbia—a group outside the individual fragmented "middle-class" students at Columbia—that woke these students up to the fact that there is a world of suffering, brutalized, exploited people, and that these people are a force willing to fight for freedom. Especially important to this realization was the power of Harlem, both manifest and dormant. Now the liberal universe—the isolated self—was shattered, and the mass occupation started by a handful of whites, the twenty-three who stayed in Low [Library], grew to be the natural response of well over a thousand people who wanted to fight back against the oppression of blacks, Vietnamese, and themselves.

From another point of view, the militancy of the SDS whites forced others to reconsider their position and eventually to join the occupation. But the SDS occupation itself hinged on that of the blacks, and the overwhelming presence of the black students and Harlem itself in proximity forced us to keep the image of the real world—away from which middle-class white students can easily slip—clear and bright in our minds. Because of the blacks, we recognized the immediacy and necessity of the struggle: Vietnam is far away, unfortunately, for most people, and our own pain has become diffuse and dull.

In addition to the vanguard position of blacks toward whites, the example and vanguard role of whites vis-a-vis other whites must also be stressed. When neutral or liberal or even right-wing students see other students, very much like themselves, risking careers, imprisonment, and physical safety, they begin to question the political reasons for which the vanguard is acting, and, concomitantly, their own position. Here, education and propaganda are essential to acquaint people with the issues, and are also the rationale for action. At no time is "organizing" or "talk" more important than before, during, and after militant action.

One of the reasons why people joined en masse was the fact that white students, with the same malaise, alienation, unhappiness about this society and their lack of options in it, and the same hatred for the war [in Vietnam] and racism, saw a way to strike back at the enemy in the actions begun by a few. This was the same enemy, the ruling class and their representatives, the Board of Trustees of Columbia, that had been oppressing blacks and Vietnamese. So, with a little class analysis, articulated by SDS, hundreds of whites saw how they had to move, for their own liberation as well as that of others . . .

Failure of "Mass Politics"

After the police bust which cleared over a thousand people from five buildings, the rebellion faced a critical turning-point. The mass of students, faculty, community people, and others spontaneously demanded a strike against classes, shutting down the university. But the political basis for this strike—its demands, tactics, and organization—was still unclear. Radicals wanted the strike to maintain the original six demands, as a means of keeping the political focus on racism and imperialism, while liberals pushed for as broad a strike as possible—"You've got a good thing here, don't blow it, eveyone's with you, but don't force your politics onto people" was a typical liberal remark.

The real danger, despite the chorus of liberal warnings, was in watering down the politics and the tactics of the strike. This the radical strike committee knew (this was the same strike committee that had been established during the liberation of the buildings, with two representatives from each building), and yet the result of the expansion of the strike committee, even with the politics of the six demands, was the eventual weakening and loss of mass base which occurred in the weeks after the bust.

In brief, the story of the expansion of the strike committee is as follows. The original committee called for a mass meeting on Wednesday night, the day following the bust. This meeting was attended by over 1,300 people, all vigorously anti-administration, and most of whom were ready to follow radical leadership. At that meeting, the strike committee proposed a two-part solution:

1) Expand the strike committee to include representatives of any new constituency groups to form on the basis of one representative to seventy members. Groups could join if they supported the original six demands.
2) Restart the university under our own auspices by running liberated courses, and eventually establishing a provisional administration.

Debate centered around the question of requirements for joining the strike committee: the radicals thought they were absolutely necessary in order to maintain some political coherence, while the liberals, centered around the graduate-faculties student council grouping, wanted, as usual, the broadest base possible, and no requirements. . . . Through a misunderstanding, I capitulated the strike committee position to a liberal one, establishing an apolitical strike committee. . . . The new committee passed almost unanimously the [original] demands, plus a seventh demand on being able to participate in restructuring, so it looked to us (the radicals) that we had "reinjected" politics back into the committee. One good aspect of the error, which should not be underestimated, was that the liberals were prevented from organizing themselves into an opposition for two whole weeks . . .

The failure to deepen and expand the radical base which had formed during the occupation of the buildings, however, lay at the root of our problems . . .

The people in the buildings had fought. Many were new to the radical movement, many were just learning. . . . If ever the phrase "practice outran theory" was true, this was such a time. People seizing buildings. . . fighting cops, committing their lives and careers to a movement for liberation—this was all new and unexplained in political terms. During the liberation of the buildings, too, the frantic pace had kept discussion on too much of a tactical level (Should we barricade? Should we negotiate with the cops?), often focused away from the broader questions that would tell people why, where this is all going, how it fits into a broader, worldwide struggle . . .

How does a mass radical movement involve greater and greater numbers in decision-making? How does it maintain its radical politics when faced with demands for coalition? These problems are still unanswered, though the experiences of Columbia and San Francisco State [where a Third World/Liberation Front/ Black Student Union Movement had been successful] do help provide some ideas.

Significance of the Columbia Uprising

In these notes I've tended to emphasize the errors we made in order to communicate some of the lessons learned during what was for all of us the most intense political experience of our lives.

The failure to establish mass, militant, long-term radical politics has at least in part been answered by the experiences of San Francisco State and other schools. . . . The victories of the Columbia struggle, however, were great. It was the most sustained and most intense radical campus struggle up to that time, around the clearest politics.

At a time when the radical movement was the most disheartened and dispirited . . . the Columbia student rebellion broke through the gloom as an example of the power a radical movement could attain. . . . Liberal politics were exposed as just so much shallow verbiage and wasted effort when compared to the power of a mass radical movement, around significant issues such as racism and imperialism. The radical "base," for the first time ever at one campus, attained a number in the thousands.

Nationwide, Columbia and Chicago [the 1968 Democratic convention where radicals also engaged in mass protests] provided the models for militancy and energy which attracted masses of students after the total failure of conventional politics this summer and fall. The content of that politics, too, the compromises and reformism . . . were juxtaposed to the thoroughgoing analysis of the Left on imperialism, racism, poverty, the class nature of the society. This all was highlighted by Columbia.

At Columbia, our two principal demands, the ending of construction of the gym in Morningside Park, and the formal severing of ties with the Institute for Defense Analysis, were, in fact, met. This laid the basis for broadening the demands this fall to ending all defense and government research, and stopping all university expansion into the community.

Perhaps the most important result of the rebellion, in terms of long-term strategy for the Movement, was the creation of new alliances with student, nonstudent, community, and working-class groups throughout the city. A chapter that had been mostly inward-looking and campus-oriented suddenly opened up and began to realize the tremendous importance of the various types of hook-ups—support, tactical alliance, coalition—which would broaden the radical movement beyond its white, "middle-class," student base . . .

More general off-campus results of the uprising, though important, are hard to estimate. Despite the distortions of the press, many people began to see that students are willing to fight militantly for good goals—ending racism, ending the war. Though no mass or general strike erupted in the nation around our demands, we feel the Columbia rebellion helped break down the antagonism of working people toward students fighting only for their own privilege (at least where the truth got through) . . .

Our strength was greatest at the time of our greatest militancy. It was also the time that we resolved to fight—to disregard all the liberal[s] warning us of the horror of the police bust and the right-wing reaction. In a sense it was a time when we overcame our own middle-class timidity and fear of violence. We, of course, were following the lead of the blacks, but we were also forging new paths where elite white students had never been before. At that time nothing could defeat us, not the police, not the jocks, not the liberal faculty, so treacherous and yet so impotent, only our own (we found out later) weakness and bad political judgement. The liberal world was paralyzed; radicals had a vision of what victory seems like.

Of course, we made mistakes, dozens of them. At the lowest points, feeling that the Movement itself had erred in irreconcilable ways (such as leaving Hamilton Hall, which we at that time did not understand as inevitable and even a source of strength), we found the strength to go on in the knowledge that somehow, history was carrying us forward. Also important was the observation that after making forty-three mistakes, forty-four wouldn't make any difference, so we threw ourselves into the next crisis.

After all, we learned almost accidentally the great truth stated by Chairman Mao Tse-tung [of China], "Dare to struggle, dare to win."

That summer of 1968, SDS tried to keep the movement alive with a "Columbia Strike School," held, ironically, in a fraternity house just off campus (fraternities were regarded as elitist by sixties activists). By fall, however, most students returned to the campus wanting things to be as they had been, with no more upheavals. The students who had been so radicalized that they could not go back to academics-as-usual had to look elsewhere. Mark Rudd was among them. He joined the Weathermen, a radical underground group committed to working against the Vietnam War by sabotage and bombing, if necessary.

In late August 1968, the Democratic Party held its presidential convention in Chicago. The Weathermen and a variety of other radical groups showed up to demonstrate outside the convention hall, to force the Democratic Party to live up to the promises it had made at the 1964 convention and afterward, as well as to admit more minority and women and radical delegates. The demonstrators clashed violently in the streets with the Chicago police; and the following March, eight radicals became the first group to be indicted under the new anti-riot provision of the 1968 Civil Rights Act (a provision which made it a crime to cross state lines to incite riots or to teach the use of riot weapons).

The radical community engaged in massive demonstrations against the trial outside the courthouse. Mark Rudd and other Weathermen participated in the four violent "days of rage" that fall of 1969. Rudd was arrested, and although the charges against him were minor, the bail was exorbitant for the time—$25,000. From the size of the bail, Rudd suspected that his trial was going to be a "show trial," as an example to other radicals, and he chose not to be a party to it. He jumped bail and disappeared into the ever-growing radical underground. Despite a nationwide manhunt and a place on the FBI's ten-most-wanted list, he succeeded in hiding out for more than seven years.

In September 1977, Rudd, then thirty years old, came out of hiding and voluntarily surrendered to authorities in New York and Chicago. The charges against him were all misdemeanors, such as second-class trespass and unlawful assembly. He was released on low bail and, in November, sentenced to a year's probation. Rudd never revealed where or how he had managed to hide for more than seven years or how he had eluded capture despite the efforts of the FBI's special squad, which shadowed his friends, tapped their telephones, and examined their mail.

At this writing, Mark Rudd is living in New Mexico and is active in the anti-nuclear movement and in the movement against U.S. involvement in Nicaragua. In March 1987, he spoke at Columbia University and announced that he had decided to step up his visible political activities, explaining that he was convinced that the war in Nicaragua would be for the eighties generation what the Vietnam War was for his.

During the time of the student strike at Columbia University, student unrest was not a phenomenon confined to the United States. That same spring, students in France launched their own movement of marches and sit-ins to protest what they regarded as undue police force in putting down demonstrations against American aggression in North Vietnam, among other things. Columnist Flora Lewis, writing in *The New York Times* on December 9, 1986, alluded to these other things when she called the militant French students of eighteen years earlier "wry rebels . . . disdainful of excess consumerism, demanding 'imagination power,' dreaming in romantic passion of remaking the world to their taste." She could have been describing a good proportion of the American student activists. There were differences between the American and French student protesters, however. The most militant leaders of the French students were more Communist-oriented than their American peers. Also, unlike their American counterparts, the French students created such upheaval that they essentially brought down the government: President Charles de Gaulle resigned the following year.

In the United States, the revolution on the campus extended past the sixties, but *just* past. It effectively ended on May 4, 1970, at Kent State University in Ohio. Kent State had been embroiled in student protest since the fall of 1968, when members of the Oakland, California, police department had arrived to recruit new trainees. At the time the Oakland police were involved in a violent struggle with the Black Panther Party, and both the

Kent State chapter of SDS and the Black United Students (BUS) mounted protest demonstrations against the recruitment drive. The following spring SDS protested against the campus ROTC program, and the administration banned SDS from the campus. Other campus radicals viewed the administration's move as an effort to suppress dissent. The situation smoldered but did not catch fire until April 30, 1970, when President Richard Nixon announced his intention to send U.S. troops into Cambodia, a country bordering Vietnam, which the enemies of South Vietnam were using as a base. Students who were against U.S. involvement in the Vietnam conflict were galvanized to action against this widening of the war. Their protests escalated over the next two days, and when the ROTC building was set afire, Ohio governor James Rhodes called out the Ohio National Guard.

This action radicalized even previously disaffected students. They resented the "occupation" of their campus by National Guardsmen. On Monday, May 4, someone began to ring an old railroad-engine bell that was traditionally used to call the students to the campus commons. Students converged from all directions. At the commons, they were met by National Guardsmen who fired tear-gas canisters into the crowd. The students threw the canisters back at them, along with rocks and other objects, as they charged at the Guardsmen. Then a barrage of shots rang out. When it was over, four students were dead.

A student named Mary Ann Vecchio was the first to reach one of the dead students. She raised her face to the sky and screamed. Her photograph (on facing page) was carried around the world, and her contorted face, with its openmouthed, soundless scream, became the pictorial epitaph of youthful innocence in the sixties.

This incident at Kent State radicalized many students who had not been part of the anti-war effort, and it seemed to revitalize the Anti-War Movement. There was a new outbreak of demonstrations against the war on campuses all across the country. More than five hundred campuses canceled classes, and fifty did not reopen at all that semester. Half of the nation's campuses

Kent State student Mary Ann Vecchio kneels by the body of a slain friend. Four young people died at Kent State University when Ohio National Guardsmen fired on student anti-war protestors.

experienced protests in one form or another, involving more than four million students. Some of these protests were violent; within a week after the Kent State killings, thirty ROTC buildings were destroyed by fire or bombs and the National Guard was called to twenty-two campuses. But while it may have revitalized the anti-war effort, the Kent State tragedy also profoundly changed the relationship in the United States between a university and its students. Some observers have said that the campus revolution of the sixties was similar in many ways to a rebellion by youth against their parents. The two sides didn't like each other much, but they were still family. When the National Guard was called to the Kent State campus, the situation dramatically changed—a force outside the "family" was suddenly in control, leaving both the students and the university powerless. The American center of higher education ceased to be a family, if indeed it ever really was one at all.

CHAPTER FOUR

THE MUSIC OF THE SIXTIES

The music of an era is like a mirror reflecting the concerns of a culture at that time. Sometimes it reflects these images in an indirect way, sometimes very directly. During World War II, for example, patriotic songs and love ballads were exceptionally popular because the war had separated many young men from their loved ones. Sometimes the music of an era tries for a more direct effect. Nine days after the stock market crash of 1929, the song "Happy Days Are Here Again" was copyrighted. In 1931, at the height of the Great Depression, one of the most popular songs was "Life Is Just a Bowl of Cherries." Clearly, the intent of both these songs was to lift the spirits of Americans. Many classic folk songs are actually labor songs, born out of the struggle by American workers to gain more rights in the workplace, especially the right to form unions. These kinds of songs were intended to bolster the resolve of labor activists.

The music of the 1960s was like the music of earlier decades in both these respects. It can be distinguished from other periods by three main characteristics.

First, it reflected the new sexual permissiveness by including obviously sexy lyrics. Until the mid-1950s, sexual passion was never directly addressed in the lyrics of popular songs, although those who titled instrumental jazz pieces seemed to hover gleefully close at times. Consider two Duke Ellington titles from the 1930s: "Warm Valley" and "T.T. on Toast." Popular song titles and lyrics always treated sex euphemistically. In 1951 Rosemary Clooney had a hit with "Come On-a My House." While she was only offering "candy" at her house, most adult listeners, at least, knew what she was really talking about.

Second, until the mid-1950s, popular music was aimed at both teenagers and their parents. There was no "youth culture" distinct from the rest of the culture. The term "generation gap" had yet to be coined.

Third, until the mid-1950s, both popular-music musicians and their audiences were overwhelmingly middle-class and white. There were black recording artists and record buyers, but they were as segregated in the music world as they were in the larger society. With a few exceptions, such as Nat King Cole and Billy Eckstine, black records were not played on major radio stations nor sold in major record stores. In the 1920s and 1930s, black records were called "race records" and were marketed only in black neighborhoods, sold in a variety of ghetto stores, from the trunks of cars, out of suitcases. In the 1940s, black music was labeled "rhythm and blues," but it still meant *black* and it still was not part of the mainstream.

All that began to change in the mid-1950s, when a number of divergent forces came together to create a new kind of music and a particular audience for that music. One major force was the mass migration of southern blacks to the North during and after World War II. An increase in "race programming" on urban radio stations reflected that population shift. Until that time, rhythm and blues had been largely inaccessible to white audiences; now, all they had to do was turn on a radio. The stations that played black music tended to be low-frequency stations situated at the ends of the dial, but a determined listener could find them. What the white listeners heard were far more realistic lyrics about life ["Money Honey" by the Drifters, 1953] and love ["Good Lovin" by the Clovers, 1953], and a sound [Chuck Berry's "Roll Over Beethoven" and "Maybellene"] that was at the opposite end of the spectrum from the mild, frequently emotionless instrumentation of white pop music.

The more adventuresome white youngsters also wanted to see how those pounding rhythms were created in live performances. In late 1955, young Elvis Presley made his first trip to New York. The official reason was a meeting with his new record company, RCA, but his real goal was to go to the Apollo Theater in Harlem to see black stars like Bo Diddley dance around on the stage, charging up the audience with his sexually explicit movements.

By 1952, white pop singers were starting to record versions, or "covers," of black R & B records, and for a while these seemed to satisfy the young white record buyers. The turning point came in 1956, when Little Richard's "Long Tall Sally" outsold Pat Boone's toned-down version. The message was clear: The kids wanted the real thing.

By that time the teenage market was beginning to form. In the generally affluent 1950s, many teenagers enjoyed the luxury of both money and spare time. The "youth cult" didn't become a real phenomenon until the early 1960s, but in the middle 1950s teenagers began to be a distinctly separate force, one that would alter the way products—including records—were marketed, and one that would become increasingly distanced from the older population. The generation gap was beginning.

Nowhere did that gap present itself more clearly than in the controversy over rock 'n' roll and over its most popular purveyor, Elvis Presley. He rode in a gold Cadillac, he dressed in gold lamé suits, he gyrated his hips so sensuously that when he appeared on television the cameras never showed him below the waist. Parents were enraged; young people were delighted. A generational tug-of-war resulted. There were attempts at censorship of rock songs on radio; law-enforcement officials raided rock'n' roll stage shows; in 1956, in Birmingham, Alabama, the local White Citizens Council launched a campaign against "bop and Negro music" and a group of WCC members tried to beat up Nat King Cole.

The story of music in the 1950s could fill a book in itself, and has in fact filled several. What is important here is to point out that the music of the 1960s was an outgrowth of previous musical trends. Several qualities of 1960s music, including black musical influences, sexually explicit lyrics, and what might be called sheer noise level, had a solid basis in the preceding decade. The negative reaction to the rock music of the 1950s led to the renaissance of folk music, and the main characteristic of folk music is that of socially relevant lyrics.

The music of the sixties was the Beach Boys and Bob Dylan, the Beatles and the Supremes, the Rolling Stones and Jimi Hendrix, the Everly Brothers, Janis Joplin, Sonny and Cher, the Doors, the Byrds, Joni Mitchell, Cream, the Who, the Jefferson Airplane [later the Jefferson Starship], and a lot more. All of these diverse musical styles reflected American culture in the 1960s. Not for nothing were the youth of the sixties later dubbed the Woodstock Generation, after the huge musical "happening" near Bethel, New York, in 1969. It is not the intention here to provide a complete survey of the music of the decade. What follows is a brief overview of the musical styles that had the greatest effect, with an emphasis on the music that encouraged the political activism for which the sixties are best remembered.

THE NEW FOLK MUSIC

Before the 1960s, folk music was definitely not in the mainstream. In the 1950s, in fact, it was closely associated with Communism and other leftist causes such as labor unionism and civil rights. For all that, however, folk music was one of the few true expressions of ordinary, often poor, people. Genuine folk songs were not written by professional songwriters but by coal miners and cotton pickers and stevedores.

The best example of a traditional folk song that was sung in the 1960s is "We Shall Overcome." According to James Fuld in *The Book of World-Famous Music,* the song was derived from two hymns: the simple melody from a hymn which was first printed in the United States in May 1794, and the words from a hymn titled "I'll Overcome Some Day," published in 1900. It included the words, 'If in my heart, I do not yield, I'll overcome some day."

The first time the words and music appeared together in print was in the Negro gospel song "I'll Overcome Someday," published in May 1945 by Martin & Morris Music Studio in Chicago. On the sheet music, credit for the original music is given to Atrong Twigg and credit for revised lyrics and music is accorded to Kenneth Morris.

Five months later, in Charleston, South Carolina, the Negro Food and Tobacco Workers went on strike, and it is said that strikers there first sang the song with the plural pronoun: "*We* will overcome." Two of the strikers later attended a labor workshop at the Highlander Folk School in Monteagle, Tennessee, and shared the song with Zilphia Horton, wife of the founder of the school, who in turn taught it to others. Guy Carawan, Frank Hamilton, and Pete Seeger, all white folksingers, added lyrics to it; Seeger is credited with changing "We *will* overcome" to the more forceful "We *shall* overcome."

Clearly one of the strengths of the song is its adaptability to a variety of situations. It became an integration song in the course of the Montgomery bus boycott. The black people who met at the Hutchinson Street Baptist Church, the command post for the boycott, sought strength and courage in song, which indeed is the traditional motivation behind folk songs. During later civil rights campaigns, the marchers and workers found they needed their songs more than ever, and "We Shall Overcome," as well as traditional spirituals, became their way of whistling in the dark, so to speak. "They could not stop our sound," recalled Bernice Johnson Reagon, who was active in the civil rights campaign in Albany, Georgia, and who was interviewed for "Eyes on the Prize," a six-part PBS-TV special on the Civil Rights Movement, first aired in January-February 1987. "They would have to kill us to stop us from singing. Sometimes the police would plead and say, 'Please stop singing.' And you would just know that your word was being heard, and you felt joy."

By 1963, "We Shall Overcome" had become the virtual anthem of the Civil Rights Movement. When President Johnson announced his signing of the 1965 Voting Rights Act in a nationally televised address, he concluded by saying, "And we shall overcome." Less than two months later, the song was on the lips of Mrs. Viola Gregg Liuzzo as she lay dying from a Ku Klux Klansman's bullet (she was shot while driving Selma-to-Montgomery marchers back from Montgomery). A month before that, a South African freedom fighter in a Johannesburg prison, John Harris, sang the song just before he was hanged; the song was subsequently banned in South Africa.

"We Shall Overcome" has been recorded by Pete Seeger, Joan Baez, and many others. It remains today the most clearly recognizable expression of the battle against oppression and is still used by demonstrators in many causes, from striking workers to anti-nuclear demonstrators. While the same first verse is used in every case, later verses depend considerably on the situation. We found a dozen, and no doubt more will be created to meet new situations.

We Shall Overcome

We shall overcome, we shall overcome,
We shall overcome someday.
Oh, deep in my heart, I do believe,
We shall overcome someday.

We are not afraid, we are not afraid,
We are not afraid, today.
Oh, deep in my heart, I do believe,
We shall overcome someday.

Other verses, in no particular order:

We are not alone . . . (today)
We'll walk hand in hand . . .
We shall live in peace . . .
We shall all be free . . .
The Lord will see us through . . .
The whole wide world around . . .
The truth will make us free . . .
We shall ban the bomb . . .
Black and White together . . .
We shall end Jim Crow . . .

It is not surprising that Pete Seeger recorded "We Shall Overcome." More than any other singer, he was—and continues to be—the personification of traditional folk music. It was he who first recorded many of the workers' songs, field songs, and sea chanteys that previously had been passed down from one generation to another by word of mouth. Always involved in leftist causes, he had been a victim of the anti-Communist "Red Scare" of the early 1950s. Anyone who had ever been a member of the Communist Party or associated with leftist causes such as labor unionism was thought to be part of a plot to overthrow the U.S. government. Public figures and entertainers came under particularly close scrutiny, and many were blacklisted—that is, refused work—on television or radio or in films. Seeger had been blacklisted, and the fact that his single "Little Boxes" was on the pop music charts in 1963 is worth noting. It was an indication that many Americans had realized that the anti-Communist witch-hunts of the 1950s had been excessive and that a society that prided itself on its freedoms had been wrong to actively deny the rights of many of its citizens based on mere suspicion.

Even more remarkable than the fact that a song sung by Seeger was a hit was its subject. "Little Boxes," written by Malvina Reynolds, was a witty attack on all that 1950s America held dear—its middle-class suburbs, its "upward mobility," its materialism, its glorification of *sameness.* The song put into words a lot of the uneasy feelings the middle-class young people coming of age in the 1960s had been vaguely aware of but unable to express.

Little Boxes

Little boxes on the hill-side
Little boxes made of ticky tacky,
Little boxes on the hill-side,
Little boxes all the same
There's a green one and a pink one
And a blue one and a yellow one
And they're all made out of ticky tacky
And they all look just the same.

And the people in the houses
All went to the university,
Where they were put in boxes
And they came out all the same,
And there's doctors and lawyers,
And business executives,
And they're all made out of ticky tacky
And they all look just the same.

And they all play on the golf course
And drink their martinis dry,
And they all have pretty children
And the children go to school,

And the children go to summer camp
And then to the university,
Where they are put in boxes
And they come out all the same.

And the boys go into business
And marry and raise a family
In boxes made of ticky tacky
And they all look just the same.
There's a green one and a pink one,
And a blue one and a yellow one,
And they're all made out of ticky tacky
And they all look just the same

(No mention of girls and what they did, but this omission is appropriate for the time. The girls married the boys and lived with them in the boxes made of ticky tacky, and bore the children who would go to the university and be put in their own little boxes—or so the fifth verse might have gone.)

"Little Boxes," which was copyrighted in 1962, was unlike traditional folk music in that it had been *written* rather than having evolved in an oral tradition. This writing of many new songs is one thing that distinguished the folk revival of the sixties.

Still, the new songs basically followed the folk-song tradition. They depended very little on a beat or rhythm—all one needed was a guitar and knowledge of a few chords to play a folk song. What they depended on most was a clever, meaningful lyric. Folk songs are poetry set to a tune. They are not for dancing but for listening to and thinking about. And in the 1960s, ideally, they were also to be acted upon. At no time were criticisms of the system, identification with the underdog, yearning for peace, revulsion against militarism, and the search for answers more clearly expressed than in the folk songs of the sixties. To quote

Joan Baez and Bob Dylan, two leaders of the folk revival. While Bob Dylan's music provided a call to arms for Sixties radicals, Joan Baez would later provide an eloquent voice for the anti-war protests in the later Sixties.

Dave Von Ronk, a folk music star of the time, "Any music is music of its time. But the music of the sixties was *about* its time, too. It dealt almost on a one-to-one basis with the experience that people were going through."

Here are a few examples:

"Blowin' in the Wind" (Bob Dylan) asked about how many deaths would be necessary before people decided there had been too many.

"Where Have All the Flowers Gone?" (Pete Seeger) was about flowers on the graves of soldiers.

"Eve of Destruction" (recorded by Barry McGuire) warned that people ought to wake up and believe that destruction was at hand.

"There But for Fortune" (recorded by Joan Baez) reminded people that they themselves had nothing to do with the economic and social circumstances into which they'd been born.

The largest number of popular folk songs written in the 1960s were written by Bob Dylan, the poet laureate of the sixties folk revival.

Dylan was a Jewish kid from Hibbing, Minnesota, who had taught himself to play the Sears, Roebuck electric guitar he had bought on credit. He began as a folksinger, singing traditional songs, but by the time he was in his early twenties and living in Greenwich Village in New York City, he had started writing his own. He arrived in New York in 1961, heading immediately for the Village, then the cradle of everything leftist and avant-garde. He had attracted a sizable following by 1962, the year his first album was released, and by 1965 he was the acknowledged spokesman of a generation. If "We Shall Overcome" was the anthem of the nonviolent civil rights struggle, then the songs of Dylan were a call to arms for the sixties radicals. Indeed, the radical group the Weathermen took their name and their creed from lines in Dylan's song "Subterranean Homesick Blues." More wide-ranging in its appeal, and more identifiable as an anthem for white activists in the sixties, was Dylan's "The Times They Are A-Changin' "(1963).

The Times They Are A-Changin'

Come gather 'round people
Wherever you roam
And admit that the waters
Around you have grown
And accept it that soon
You'll be drenched to the bone.
If your time to you
Is worth savin'
Then you better start swimmin'
Or you'll sink like a stone
For the times they are a-changin'.

Come writers and critics
Who prophesize with your pen
And keep your eyes wide
The chance won't come again
And don't speak too soon
For the wheel's still in spin
And there's no tellin' who
That it's namin'.
For the loser now
Will be later to win
For the times they are a-changin'.

Come senators, congressmen
Please heed the call
Don't stand in the doorway
Don't block up the hall
For he that gets hurt
Will be he who has stalled
There's a battle outside
And it is ragin'.
It'll soon shake your windows

And rattle your walls
For the times they are a-changin'.

Come mothers and fathers
Throughout the land
And don't criticize
What you can't understand
Your sons and your daughters
Are beyond your command
Your old road is
Rapidly agin'.
Please get out of the new one
If you can't lend a hand
For the times they are a-changin'.

The line it is drawn
The curse it is cast
The slow one now
Will later be fast
As the present now
Will later be past
The order is
Rapidly fadin'
And the first one now
Will later be last
For the times they are a-changin'.

The rock revival of the late sixties led to the death of the folk revival. On the simplest level, it might be argued that for all their articulate and meaningful lyrics, folk songs failed to satisfy a very important need: the need to move. People could be expected to sit and listen intently only for so long; at some point they wanted to get up and dance. Dylan recognized this need quite early on, and in fact folk purists charged that he left "the folk" in 1965 when he appeared at the Newport Folk Festival with the electric Paul Butterfield Blues Band. But it can also be argued that adding rock 'n' roll instrumentation to folk songs was the single most important factor in keeping folk music vital until the end of the sixties.

Dylan has gone through many other changes since, both personally and musically. In the early seventies, he went to Jerusalem in search of his "Jewish identity." Later, he studied at a Bible school in California and recorded three albums of gospel-rock. The first, *Slow Train Coming* (1979), sold one million copies and was declared a platinum album, but the next two didn't even sell the one million dollars worth of copies necessary to be declared gold records. Next, he became associated with an ultra-Orthodox Jewish sect, the Lubavitcher Hasidim, and recorded another album, *Infidels,* which continued the biblical theme with an overlay of extreme conservatism. In 1984, he told an interviewer for *Rolling Stone* that he thought politics was "an instrument of the Devil" and that there was no hope for peace in the world. Despite this fatalistic view, he believes that the sixties did change society for the better, and since most of the movements of the sixties were political, it would seem that politics are not *all* bad.

MOTOWN

The music of Detroit's Motown provided the beat that was missing in folk music, although its lyrics were pretty forgettable. The Detroit Sound was nothing if not danceable, and the success of Motown Records was a logical outgrowth of black music's movement into the mainstream—or the movement of the mainstream audience toward black music—that had started in the 1950s.

Originally called Hitsville, USA, and started on the proverbial shoestring by Berry Gordy in 1958, the company changed its name to Motown in 1962, the year it became a musical phenomenon. Using young talented kids from Detroit's black neighborhoods, a formula sound that emphasized a steady, driving beat, teenybopper lyrics about love, and a solid dose of showmanship, Motown produced five hit records in 1962. Except for a lull in the late 1960s, its records continued to dominate the charts until 1971. A few of its hits were:

Smokey Robinson and the Miracles' "Ooo Baby Baby" and "You've Really Got a Hold on Me"

The Marvelettes' "Please Mr. Postman" and "Beechwood 45789"

Mary Wells' "You Beat Me to the Punch" and "The One Who Really Loves You"

The Supremes' "Where Did Our Love Go?," "Baby Love," and "Come See about Me"

The Contours' "Do You Love Me?"

Motown's acts were almost all groups: the Temptations, the Supremes, Smokey Robinson and the Miracles, Martha and the Vandellas. They sang harmony and onstage they moved in intricately choreographed routines. They were unfailingly well-groomed; the girl groups like the Supremes were unstintingly glamorous and weren't allowed to leave the Motown tour bus unless they were in full makeup. Until the late 1960s they publicly had nothing whatsoever to do with any of the social and political movements that were going on in the outside world. In fact, for most of the decade Motown policy was to avoid politics entirely.

In the company's early days, this was a productive policy. Berry Gordy was aiming to attract the white crossover audience, and he did not want his performers judged by anything but their music. Given the complexion of its performers, Motown remained as racially invisible as possible throughout the years of the major Direct Action Civil Rights Movement. Gordy didn't want his performers associated with controversy of any kind.

Motown publicity people sat in on all interviews, and quickly headed off any questions about civil rights or politics. Even the Black Is Beautiful Movement of the later 1960s had little effect on Motown, although girl groups like the Supremes did wear Afro wigs on occasion once Afros were "in."

In the summer of 1967, blacks rioted in Detroit's ghetto neighborhoods. The Motor Town Revue happened to be performing in the city at the time, and it left town immediately. Motown was not going to be associated with black riots. But the following year the company began to respond to the way the wind was blowing. Late in 1968, the Supremes recorded two songs with "socially relevant" lyrics about out-of-wedlock birth: "Love Child" and "I'm Livin' in Shame." The Temptations included a cut called "War" on their album *Psychedelic Shack,* whose title reflected the popularity of psychedelic art and drugs. While "War" did not mention Vietnam, it talked about war causing unrest among the young. Several thousand people wrote Motown asking that the track be released as a single. Motown responded by having Edwin Starr, not the Temptations, record the song for release. Starr's singing was more soulful than that of the Tempts, and he put a lot of soul into his rendering of the song which asked what war was good for.

These records of Motown's were few, they were late in coming, and they were clearly exceptions to the Motown rule. There is, in fact, some evidence that Motown's influence waned in the late sixties because it lacked social relevance. In a sense, this is an unfair charge. Had the company taken an activist stance in the early sixties, it might never have succeeded in making the crossover to the white audience. Yet once it had succeeded the company and its performers were criticized for not being relevant. Joe Billingslea, one of the Contours, described this catch-22 situation well to Gerri Hirshey, author of *Nowhere to Run: The Story of Soul Music.* "Motown got caught in some funny crossfire. Here's a bunch of black kids going flat-out after the American dream, you dig? The nice house, the clothes, the car. Just what everybody else has always gone for. But with what was going on, the riots, the Vietnam mess, it was the *down* side of the dream. And so just when some cat gets enough to afford the Continental—bang—it's not *cool* to drive it, disrespectful of the movement or whatever." The very things that white middle-class kids could denigrate because they'd already had them—the little boxes and the golf courses—were now out of reach for blacks because they were politically inappropriate.

While Motown never again dominated the charts the way it had from 1962 to 1971, the company continued to be successful. At various times in the seventies and eighties it was the label of the Jackson Five, Stevie Wonder, the Commodores, Lionel Ritchie, and many other stars. But it continued to stay far away from politics.

THE BRITISH INVASION

Like the Motown Sound, most of the musical trends in the 1960s were basically nonpolitical. Some argue that by the time the Beatles invaded the United States in 1964, the folk revival was already beginning to wane. The quiet, pastoral nature of folk music just didn't appeal to the hyperactivity of many sixties youth. People wanted music that was more exciting and sophisticated. That sound was duly produced not only by Motown but by four long-haired youths from Liverpool whose major musical influences had been black American rhythm and blues.

The Beatles burst onto the American scene with a sound that was, to begin with, loud. Both their instruments and their voices were highly amplified. But behind the loudness was a real musical sophistication, first in the melodies and instrumentation and later in the lyrics, which were a sort of avant-garde poetry. Their music was sufficiently complex to interest musicians in symphony orchestras, who would later record many of their songs. The Beatles were also sticklers for quality. While it had been the custom to issue albums with only one or two really good

The Beatles perform at a charity concert during their phenomenally successful U.S. tour. Their success would pave the way for the British Invasion in music.

songs, the Beatles albums had six, or nine, or even more songs good enough to be released as singles.

About the only thing their lyrics had in common with folk-singers like Bob Dylan was their celebration of youth. Unfortunately, they shared something else with Dylan. While one of Dylan's songs gave the name and creed to the radical Weathermen, one of their song titles was adopted by Charles Manson, a charismatic psychotic. Manson predicted that black militants would take over the United States and he described that situation as "Helter Skelter," a Beatles song title. When on August 8, 1969, members of Manson's "family" of followers murdered actress Sharon Tate and several other people in a house in the Hollywood Hills, they wrote "Helter Skelter" on the walls in blood.

On the whole, their lyrics were not political. The Beatles had little or nothing to say about war, hunger, racial discrimination. They were more intent on poking fun at the establishment, as in "Taxman," than in launching any moral attacks on it. Their social consciousness was confined primarily to idealistic generalities—"All You Need Is Love." As the sixties wore on, their lyrics did express other cultural currents: the trend toward Eastern religions, as in "Within You, Without You," and the new drug culture, as in "Lucy in the Sky with Diamonds" (young people immediately noticed the acronym LSD contained in the title), and "A Day in the Life" ("I'd love to turn you on").

The Beatles paved the way for other English groups that much more boldly reflected the sixties loss of sexual innocence—the Rolling Stones with "I Can't Get No Satisfaction," for example. The Stones seemed to personify elegant decadence. Song titles such as "Stray Cat Blues" (the Stones were also heavily influenced by black American blues), "No Expectations," and "Sympathy for the Devil," as well as album titles such as *Let It Bleed* were calculated to shock. There was a lot of that in the sixties, identification with the underdog and the anti-hero and anything that wasn't part of the 1950s suburban complacency. Compare names of musical groups from the early sixties with those of the late sixties:

Early sixties: the Passions, the Mystics, the Chiffons, the Angels.

Late sixties: the Outsiders, the Young Rascals, the Animals, the Grateful Dead, the Fugs.

The sounds of these late sixties groups were as harsh as their names—indeed, harsh as acid. By 1967 the country's musical center had shifted from Motown to Philadelphia (for blacks) and San Francisco (for whites). Grace Slick of the Jefferson Airplane, Janis Joplin, Jimi Hendrix, Jim Morrison and the Doors personified the San Francisco music scene, where the solid establishment of the new drug culture had combined with the revival of rock to produce acid rock, the aural equivalent of an LSD trip.

But somehow, as the 1960s came to a close, there was room for all the musical styles of the decade at Woodstock, the three-day musical happening that gave its name to the entire sixties generation. It took place in August 1969 in a farmer's field near the small town of Bethel, in the Catskill Mountains in upstate New York, fifty-five miles from Woodstock (the festival was moved from Woodstock at the last minute, but took the name along). Billed as three days of peace and music, it attracted half a million young people united in the belief that peace and flowers and music were far better than war and guns and dissension.

The individuals and groups who performed at Woodstock included Joan Baez, Blood, Sweat and Tears, the Paul Butterfield Blues Band, the Band, Creedence Clearwater Revival, Canned Heat, Country Joe and the Fish, Crosby, Stills and Nash, Joe Cocker, Arlo Guthrie, the Grateful Dead, Tim Hardin, Jimi Hendrix, Richie Havens, Keef Hartley, the Incredible String Band, Janis Joplin, the Jefferson Airplane, the Joshua Light Show, Melanie, Mountain, Quill, John Sebastian, Ravi Shankar, Sly and the Family Stone, Bert Sommer, Santana, Sweetwater, Ten Years After, Johnny Winter, and the Who. Together they rep-

Half a million young people gather on Max Yusgar's farm for the Woodstock Music Festival, the three-day celebration that would give the Sixties generation its name.

resented the broad spectrum of sixties musical styles, though the roster was light on "pop"—no Beach Boys, Everly Brothers, Sonny and Cher, or Motown acts. Sly and the Family Stone were the single group to represent the hard-edged Philadelphia Sound that helped to eclipse Motown for a time. Ravi Shankar was the single representative of the pure Eastern music sound.

Actually, the list of performers turned out to be less impressive than the audience itself, who were the real stars of Woodstock.

The planners and promoters of the Woodstock Music Festival had never in their wildest dreams expected half a million people. When they, and others, began to realize that this festival was going to turn into a "happening," they not only scrambled to accommodate the huge crowd—whose number was equivalent to the population of the fourth largest city in the United States—but also fell prey to some of the same problems that many sixties young people had devoted the decade to fighting. In a 1979 book tilted *Barefoot in Babylon: The Creation of the Woodstock Music Festival, 1969,* Robert Stephen Spitz reports that acts of remarkable generosity coexisted with extraordinary displays of greed: while three hundred hippies worked to build the stage in exchange for two meals a day and all the pot they could smoke, Abbie Hoffman, a leader of the Yippies (Youth International Party), was asking for $50,000 from the organizing committee in order not to put LSD in the festival's water supply.

The huge audience that assembled on Max Yasgur's farm near Bethel, on the other hand, seemed to have few worries and absolutely no desire to take advantage of the situation. They simply wanted to be part of the "happening."

They backed up traffic for miles around, and when they couldn't get through in their cars they abandoned them and walked the rest of the way. They shared their food, blankets, drugs, and bodies with one another. A couple of babies were actually born on Yusgar's farm.

The small town's stores were overwhelmed. At Vassmer's General Store, the two owner-brothers let people in forty or fifty at a time. The first item they ran out of was potato chips. Fifteen years later, the brothers, Art and Fred Vassmer, spoke of Woodstock with awe: "I'll tell you something," said Art Vassmer to a *New York Times* reporter in August 1984, "we cashed I don't know how many checks, and you know what, not one of them bounced."

Thousands of people went skinny-dipping. Thousands more smoked pot and took acid. But there was no violence, no thievery, no fighting. Police made drug arrests, and there were two drug-related deaths and one accidental death, but there were no cases of one human being attacking another. In fact, Woodstock was a powerful demonstration of how a huge number of people could handle themselves well, with peace and love in their hearts.

Say "Woodstock" now and the face of nearly everyone who was old enough to know it happened will light up. And nearly everyone who was old enough to be there will *claim* to have been. Wrote Richard Chavet in a 1984 op-editorial in *The New York Times,* "I didn't go to Woodstock, but I said I did, which is almost the same thing."

Unfortunately, the era of sixties music did not end without producing a violent footnote. On December 6, 1969, the Rolling Stones staged a free concert at Altamont Speedway outside of San Francisco. At the suggestion of the manager of the Grateful Dead, the Stones invited members of the Hell's Angels motorcycle club to act as a security force. Pumped up by the crowd, and by their sense of self-importance, the Angels were eating acid by the handful. Instead of keeping the peace, they fought with one another and with the crowd. The Stones were into their fourth song when their Angel "security force" beat up its first victim. About three songs later another man lay dead. When it was over, Mick Jagger said, "I'd rather have had the cops." There would be no more free concerts for a while—by any performers.

In one of the tidier moments of history, much of sixties music came to an end in the last year of the decade and the first year of the next. The Motown Sound seemed to lose its way, though the group of brothers from Gary, Indiana, called the Jackson Five, would revive it in the early seventies. The Beatles broke up in 1969 and John, Paul, George, and Ringo went their separate ways. Ringo Starr didn't establish an individual sound later on. George Harrison went more deeply into Eastern music, following his mentor, the sitarist Ravi Shankar. Paul McCartney, with his wife, Linda, and their group, Wings, went on to develop such a distinct musical identity that there are teenagers today who are surprised to learn that he was once with "another group." John Lennon, with his wife, Yoko Ono, also developed a unique individual style and became the "musical conscience" of the seventies in much the same way as Dylan had in the sixties. One of his most popular titles, "Give Peace a Chance," became the anthem of the Peace Movement. He was murdered by a deranged fan in 1980. Jimi Hendrix died of a drug overdose in London on September 18, 1970, and sixteen days later Janis Joplin also died of a drug overdose in a motel in Los Angeles. Both were twenty-seven years old.

It is interesting that the Woodstock Festival came to put its stamp on the sixties generation. After all, given some of the negative reactions to the sixties, someone could have dubbed the young people of the time the Altamont Generation. That Woodstock was chosen indicates that, for all its drawbacks and its excesses, the sixties generation struck a responsive chord. People who hated the drugs, the free love, the anti-hero worship, and the anti-establishment sass responded in spite of themselves to the love and the flowers, to the earnest talk of peace and the honest "we-ness" instead of "me-ness," and—the anti-materialism of the sixties notwithstanding—to the no bounced checks at Vassmer's General Store. Even the people who disapproved of most of the movements of the decade nevertheless responded to its music.

CHAPTER FIVE

THE BLACK POWER MOVEMENT

The black cultural nationalism which took hold on college campuses in the sixties was one manifestation of the Black Power Movement that arose in the middle of the decade. That movement was a response to both the successes and the failures of the Direct Action Civil Rights Movement. The Civil Rights Movement had gained important rights for black people, perhaps the most important being the right to vote. It had also shown that organized, concerted action could produce results. But these gains had been won at great cost, not only in terms of lost lives but of lost hope that whites would ever really accept blacks as equals.

Having won the legal victories it had sought, by the middle sixties the Direct Action Civil Rights Movement began to lose its strength. What replaced it was a new sense among blacks that integration was not as important as separate development for blacks, that mere laws were not going to change white people's attitudes, that racism was so deeply embedded in the American system that there was no point trying to work within that system.

Like the other movements discussed in this book, the Black Power Movement had its roots in earlier times. Using a general definition of Black Power as black nationalism and self-determination, one can trace those roots back to the first days of slavery. Slaves certainly did not choose to come to America, but as time went on, blacks, both slave and free, began to consider America their home, though there were always some who, believing that white America would never accept blacks as equals, yearned to go back to Africa.

In the 1820s, some fifteen thousand American blacks, mostly freed slaves, founded the African nation of Liberia, with financing by whites who considered slavery evil, but could not imagine blacks being assimilated into American society. Nearly a century later, Marcus Garvey, a Jamaican who immigrated to the United States in 1916, founded the Universal Negro Improvement Association (UNIA) and attracted many urban black followers with his "Back to Africa" program for the resettlement of New World blacks in their ancestral homeland. To finance his program, he founded several black businesses in the United States, but he became embroiled in legal and financial problems and was eventually convicted of mail fraud and deported. There is some suspicion that his growing movement of black people was seen as a threat by the U.S. government.

Some two decades later, the Great Depression provided a ripe environment for the renewal of black separatist feeling. In Chicago in the 1930s, a black man who called himself Elijah Muhammad founded a religious sect loosely based on the Islamic faith practiced primarily in the Middle East, Africa, and Malaysia. The major tenets of the Nation of Islam were racial separatism and black supremacy. Elijah Muhammad called whites "devils" and claimed that blacks were the true children of God. Preaching clean living and dignity, he attracted a small following, particularly among blacks in prison. He also told blacks that they should cast off their last names because they were "slave names" given to their slave ancestors by whites. Many converts to the Nation of Islam took African last names, or they simply used an "X" because they did not know who their African forebears were.

In 1961, black historian E. Franklin Frazier published a book about the movement. He called the followers of the Nation of Islam "Black Muslims," to distinguish them from Muslims, followers of the world religion Islam, and the name stuck. Frazier wrote the book because suddenly in the 1950s the Nation of Islam had begun to grow quickly. He attributed this growth primarily to one man: Malcolm X.

Born Malcolm Little in 1925, Malcolm had taken an "X" as his last name after converting to the Nation of Islam while in prison. On his release from prison, he took an active role in proselytizing for the movement and rose quickly within it, inspiring many urban blacks to join the Nation, and many others to gain a new pride in their blackness. By the early 1960s he had become so famous that other Black Muslim leaders were jealous of him. Internal politics led to his leaving the Nation of Islam in 1964.

During the next year he traveled to Africa and discovered that true Islam was not racist. He then formed the Organization of Afro-American Unity, which would stress black nationalism and active self-defense but would not be anti-white in nature. But on February 21, 1965, while speaking before a meeting of his new OAAU, he was assassinated. The men who were convicted of the crime were Black Muslims, although some people charged that the FBI or CIA might have been behind the killing, so influential a spokesman for black nationalism had Malcolm X become.

Without Malcolm X to lead it the OAAU dissolved. The Nation of Islam also lost much of its influence and concentrated the little it retained on establishing Black Muslim businesses in ghetto communities. With the death of Elijah Muhammad in

1975, the Nation of Islam split into two factions, neither of which has played any significant role in black American life since. The name and the memory of Malcolm X have remained well known, and over the years his stature as a black hero has increased. In fact, in death he has been more influential than he was while alive.

STOKELY CARMICHAEL AND THE CALL FOR "BLACK POWER!"

The assassination of Malcolm X further increased the militancy of the Student Nonviolent Coordinating Committee members who had renounced nonviolence. In their view, too many blacks had been killed; in response to such violence, blacks had a right—in fact, a duty—to defend themselves. In the spring of 1966, Stokely Carmichael led a militant faction within SNCC to take control of the organization and wasted little time thereafter in declaring a new militant policy.

Carmichael was born June 21, 1941, in Port of Spain, Trinidad. In 1952, when he was eleven, his family moved to New York; Stokely, an excellent student, attended the prestigious Bronx High School of Science. By the time he graduated from high school, the student sit-in movement had begun in the South. In order to be closer to the sit-in movement, he turned down scholarship offers from northern white colleges and decided to attend a black school, Howard University in Washington, D.C.

While at Howard, Carmichael joined SNCC and threw himself into its activities. During the course of the Freedom Rides in 1961, the Mississippi Summer Project of 1964, and a voter-registration drive in Selma, Alabama, in the summer of 1965, Carmichael was beaten several times—both by white mobs and by the police—and arrested a score of times. In the summer of 1965 he suffered a nervous breakdown, and that was the turning point for him. He became much more militant and determined that SNCC should be, too. In June 1966 he won national fame by issuing a call for "Black Power!"

Immediately, many people confused the concept of Black Power with the strident and racist position of the Black Muslims. The editors of *The New York Review of Books* asked Carmichael to explain what he meant by "Black Power!" His article, which appeared in the September 1966 issue of the *Review*, is excerpted on the following pages.

WHAT WE WANT

For too many years, black Americans marched and had their heads broken and got shot. They were saying to the country, "Look, you guys are supposed to be nice guys and we are only going to do what we are supposed to do—why do you beat us up, why don't you give us what we ask, why don't you straighten yourself out?" After years of this, we are at almost the same point—because we demonstrated from a position of weakness. We cannot be expected any longer to march and have our heads broken in order to say to whites: Come on, you're nice guys. For you are not nice guys. We have found you out.

An organization which claims to speak for the needs of the community—as does the Student Nonviolent Coordinating Committee—must speak in the tone of that community, not as somebody else's buffer zone. This is the significance of Black Power as a slogan. For once, black people are going to use the words they want to use—not just the words whites want to hear. And they will do this no matter how often the press tries to stop the use of the slogan by equating it with racism or separatism . . .

[The] concept of Black Power is not a recent or isolated phenomenon: it has grown out of the ferment of agitation and activity by different people and organizations in many black communities over the years. Our last year of work in Alabama added a new concrete possibility. In Lowndes County, for example, Black Power will mean that if a Negro is elected sheriff he can end police brutality. If a black man is elected tax assessor, he can collect and channel funds for the building of better roads and schools serving black people—thus advancing the move from political power into the economic arena. In such areas as Lowndes, where black men have a majority, they will attempt to use it to exercise control. This is what we seek: control. Where Negroes lack a majority, Black Power means proper representation and sharing of control. It means the creation of power bases from which black people can work to change statewide or nationwide patterns of oppression through pressure from strength—instead of weakness. Politically, Black Power means what it has always meant to SNCC: the coming-together of black people to elect representatives and *to force those representatives to speak to their needs.* It does not mean merely putting black faces into office. A man or woman who is black and from the slums cannot be automatically expected to speak to the needs of black people. Most of the black politicians we see around the country today are not what SNCC means by Black Power. The power must be that of a community, and emanate from there.

Ultimately, the economic foundations of this country must be shaken if black people are to control their lives. The colonies of the United States—and this includes the black ghettos within its borders, North and South—must be liberated. For a century, this nation has been like an octopus of exploitation, its tentacles stretching from Mississippi to Harlem to South America, the Middle East, southern Africa, and Vietnam; the form of exploitation varies from area to area but the essential result is the same—a powerful few have been maintained and enriched at the expense of the poor and voiceless colored masses. This pattern must be broken. As its grip loosens here and there around the world, the hopes of black Americans become more realistic. For racism to die, a totally different America must be born.

This is what the white society does not wish to face; this is why that society prefers to talk about integration. But integration speaks not at all to the problem of poverty—only to the problem of blackness. Integration today means the man who "makes it," leaving his black brothers behind in the ghetto. It has no relevance to the Harlem wino or to the cottonpicker making three dollars a day.

Integration, moreover, speaks to the problem of blackness in a despicable way. As a goal, it has been based on complete acceptance of the fact that in order to have a decent house or education, blacks must move into a white neighborhood or send their children to a white school. This reinforces, among both black and white, the idea that "white" is automatically better and "black" is by definition inferior. This is why integration is a subterfuge for the maintenance of white supremacy. It allows the nation to focus on a handful of Southern children who get into white schools, at great price, and to ignore the 94 percent who are left behind in unimproved black schools. Such situations will not change until black people have power—to control their own school boards, in this case. Then Negroes become equal in a way that means something, and integration ceases to be a one-way street. Then integration doesn't mean draining skills and energies from the ghetto into white neighborhoods; then it can mean white people moving from Beverly Hills into Watts, white people joining the Lowndes County Freedom Organization. Then integration becomes relevant . . .

White America will not face the problem of color, the reality of it. The well-intended say: "We're all human, everybody is really decent, we must forget color." But color cannot be "forgotten" until its weight is recognized and dealt with . . .

Whites will not see that I, for example, as a person oppressed because of my blackness, have common cause with other blacks who are oppressed because of blackness. This is not to say that there are no white people who see things as I do, but that it is black people I must speak to first. It must be the oppressed to whom SNCC addresses itself primarily, not to friends from the oppressing group.

From birth, black people are told a set of lies about themselves. We are told that we are lazy—yet I drive through the Delta area of Mississippi and watch black people picking cotton in the hot sun for fourteen hours. We are told, "If you work hard, you'll succeed"—but if that were true, black people would own this country. We are oppressed because we are black—not because we are ignorant, not because we are lazy, not because we're stupid (and got good rhythm), but because we're black . . .

The need for psychological equality is the reason why SNCC today believes that blacks must organize in the black community. Only black people can convey the revolutionary idea that black people are able to do things themselves. Only they can help create in the community an aroused and continuing black consciousness that will provide the basis for political strength. In the past, white allies have furthered white supremacy without the whites involved realizing it—or wanting it, I think. Black people must do things for themselves; they must get poverty money they will control and spend themselves, they must conduct tutorial programs themselves so that black children can identify with black people. This is one reason Africa has such importance: the reality of black men ruling their own nations gives blacks elsewhere a sense of possibility, of power, which they do not now have . . .

Black and white can work together in the white community where possible; it is not possible, however, to go into a poor Southern town and talk about integration. Poor whites everywhere are becoming more hostile—not less—partly because they see the nation's attention focused on black poverty and nobody coming to them . . .

Black people do not want to "take over" this country. They don't want to "get Whitey"; they just want to get him off their backs, as the saying goes. It was, for example, the exploitation by Jewish landlords and merchants which first created black resentment toward Jews—not Judaism. The white man is irrelevant to blacks, except as an oppressive force. Blacks want to be in his place, yes, but not in order to terrorize and lynch and starve him. They want to be in his place because that is where a decent life can be had.

But our vision is not merely of a society in which all black men have enough to buy the good things in life. When we urge that black money go into black pockets, we mean the communal pocket. We want to see money go back into the community and used to benefit it. . . . The society we seek to build among black people, then, is not a capitalist one. It is a society in which the spirit of community and humanistic love prevail. The word "love" is suspect; black expectations of what it might produce have been betrayed too often. But those were expectations of a response from the white community, which failed us. The love we seek to encourage is within the black community, the only American community where men call each other "brother" when they meet. We can build a community of love only where we have the ability and power to do so: among blacks.

. . . The reality is that this nation is racist; that racism is not primarily a problem of "human relations" but of an exploitation maintained—either actively or through silence—by the white society as a whole. Can whites, particularly liberal whites, condemn themselves? Can they stop blaming us, and blame their own system? Are they capable of the shame which might become a revolutionary emotion?

. . . We won't fight to save the present society, in Vietnam or anywhere else. We are just going to work, in the way *we* see fit, and on goals *we* define, not for civil rights but for all our human rights.

The Black Power slogan created controversy but spurred little concrete policy or action. For all his articulateness, Stokely Carmichael did not himself formulate a plan on which blacks could act. It could be said that Carmichael, and his supporters in

SNCC, intended the slogan to be a rallying point, not a program. But having issued it, he found himself spending most of his time explaining it, not rallying blacks around it. And no matter how often he explained it, he could not calm the fear of many that it was a call to violent revolution.

Black moderates attacked the slogan, and SNCC as well. SNCC also came under increased scrutiny from white authorities; in Philadelphia, for example, police raided SNCC headquarters looking for nonexistent bombs. As the chief spokesman for Black Power, Carmichael was constantly in the spotlight, and this caused jealousy within the ranks of SNCC. By the spring of 1967 he was tired of the pressure and eager to give up his chairmanship. He was replaced by H. Rap Brown, who was even more militant and who changed the "N" in SNCC from Nonviolent to National.

In July 1967, Carmichael left the United States on a trip to twelve countries, primarily in Africa. Wherever he went, he talked about the brotherhood of American blacks with other oppressed colored peoples in the world. From 1968 to 1969 he served as prime minister of the Black Panther Party in California but he resigned because he disagreed with their formation of coalitions with white radicals. In March 1968, he married Miriam Makeba, a black singer from South Africa, and often traveled with her as she performed around the world. In 1969, Carmichael and his wife established a home in Conakry, Guinea, and he devoted his energies primarily to African affairs, participating in what he called "the reality of black men ruling their own nations," an idea which he espoused in his article for *The New York Review of Books*.

THE BLACK PANTHER PARTY

The Black Panther Party for Self-Defense was formed in September 1966, four months after Stokely Carmichael issued his call for "Black Power!" Despite its similar name, it had no relationship to the Black Panther political party founded in Lowndes

County, Alabama, in 1965, to which Carmichael made reference in the previous article. The Black Panther Party for Self-Defense was conceived by two Oakland, California, men, Huey Newton and Bobby Seale, in response to riots by black youths in Oakland (the black community across the bay from San Francisco). The riots had been unorganized expressions of rage; property had been destroyed, the residents terrified, and the community left in even worse shape than it had been in before. The Oakland police, attempting to quell the riots, had arrested and beaten local residents who had not participated, leading to new charges of police brutality by a community that believed, as did the people of other poor black urban areas, that the police existed not to protect them but to prey on them. Newton and Seale believed there was a way to harness and organize the youths' anger for constructive purposes and to simultaneously fight back against police brutality.

They decided to start a self-defense organization, choosing the black panther as its symbol because, as Newton put it, "The nature of the panther is that he never attacks. But if anyone attacks him or backs him into a corner, the panther comes up to wipe that aggressor or that attacker out, absolutely, resolutely, wholly, thoroughly, and completely." Seale was chairman and Newton was minister of defense. They wrote a program for the party that was both relevant to the needs of the black people of Oakland and easy to understand. The resulting ten major points in the October 1966 Black Panther "Party Platform and Program" are credited chiefly to Newton.

WHAT WE WANT
WHAT WE BELIEVE

1. *We want freedom. We want power to determine the destiny of our Black Community.*

We believe that black people will not be free until we are able to determine our destiny.

2. *We want full employment for our people.*

We believe that the federal government is responsible and obligated to give every man employment or guaranteed income. We believe that if white American businessmen will not give full employment, then the means of production should be taken from the businessmen and placed in the community so that the people of the community can organize and employ all of its people and give a high standard of living.

3. *We want an end to the robbery by the white man of our Black Community.*

We believe that this racist government has robbed us and now we are demanding the overdue debt of forty acres and two mules. Forty acres and two mules was promised 100 years ago as restitution for slave labor and mass murder of black people [Actually, it was one mule, and this restitution was never promised, merely suggested by some nineteenth-century Abolitionists.] We will accept the payment in currency which will be distributed to our many communities. The Germans are now aiding the Jews in Israel for the genocide of the Jewish people. The Germans murdered six million Jews. The American racist has taken part in the slaughter of over fifty million black people; therefore, we feel that this is a modest demand that we make.

4. *We want decent housing, fit for shelter of human beings.*

We believe that if the white landlords will not give decent housing to our black community, then the housing and the land should be made into cooperatives so that our community, with government aid, can build and make decent housing for its people.

5. *We want education for our people that exposes the true nature of this decadent American society. We want education that teaches us our true history and our role in the present-day society.*

We believe in an educational system that will give to our people a knowledge of self. If a man does not have knowledge of himself and his position in society and the world, then he has little chance to relate to anything else.

6. *We want all black men to be exempt from military service.*

We believe that black people should not be forced to fight in the military service to defend a racist government that does not protect us. We will not fight and kill other people of color in the world who, like black people, are being victimized by the white racist government of America. We will protect ourselves from the force and violence of the racist police and the racist military, by whatever means necessary.

7. *We want an immediate end to POLICE BRUTALITY and MURDER of black people.*

We believe we can end police brutality in our black community by organizing black self-defense groups that are dedicated to defending our black community from racist police oppression and brutality. The Second Amendment to the Constitution of the United States gives a right to bear arms. We therefore believe that all black people should arm themselves for self-defense.

8. *We want freedom for all black men held in federal, state, county and city prisons and jails.*

We believe that all black people should be released from the many jails and prisons because they have not received a fair and impartial trial.

9. *We want all black people when brought to trial to be tried in court by a jury of their peer group or people from their black communities, as defined by the Constitution of the United States.*

We believe that the courts should follow the United States Constitution so that black people will receive fair trials. The Fourteenth Amendment of the U.S. Constitution gives a man a right to be tried by his peer group. A peer is a person from a similar economic, social, religious, geographical, environmental, historical and racial background. To do this the court will be forced to select a jury from the black community from which the black defendant came. We have been, and are being tried

On May 2, 1967, members of the Black Panther Party for Self-Defense leave the capitol building in Sacramento, California, where party chairman Bobby Seale (FAR RIGHT, in beret) read the Panthers' first message to the American people.

by all-white juries that have no understanding of the "average reasoning man" of the black community.
10. *We want land, bread, housing, education, clothing, justice and peace. And as our major political objective, a United Nations–supervised plebiscite to be held throughout the black colony in which only black colonial subjects will be allowed to participate, for the purpose of determining the will of black people as to their national destiny.*

When, in the course of human events, it becomes necessary for one people to dissolve the political bonds which have connected them with another, and to assume, among the powers of the earth, the separate and equal station to which the laws of nature and nature's God entitle them, a decent respect to the opinions of mankind requires that they should declare the causes which impel them to the separation.

We hold these truths to be self-evident, that all men are created equal; that they are endowed by their Creator with certain unalienable rights; that among these are life, liberty, and the pursuit of happiness. *That, to secure these rights, governments are instituted among men, deriving their just powers from the consent of the governed; that, whenever any form of government becomes destructive of these ends, it is the right of the people to alter or to abolish it, and to institute a new government, laying its foundation on such principles, and organizing its powers in such form, as to them shall seem most likely to effect their safety and happiness.* Prudence, indeed, will dictate that governments long established should not be changed for light and transient causes; and, accordingly, all experience hath shown, that mankind are more disposed to suffer, while evils are sufferable, than to right themselves by abolishing the forms to which they are accustomed. *But, when a long train of abuses and usurpations, pursuing invariably the same object, evinces a design to reduce them under absolute despotism, it is their right, it is their duty, to throw off such government, and to provide new guards for their future security.*

With its many references to the Declaration of Independence and the U.S. Constitution, the Black Panther Party Platform can be read in part as a cry against injustice; but Newton and Seale were not so naive as to believe that this would have much impact. They realized that what *would* attract members was the radical proposal that all blacks arm themselves. And in the next few months they did attract members from the frustrated and disaffected youth of Oakland. In the spring of 1967, they made a bold demonstration of their willingness to act on the seventh point of their platform. Having read that the California legislature was considering a gun-control bill, and believing that the bill was aimed at groups like their own, the Panthers decided to take a unique, public stand against the bill. On May 2, 1967, thirty Panthers, including six women, armed to the teeth, walked into the capitol building at Sacramento and entered the assembly room. Reporters and photographers scrambled to cover the story. With microphones thrust at him from all angles and flashbulbs popping around him, Chairman Bobby Seal read "Executive Mandate Number One," the party's first message to the American people. It denounced the proposed legislation as "aimed at keeping the black people disarmed and powerless at the very same time that racist police agencies throughout the country are intensifying the terror, brutality, murder, and repression of black people."

That demonstration, needless to say, brought the Black Panther Party a lot of publicity. It also brought a lot of new members to the party, as well as overtures from white radical groups who wanted to join forces. When the Panthers agreed to work with these groups, they incurred the enmity of black cultural nationalist groups who wanted nothing to do with whites. In addition, that demonstration at Sacramento also focused the attention of local and national law-enforcement agencies on the Panthers.

In October 1967, Oakland police and members of the Black Panther Party were involved in a shoot-out that resulted in the death of a patrolman and the arrest of Huey Newton for murder. In April 1968, in another shoot-out in Oakland, one of the original Panthers, seventeen-year-old Bobby Hutton, was killed. Eldridge Cleaver was wounded and arrested.

ELDRIDGE CLEAVER

Eldridge Cleaver, born in 1935, was probably the most popular and romantic figure in the Black Panther Party. When Bobby Seale and Huey Newton formed the Panthers, he was in one of the many prisons he had served time in over the course of fourteen years; he had entered his first prison at the age of nineteen. Eventually, he had begun to question the meaning of his life and had started reading books, and writing. He also joined the Black Muslims, who seemed to have particular success in converting black prisoners; but after the assassination of Malcolm X in 1965, Cleaver left the Nation of Islam. The only constant in his life was writing.

A civil rights lawyer named Beverly Axelrod became interested in his writings and showed some of his manuscripts to the editors of *Ramparts,* a radical magazine published in New York. The editors, and several liberal white writers, were so impressed with Cleaver's work that they pressured the California prison authorities to release him, resulting in his parole in November 1966.

Cleaver immediately sought out the Black Panthers. He had watched their armed appearance in Sacramento on television, and Huey Newton had become his new hero. By the spring of 1967 he was minister of information of the Black Panther Party. He also had a book contract with Grove Press in New York. His first book, *Soul on Ice,* was published in February 1968; a collection of essays on the Beatles, spectator sports, life in Folsom Prison, the Black Muslims, rape, and a variety of other subjects, it made him internationally famous and celebrated by radicals, black and white, as a black man who had been brutalized by the racist American system and who was able to articulate his brutalized state.

Two months later, as a result of his participation in the shoot-out in which Bobby Hutton died, Cleaver's parole was revoked. The California Superior Court soon reinstated his parole, however, saying that it had been revoked not because he had violated it but because his political ideas were unpopular with the authorities. Free again, Cleaver worked to forge an alliance between the Panthers and the Peace and Freedom Party, an organization of whites opposed to the Vietnam War. The two groups formed a new California Peace and Freedom Party and ran a slate of candidates for national office that presidential election year. Cleaver was its candidate for president of the United States.

On July 3, 1968, Cleaver appeared on a local radio call-in show, "Night Call," emceed by Dell Shields. Following are excerpts from that program.

ELDRIDGE CLEAVER ON "NIGHT CALL"

Shields: Mr. Cleaver, just who and what are the Black Panthers?
Cleaver: The thing that really makes the Black Panther Party stand out from the other groups that originated in black communities is the fact that we feel it is necessary to use guns in a defensive manner against the aggression by the police department, vigilante groups, and so forth. Because we have used these guns for our defense, this is what most people have come to

associate with the Black Panther Party, but this is only one point of our platform. We have a ten-point platform that outlines the basic grievances and the basic desires and needs as we see them; and we seek to organize the black people in the black community who never have been organized before—that is, the so-called lower-class people . . .

Shields: Would you define the defensive program of the Black Panthers in terms of guns? Do you promote vigilante parties or do you—

Cleaver: No, we don't promote vigilante parties and we don't approve of them. We feel that the primary problem concerning black people today is the problem of being organized and the chief impediment to our interest in organizing the black community comes from the activities of the police department. The police department functions like an occupying army in the black community, and it intimidates black people: It disturbs meetings, it prevents black people from having peaceful assemblies; and the very presence of the police with the history they have concerning black people makes them an undesirable element in our community. We seek to remove them from our community because they are constantly killing, brutalizing people, and terrorizing people; and we feel that before progress can be made that this point has to be dealt with. So we call for the immediate withdrawal of the racist white policemen from our communities and we call for an enactment of the principle that those who police our community must live in our community . . .

Shields: Has [*sic*] the police department and the Black Panthers ever sat down at the same table and attempted to negotiate any of the problems?

Cleaver: There has been very minimal direct contact, such as when we have had occasion to put on benefits and rallies at the auditorium where security has to be discussed; but they prefer to do that behind closed doors . . .

Caller from Cleveland, Ohio: I would like you to tell me a little more about the Peace and Freedom Party which the Black Panther Party is working with.

Cleaver: The Peace and Freedom Party is composed primarily of white people who have been disgusted by the two-party system: the Republican Party and the Democratic Party and the type of corrupt politics that they have been practicing ever since they have come into existence. So, they have broken away from those two parties and formed a third party, which seeks to align itself with the legitimate aspirations of the black community and with the anti-war movement in this country. It seeks to chart a new direction in national politics, and we [Black Panther Party] felt that this was a positive sign coming out of the white community, and we saw no reasons why we shouldn't work with them since we shared some of the same goals and attitudes toward the status quo . . .

Caller from Memphis, Tennessee: Do you think you'll get rid of [Governor] Reagan out in California?

Cleaver: If we don't get rid of Reagan we can't survive. Our survival depends on getting rid of racist politicians like him . . .

Caller from Portland, Oregon: I think violence always gets violence, and I realize he [Cleaver] feels that they have been wronged; but I believe that in his case, whereas the police have wronged him, he should have redress. But I would like to ask if he has read the life of Gandhi. . . . Don't you believe that he did such a great deal more with nonviolence?

Cleaver: Yes, I have read the life of Gandhi. I read the history of the Indian Revolution and the liberation struggle, and Gandhi is one of the greatest statesmen in our history. . . . He liberated his country with nonviolence, but he was dealing with people other than these racist Yankees that we are dealing with here. He was dealing with a minority of occupying forces and we are dealing with the majority of very complacent people who surround us and have us dispersed throughout their population, and who have a tradition of murdering and cheating us in a very brutal and violent fashion and who don't seem to recognize the handwriting on the wall and the times in which they live and the fact that black people have suffered beyond any more tolerance of a continuation of these conditions. . . . Don't come to the black community and teach to victims of this violence to be nonviolent; but teach the perpetrators of this violence to be nonviolent, and then we can talk about it . . .

Caller from Winston-Salem, North Carolina: I would just like to make a couple of points to you, sir. One thing is that I think it is a very clever rearrangement and matter of semantics in relation to words [that you use to] justify your cause as being a defensive maneuver. What I think is that you are considering the very presence of the white mother country, as you call it, a sufficient reason for the black community to take an offensive stand with your Black Panther Party. The second point is—and let's get pragmatic for a minute—if you are going to talk about violence, let's leave the part of racism out of it for a minute . . .

You talk about revolutionary changes. . . . Alright, first of all you have got to consider when you talk about violence what is the population of Negroes in the U.S., and you've got to consider that you are outnumbered almost ten to one. Also, you have to consider how many weapons factories in the U.S. are Negro controlled, how many iron factories, how many bullet factories. How many food production outlets do you control, how many farm development centers, how many grocery stores? Do you own a trucking company for getting your men and machines from place to place? Supposing the revolution ever takes place, do you own any airlines for fast communication; how many communications systems are under black control? . . .

Cleaver: Let me ask you a question—are you a white man or a black man?

Caller: I am a white man, sir.

Cleaver: I thought so. Well, let me tell you this. You can count off your statistics about everything you can control, and if you had it sewn up tight then you shouldn't even be concerned about what black people can do in this country. But we know that with all your numbers and with all your materials and superiority, and with all these things you have going for you, you are in big trouble all over the planet earth—dig it? We know that and we don't look upon this situation as being confined to the geographical borders of the U.S. or the North American continent. We look upon this in a worldwide context, and in the worldwide context you are very much in the minority and we are with the majority. So you don't just have twenty million black people to deal with, you have seven hundred million Chinese to deal with, you have three hundred million Africans to deal with, you have unnumbered millions and millions and millions and millions of mad black, brown, yellow, and red people to deal with and you know that.

—Wait a minute, now, let me finish. You talked, now let me talk—dig it? We don't care about your atomic bombs, we don't care about your tanks and your guns and how many guns you have because when the push comes to the shove we will do the same thing that the Viet Cong is doing in Vietnam: We will lay and wait and we will take your guns from you and we will use your guns against you. Your plants and your factories are right here in our neighborhoods. You put them there because you didn't want them in your own neighborhood because they give out that smoke and those foul smells. These things are here and we will move against those things—dig it—and disrupt the economy of this country and force you to destroy all of your liberties and all the beautiful things you love. Because in order to destroy the twenty million black people in this country you are going to have to destroy this country, and we say that if we can't have freedom here, then let it be destroyed, because you don't deserve it. If we can't be free, then you don't even deserve to talk of freedom and your numbers and all of that don't move nobody but you, and you're moving in a fog and there ain't nobody digging it but you.

[This exchange between Cleaver and the caller from Winston-Salem went on, neither one conceding anything to the other. Cleaver had the last word, as guests on radio call-in shows usually do.]

Caller from Baltimore, Maryland: Mr. Cleaver, if you are so unhappy with America, why don't you go back to Africa if this nation is so unsatisfactory for you?
Cleaver: I think that after we send you back to Europe we might go back to Africa.
Caller: Oh really. Well let me say one more thing to you, sir. You say that there are crimes being committed against black people. The crime rate amongst the Negro is the highest as far as the U.S. is concerned, and I say that the black people are committing crimes against white people.
Cleaver: Well, you can say that if you want to, but I say that the crime rate, or what you say is the crime rate, is not nearly high enough. Black people are put into a position where they either have to go out and beg you white people to survive or else they have to go out and take it. So I say if they are not able to get it in any other way, that they should push the crime rate to high heaven and take everything you got because you don't deserve it, because you have an anti-human attitude toward other people.
Caller: I do not have an anti-human attitude and I say, sir, that if anyone wants to work they can work.
Cleaver: Do you know that there are millions of people in this country who want work and who can't find jobs?
Caller: There are plenty of jobs that are available.
Cleaver: Well, why don't you go down to one of the unemployment offices and tell those people who are standing in line that there are plenty of jobs available, why don't you do that?
Caller: Well, the jobs are available, but we can't get any help, and I think that the way you advocate violence is a terrible thing, and I certainly don't think you are helping the situation. You

are not bringing black people and white people together.
Cleaver: Well, we want to bring people together who have their hands together and it wouldn't be any good to bring people together who have their hands sewn together, you know.
Caller: Well, I am going to hang up, but this is the first time I have had the opportunity to talk to a criminal. Thank you.
Cleaver: My pleasure.
Caller from Seattle, Washington: Mr. Cleaver, is it possible that the white and the black can live together?
Cleaver: I think . . . that ultimately it will be possible for black people and white people to live together. I think that that would be up to white people because black people are willing to live side by side with other people. But the question is this: How are we to move to survive against a hostile population that on the one hand sends in a few of its numbers to talk nonviolence to us and to talk brotherhood to us and to talk about living together, where on the other hand the very working and functioning of the system daily is grinding black people down and keeping them down. And while other people's standards of living are going up, ours is falling and standing still. It means it is very difficult for us to be concerned about brotherhood when we see the operation of this country destroying us . . .
Shields: I just want to ask one question in terms of the defensive measures of the Black Panther Party. If the Black Panther Party was to decide to forego the idea of defensive measures, do you think there would be more acceptance of the Party?
Cleaver: Yes, I think that a lot of people would read that as a good sign; but I think it would actually be a great disservice to the black people and mankind. If we were to abandon our position of calling for a cessation of the brutality against black people, then we would be in effect endorsing evil. We say it is the duty of people to stand up to and implacably oppose all manifestations of inhuman behavior.

Cleaver used his candidacy for president on the Peace and Freedom Party ticket to get support for Huey Newton, who was then on trial for murder. The publicity Cleaver and others attracted was instrumental in getting Newton's charge reduced from first-degree murder to manslaughter and in getting him freed on bail pending a new trial. Meanwhile, Cleaver was scheduled to go to trial for his part in the 1968 shoot-out that winter. Convinced that he would be convicted and sent back to prison, he left the country.

He went first to Cuba, then to Algiers, where his wife, Kathleen, joined him. At first, Cleaver remained actively involved in the Black Panther Party, depending on a group of loyal followers to speak for him. But when in the fall of 1970 Huey Newton, free on bail, began to take steps to disassociate the Panthers from the Weathermen, the most violent faction of the white radical movement, Cleaver denounced his former hero as anti-revolutionary. Newton countered with his own criticisms of Cleaver, and the following March a confrontation between Cleaver and Newton supporters in New York ended in the death of one of Cleaver's men. Cleaver ended his association with the Panthers.

He remained based in Algeria and traveled to a number of Third World and Communist countries for the next several years, hoping to influence the liberation movements of other nonwhite peoples, but he was largely unsuccessful. As an American he had a different worldview from that of the people he tried to influence. Eventually, he decided to return to the United States. In 1979, after long negotiations with U.S. and California authorites, he agreed to plead guilty to assaulting an Oakland policeman in the shoot-out more than ten years earlier, and won an assurance of the dismissal of the old murder charge against him. He returned to California and was placed on probation and ordered to do two thousand hours of community service.

Not long afterward, he announced that he was a "born-again Christian" and wrote a book about his religious experience, which did not sell as well as the writings he had done when he was an angry revolutionary. He also became a political conservative. While he encountered a considerable amount of derision because of this turnaround, he never apologized for it. In fact, he pointed out that his freedom to change his mind was one reason why he had decided that despite its flaws, the American system was the best. In 1982, he told a group of Yale University students that America was the "freest and most democratic country in the world."

The Black Panther Party maintained its strength through the end of the sixties. In spite of its numerous problems with the police, it had captured the imagination of a number of poor urban blacks, whose spirits were lifted by the idea of proud, unafraid black people directly challenging white authorities. It had also come to symbolize a cultural phenomenon of the late sixties that writer Tom Wolfe called "radical chic": a desire of the upper classes to identify with what they imagined to be the exotic, more vital lifestyle of the lower classes. When in 1969 the Panthers began a national campaign to raise funds for the defense of twenty-one members who were to stand trial, New York's social elite, who had already held fund-raising parties for California migrant workers and the Irish Republican Army, took on the Panthers' cause. The most famous of these parties took place at composer/conductor Leonard Bernstein's Park Avenue duplex and was attended by a star-studded cast.

The March 1971 shoot-out in New York between Cleaver's and Newton's followers brought the party's brief career as the darling of the socialites to an abrupt end. In fact, that violent confrontation signaled the demise of the Black Panther Party. Its ranks depleted by police raids, arrests, imprisonments, and trials, and divided by ideology, the party ceased to be a major force by the early 1970s.

Bobby Seale left the Panthers in 1974 and moved to Philadelphia, where he worked as a musician, a stand-up comic, and a radio disc jockey before getting a job as the director of a youth training program.

Huey Newton won acquittal on murder charges in 1970, and with state and federal funds started a community education and nutrition program in Oakland. It is alleged that, under the influence of cocaine, he killed a teenage girl in 1974. Like Eldridge Cleaver before him, he jumped bail and spent three years in Cuba before returning to the United States to try to straighten out his legal problems. He managed to do so and until 1983 continued to operate the education and nutrition program he had started in 1973 (his followers had carried on in his absence). In April 1985, he was arrested on charges of embezzling funds from the program. A search of his home after his arrest turned up unregistered guns, and he was also charged with possession of illegal weapons. He was convicted and began serving a sentence of sixteen months to three years in March 1987.

The Black Power Movement ultimately failed because it represented an outright threat to the white power structure and thus brought down upon itself the wrath of the FBI and the local police forces. It failed, too, because it never attracted the support of the majority of black people. The average black person wanted a job, a decent place to live, an education, an equal chance to make it in America. He or she did not want to carry a gun, or take an African name, or participate in any world revolution. He or she understood issues such as voting rights and civil rights, but was not so sure about revolutionary socialism and cultural nationalism. When people like Malcolm X were killed, and people like Carmichael and Cleaver and Newton were imprisoned or forced into exile, no one stepped in to take their places.

The Black Power Movement did, however, have an influence. Earlier, the term *black* was not regarded as a polite term—the preferred term was *Negro*. During the sixties, the idea of Black Pride came into being, and *black* became the preferred term. The Black Power Movement, like the cultural nationalism movement, also awakened people, black and white, to a larger world-view, and set them to thinking in more global terms, especially about other nonwhite countries. Thus, while the movement did not appreciably increase black power, it did increase black pride and helped to build a new sense of identity.

CHAPTER SIX

THE PEACE MOVEMENT

The campaign against U.S. involvement in the Vietnam War was certainly a major movement in the sixties, but we have chosen to call this chapter "The Peace Movement" so as to include the people and the organizations who were against all war—believing in nonviolence, no matter what the situation. The 1960s saw a minor movement dubbed "Flower Power" in which hippies, mostly young women in long hair and long skirts, made a practice of handing out flowers to passersby, especially to police officers and pro–Vietnam War demonstrators. The slogan "Make Love, Not War" was coined in the sixties, as was the slogan "War Is Not Healthy for Children and Other Living Things." One television campaign ad, aired only once during the 1964 presidential campaign between the conservative Republican Barry Goldwater and the liberal Democrat Lyndon B. Johnson, is still remembered for its strong effect. In the first scene it showed a little girl pulling the petals from a daisy one by one. In the second scene it showed the mushroom-shaped cloud of an atomic bomb.

The focus of the Peace Movement in the 1960s was, however, less on nuclear war than on U.S. involvement in Vietnam.

Why were we in Vietnam? On the simplest level, the United States government was trying to stem the worldwide tide of Communism. By the 1960s, Southeast Asia, especially the countries of Laos, Cambodia, and Vietnam, had become a major battlefield for democracy and Communism. The three countries had been under French domination (the area had been called French Indochina) since the late 1800s. Around 1916, Communist-inspired organizations began to work to overthrow French rule and succeeded in gaining a foothold in the north. They were largely unsuccessful in further expanding their influence until World War II. Before the Japanese lost the war, they managed to force the French out of the area. Treaties signed after the war was over divided what was formerly French Indochina in half: China, which had allied itself with Britain and the United States in the war, would control the northern half; Britain, the southern.

In North Vietnam the Chinese promptly recognized the Viet Minh government, a coalition of Communists, democrats, and socialists. Ho Chi Minh, president of the Viet Minh, then declared the establishment of the Democratic Republic of Vietnam. The British put the French back into power in the South. At conferences between the Viet Minh and the French, both sides demanded unity for the divided country, but neither side was willing to give up control. At issue was the type of government that would operate the reunited country—Communist or democratic. Unable to resolve the issue peacefully, the two sides were soon at war.

The situation in Vietnam was only one battlefront in a larger, global struggle that began after World War II. During that war, Communists and democrats had fought together to defeat the Nazis in Europe and the Japanese in Asia. After the war, they split apart and another "war" began: the Cold War. This was a war of ideology between Communism and democracy, with each side trying to extend its influence in other parts of the world, while trying to keep the other side from gaining any more influence. As early as 1950, the United States began sending money and supplies to help the French in Vietnam. After the French suffered a disastrous defeat at Dienbienphu in North Vietnam in 1954, they withdrew from the area altogether, leaving the government of Ngo Dinh Diem, who favored democracy and who declared South Vietnam a separate republic, the Republic of Vietnam. The United States and other Western nations supported the Diem government, as they had the French.

Over the next seven years, Ho Chi Minh consolidated his support and his territory and sent guerrilla troops into the South to try to topple President Diem's government. Diem tried to rout these guerrilla forces, whom he called Vietcong (Vietnamese Communists). In doing so, his troops often arrested or killed innocent people, and Diem was accused of conducting anti-Communist "witch-hunts." These accusations, together with the corruption in his government, weakened his position. He appealed to the United States for help, and President Lyndon B. Johnson agreed to increase U.S. aid. In the same year President Ho Chi Minh of the Democratic Republic of Vietnam in the North secured the help of Communist China in its fight against the Republic of Vietnam in the South.

Diem was assassinated by a group of his own generals in November 1963. Over the next two years, no less than twelve other governments were established in the Republic of Vietnam, and were all swiftly toppled. As each new government collapsed, the United States found itself shouldering more and more of the burden of the war. The United States government decided that the only way to get out of the conflict was to win it, quickly, and on March 2, 1965, the U.S. began to bomb North Vietnam on a round-the-clock basis. In effect, the United States was at war with the Democratic Republic of Vietnam.

But the U.S. was not *officially* at war. According to the U.S. Constitution, in order for that to happen, the president must ask

Congress to declare a state of war and Congress must vote to grant his request. Those procedures had not taken place; in fact, they never did take place during the years of U.S. involvement in Vietnam.

Some individuals and groups had been against the U.S. role in Vietnam from the start; now, they believed it was time to launch a popular movement against it. They hoped to attract individuals and groups with a series of "teach-ins" at colleges and universities throughout the United States and abroad. While the term "teach-in" was obviously related to the "sit-in" that the Direct Action Civil Rights Movement had used so effectively, the early teach-ins were not marked by the confrontations of the early sit-ins. The organizers of the teach-ins invited spokesmen for opposing views to participate, and the events were, in the main, polite academic exchanges. On May 15, 1965, a National Teach-In was held in Washington, D.C., an all-day event featuring a dozen speakers. Following are excerpts from an exchange that took place between Robert A. Scalapino, professor of political science at the University of California at Berkeley, who supported U.S. policy in Vietnam, and Hans J. Morgenthau, professor of political science and director of the Center for the Study of American Foreign Policy at the University of Chicago, who spoke against the government's policy.

NATIONAL TEACH-IN, WASHINGTON, D.C. MAY 15, 1965

Professor Scalapino: Now, I think that when it comes to the basic issues that confront us today . . . we are confronted, at least theoretically, with three broad alternatives: Withdrawal. Negotiation. Or escalation.

It seems to me clear that the arguments against withdrawal

...erful and so strong that at least as yet they have not ...d.

...ly that withdrawal would reduce American cred... her allies and neutrals round the world, but it is also ... would be a green light to the new national liberation ...ovements which are even now getting under way. I do not need to remind you that Peking has broadcast repeatedly its intent to support the Thai national liberation movement and has already launched the first propaganda with this matter in [mind].

If socioeconomic interests are the critical question, we would have some curious new kinds of analyses to make. We cannot ignore the ingredient of power. And central to this, it seems to me, is the fact that for more than five years Peking and Moscow have been arguing vigorously about the way to handle American imperialism. That argument, which has gone down to this present month, is roughly speaking as follows, and I think you know it well:

American imperialism, argues Peking, is a paper tiger. Push and attack—it will retreat. It is not to be taken as a nuclear blackmail threat. The problem with the Russians, argues Peking, is that they have been too sensitive to American power, too willing to compromise, too unwilling to push the revolutionary movement forward.

It seems to me that, above all, withdrawal—withdrawal would prove that Peking was right and make it virtually impossible for moderation to prevail inside the world Communist movement. For if the strategy of pushing American power and forcing it into a unilateral retreat works—if it works in Vietnam, it will work elsewhere and be tried elsewhere . . .

Let me move to this question of negotiation: I suspect the overwhelming majority of people in this room, and listening to us, favor negotiation. And I suspect that the critical issue, therefore, to come is: Who is willing to negotiate and on what terms.

Up to date, and we can certainly hope that this will change, the Chinese have indicated very little willingness to negotiate. . . . And we are still hoping that at least Hanoi [capital of the Democratic Republic of Vietnam in the North] will come forward and break its tie, now more than two years old, with Peking and move into a new orbit of independence.

The whole history of Vietnam indicates that while there has always been a stout resistance to China on the one hand there has always been a strong element willing to cooperate with China on the other. And this brings to me—I think—the focus of this problem: namely, the question of the containment of China. . . . I suggest that the pressures which Communist China is putting upon the small neutralist countries today—unless they are counteracted by some balance of power in this region—will be anti-nationalist and increasingly satellite in character.

These are small states, the survival of which depends upon some balance of power—a balance of power, I say, that must be a combination of both Western and Asian power, that must represent a fusion, for today it is critical that we come into line with such major societies in Asia as Japan and India, and I would hope some day, Indonesia. For these are societies with whom we can work in forwarding the social, economic, and nationalist revolutions . . .

I say that this policy can run along these lines:

First, our broad objective should be a neutral, nonaligned Asia that is truly neutral and nonaligned, not the Communist version of the Vietcong.

Secondly, we should, of course, negotiate. But we should make it clear that we are not negotiating just with labels, that we are negotiating with men representing forces. We should negotiate with the Communists in South Vietnam as Communists, and we should negotiate with the other elements in terms of whatever representation they truly represent. It must be remembered that the Buddhists are the largest functional group in South Vietnam and they certainly dwarf the Vietcong in numbers and supporters.

And lastly I would say this, that I think that as long as we maintain two open channels not only for the neutrals but for the Communists, one in which we urge social, economic, cultural exchange, one in which we urge peaceful coexistence, one in which we desire the exchange of scholars, journalists, and economic development—yes, with China, as with others. And the other channel in which we say we will not surrender unconditionally, we will not be driven out by a philosophy that regards compromise as evil as long as it takes that stand, as long as we keep these channels open and operative in an imaginative sense, I do not see how we can fail in the long run to reach a solution to our problems.

Professor Morgenthau: Let me suppose that Professor Scalapino's analysis of the facts in Southeast Asia is correct in every particular—a mere hypothetical assumption on my part.

What would the consequences for American policy be?

Professor Scalapino speaks very softly about the establishment of a balance of power. I speak very crudely about war against China.

For I see here one of the basic inner contradictions of our policy which makes, as speakers have reminded us this morning and this afternoon, those problems so terribly complicated.

It is because we set ourselves goals in Asia and we have done so, I should say in parting, for half a century, which cannot be achieved with the means we are willing to employ.

And as it is in philosophy and in pure logic, if you pose a wrong question you find it extremely complex to give a simple and correct answer.

And the uneasiness in the country of which this assembly is an impressive manifestation, I think stems from this instinctive recognition that there's something basically wrong in the modes of thought and action of our government, that there is an essential contradiction or a number of contradictions between what we profess to want and the policies we want to employ and the risks which we want to take.

And I submit again, as I have done this morning, and have done before in lectures many times, that if you really want to achieve in Asia what the spokesmen for our government say they want to achieve, you must be ready to go to war with China, with all that that implies.

I would also say a word . . . about negotiations. Much has been made of our willingness to negotiate. There is, of course, no doubt, and Mr. McGeorge Bundy [Special Assistant to President Johnson for National Security Affairs] didn't need to emphasize it, that our Government wants a peaceful solution. No decent government which isn't out of its mind would want anything else.

But this is not the point. The point is not what you intend, but the point is what you do regardless of your intentions. The history of the world is full of instances where well-meaning, highly-principled people have brought unspeakable misery upon their own nation in spite of good intentions, because it used the wrong policies.

Let me turn to the problem of negotiations. Of course we want a negotiated settlement, and I'm sure there are people in our government who pray for a negotiated settlement. If only the other side would make a move.

But those people cannot see that the implicit conditions which we have made—the unspoken conditions—make a negotiated settlement at the moment impossible.

For, first of all, we refuse to negotiate with the Vietcong.

Secondly, we make it an implicit condition that we remain—at least for the time being—in South Vietnam—that is to say, as long as no stable government is established there, which will take a very long time.

Now the other side is fully aware of the blind alley in which we find ourselves in South Vietnam. We don't have the courage to retreat and we don't dare to advance too far.

And so obviously from the point of view of Peking, which

hasn't lost a single man in that conflict and has only lost, as far as we can tell, one gun, which Mr. McNamara [Secretary of Defense] showed the other day in a press conference.

Of course from the point of view of Peking, nothing better could happen than the United States waging a war in Vietnam which it is not able to win and which it cannot afford to lose.

Why should Peking under such circumstances recommend negotiations?

Negotiations are possible only under the conditions such as when one recognizes the inevitable facts of life in Asia which, as I have said before, can only be changed by war.

Professor Scalapino: If I may risk a simplification of Professor Morgenthau's thesis: It seems to me that he is coming pretty close to saying that either war or withdrawal from Asia is inevitable for the United States—and that we must either get out or we must go to war with China.

I may be misinterpreting him, but that's the way I read his remarks and he'll have a chance to rebut this if I'm wrong.

Now, I would just like to reiterate what's been said by other people here. I don't believe in historical inevitability. But if I did, I would put this in precisely the opposite framework. I would say that withdrawal at this point will mean war. Because I think it will inevitably settle, at least for the time being, the issue of how to meet American imperialism, as the Communists put it.

I think it will inevitably cause the launching not of a thousand ships, but a thousand revolts not just in Asia, but wherever this movement can get under way. And I think that that means war. Under what conditions, I cannot predict, nor can you.

Now it seems to me that that's the critical issue.

We are engaged in the hard, difficult, complex task of trying again to build a containment policy, if you will, but one that is more broad than in the past. And I would simply end my answer to Mr. Morgenthau's comment by suggesting that if you take the last ten years, I think that the United States, itself a late-developing society in terms of world leadership, has learned a great deal; has moved a great distance.

Ten years ago we were still saying—some of us, not I, but some—that neutralism was immoral. Today, we are prepared—and I think this is true of both of our major parties—to work with and underwrite when we can, neutral and nonaligned states.

We have people—and this point ought to be underlined and reemphasized—who are not reactionary; who are not committed to the past, and who have found that between us and the Communists they'd rather take their chances on socioeconomic reform and development with us.

And I maintain that in some of the areas where the American commitment has been heaviest in Asia, the standard of living is going up most rapidly.

This is important, not because I want to whitewash American policy, I think we've made many mistakes in the past, we're still making some—but I think the time has come both to face up to alternatives and at the same time to point out again and again that, if we can't do something to preserve a certain openness in these societies, then, it seems to me, the balance of power will be abruptly changed and global war will ensue.

Arguments about U.S. policy in Vietnam remained on a generally polite level until the following year, when the military draft began to affect the students taught by professors such as Scalapino and Morgenthau. Before 1966, students were automatically exempt from being ordered to do military service. But by 1966 the U.S. armed forces had so deeply committed their manpower to the Vietnam conflict that the Selective Service System changed its policy toward student deferments. Henceforth, only students with good grades would be deferred; students with low grades would lose their exemption. The Selective

As American involvement in the war in Vietnam escalated, anti-war protest swept the country. ABOVE, a student at the University of Washington in Seattle burns his draft card to protest Dow Chemical's manufacturing of napalm. BELOW, thousands of demonstrators gather at a rally opposite the Lincoln Memorial in Washington, D.C.

Service System inaugurated a series of academic tests; in May and June of each year, students in the lower portions of their classes could take these tests, and if they passed, they could be deferred until the next year. If they failed, they would be eligible for the draft.

Needless to say, these changes attracted a lot of college students to the anti-war effort. In fact, they represented a movement within a movement—the anti-draft movement within the anti-war movement. There were some students in this movement who hardly knew where Vietnam was and had absolutely no opinion on U.S. policy there until they found out that their poor grades might get them drafted into the military and sent to Vietnam. There were also many students with good grades who resented this military invasion into the academic world, especially when they learned that in many cases the military had been working closely therein all along.

We have already discussed the student protests against the role of higher-education institutions in the military-industrial complex. That role was largely indirect, taking the form of military research. But now, students were infuriated to learn that the Selective Service System was taking direct credit for the fact that some of them were in institutions of higher learning in the first place!

The students learned of this connection in a variety of ways, among them through a pamphlet called "Channeling" that was distributed on college campuses in the latter part of the 1960s by a group that called itself the Peace and Liberation Commune Press (P & LCP). Pamphleteering was a major activity of peace movement groups and those involved in other political movements, for they did not trust mainstream newspapers to print their views. In fact, there was probably as much pamphleteering done in the 1960s as during the years preceding the American Revolution, when pamphlets were the main expression of public opinion. Along with some five hundred "underground newspapers" committed to radical politics, there were hosts of groups that printed and distributed pamphlets, many of them intent on exposing the activities of the government or the military-industrial complex. The bulk of the "Channeling" pamphlet consisted of "an unedited, official Selective Service System document" called "Channeling." According to the P & LCP, this was one of ten documents in an "Orientation Kit" put out in July 1965 by the Selective Service System. "It was withdrawn, perhaps because of the outrage it engendered. However, the SSS still presents material from the 1965 pamphlet in an abbreviated and less candid form. Its policy is unchanged. See The Selective Service: Its Concept, History and Operation, September 1967, p. 27, 28 (U.S. Govt. Printing Office: 1967-0-267-285)."

What followed was the six-page SSS document, with the "outrageous" statements underlined. We have reprinted primarily the paragraphs containing the underlined statements, as well as the P & LCP summation of why the document was so "outrageous."

"CHANNELING"

One of the major products of the Selective Service classification process is the channeling of manpower into many endeavors, and occupations: activities that are in the national interest. This function is a counterpart and amplification of the System's responsibility to deliver manpower to the armed forces in such a manner as to reduce to a minimum any adverse effect upon the national health, safety, interest, and progress. By identifying and applying this process intelligently, the System is able not only to minimize any adverse effect, but to exert an effect beneficial to the national health, safety and interest . . .

While the best known purpose of Selective Service is to procure manpower for the armed forces, *a variety of related processes takes place outside delivery of manpower to the active armed forces.*

Many of these may be put under the heading of "channeling manpower." Many young men would not have pursued a higher education if there had not been a program of student deferment. Many young scientists, engineers, tool and die makers, and other possessors of scarce skills would not remain in their jobs in the defense effort if it were not for a program of occupational deferment. Even though the salary of a teacher has historically been meager, many young men remain in that job seeking the reward of deferment. The process of channeling manpower by deferment is entitled to much credit for the large amount of graduate students in technical fields and for the fact that there is not a greater shortage of teachers, engineers, and other scientists working in activities which are essential to the national interest.

More than ten years ago, it became evident that something additional had to be done to permit and encourage development of young scientists and trained people in all fields. A million and a half registrants are now deferred as students . . .

The opportunity to enhance the national well-being by inducing more registrants to participate in fields which relate directly to the national interest came about as a consequence, soon after the close of the Korean episode, of the knowledge within the system that there was not enough registrant personnel to allow stringent deferment practices employed during war time to be relaxed or tightened as the situation might require. Circumstances had become favorable to induce registrants, by the attraction of deferment, to matriculate in schools and pursue subjects in which there was beginning to be a national shortage of personnel. These were particularly in the engineering, scientific, and teaching professions.

This was coupled with the growing public recognition that *the complexities of future wars would diminish further the distinction between what constitutes military service in uniform and a comparable contribution to the national interest out of uniform.* Wars have always been conducted in various ways, but appreciation of this fact and its relationship to preparation for war has never been so sharp in the public mind as it is now becoming. The meaning of the word "service," with its former restricted application to the armed forces, is certain to become widened much more in the future. This brings with it the ever increasing problem of how to control effectively the service of individuals who are not in the armed forces.

In the Selective Service System, the term "deferment" has been used millions of times to describe the method and the means used to attract to the kind of service considered to be most important, the individuals who are not compelled to do it. *The club of induction has been used to drive out of areas considered to be less important to the areas of greater importance in which deferments were given,* the individuals who did not or could not participate in activities which were considered essential to the Nation. The Selective Service System anticipates evolution in this area. It is promoting the process by the granting of deferments in liberal areas where the national need would clearly benefit . . .

Patriotism is defined as "devotion to the welfare of one's country." It has been interpreted to mean many different things. Men have always been exhorted to do their duty. *But what that duty is depends upon a variety of variables,* most important being the nature of the threat to the national welfare and the capacity and opportunity of the individual. Take, for example, the boy who saved the Netherlands by plugging the dike with his finger.

At the time of the American Revolution the patriot was the so called "embattled farmer" who joined General Washington to fight the British. The concept that patriotism is best exemplified by service in uniform has always been under some degree of challenge, but never to the extent that it is today. *In today's complicated warfare when the man in uniform may be suffering far less than the civilians at home, patriotism must be interpreted far more broadly than ever before.*

This is not a new thought, but it has had new emphasis since the development of nuclear and rocket warfare. Educators, scientists, engineers, and their professional organizations, during the last ten years particularly, have been convincing the American public that *for the mentally qualified man there is a special order of patriotism other than service in uniform*—that for the man having the capacity, dedicated service as a civilian in such fields as engineering, the sciencies, and teaching constitute the ultimate in their expression of patriotism. A large segment of the American public has been convinced that this is true . . .

In the less patriotic and selfish individual [this process] engenders a sense of fear, uncertainty, and dissatisfaction which motivates him, nevertheless, in the same direction. He complains of the uncertainty which he must endure; *he would like to be able to do as he pleases;* he would appreciate a certain future with no prospect of military service or civilian contribution, but he complies with the needs of the national health, safety, or interest—or he is denied deferment . . .

The psychology of granting wide choice under pressure to take action is the American or indirect way of achieving what is done by direction in foreign countries where choice is not allowed. Here, choice is limited but not denied, and it is fundamental that an individual generally applies himself better to something he has decided to do rather than something he has been told to do . . .

The device of pressurized guidance, or channeling, is employed on Standby Reservists of which more than 2½ million have been referred by all services for availability determinations. The appeal to the Reservist who knows he is subject to recall to active duty unless he is determined to be unavailable is virtually identical to that extended to other registrants . . .

From the individual's viewpoint, he is standing in a room which has been made uncomfortably warm. Several doors are open, but they all lead to various forms of recognized, patriotic service to the Nation. Some accept the alternatives gladly—some with reluctance. The consequence is approximately the same . . .

A quarter billion classification actions were needed in World

War II for the comparatively limited function of the Selective Service System at that time. *Deciding what people should do, rather than letting them do something of national importance of their own choosing, introduces many problems* that are at least partially avoided when indirect methods, the kind currently invoked by the Selective Service System, are used . . .

Summation: Ontology and the Military-Industrial Complex

The draft is familiar enough, but it is not well-known that the government uses the threat of the draft and the deferment system to obtain personnel for the industrial part of the military-industrial complex. And by determining the choice of career, the government determines the curriculum choices of the young. In this way it channels their thoughts, their feelings and their motions during the formative years at college . . .

Channeling is accomplished for the most part by Defense Department agencies other than the SSS. It is easier to use the carrot than "the club of induction." Thus, most of the high-paying jobs which open for graduates are for engineers, researchers, and administrators in industries whose existence depends on defense contracts. Similarly, Defense Department money pays for and decides the uses of two-thirds of the scientific research in this country, including the work done on college campuses. And all this to keep the U.S. ahead in the race to accumulate overkill.

Channeling did not begin with Vietnam and it will not end with Vietnam. Vietnam is a symptom of the problem, a war without identifiable human goals. It is only in part an exploitive war caused by a "conspiracy of American imperialists." It is instead an absurd war. It is a trans-human institutional phenomenon of the MIC [military-industrial complex]. No one runs the MIC, it runs us. Its motions are not determined by the objectives of any human being or group of human beings . . .

The MIC is to our age what the Church was to earlier ages. Where for ages there was absurdity and obedience in the name of God, now there is absurdity and obedience in the name of defense. Overkill is as impossible as the Trinity but one must believe in it. Whereas once the University's task was to train priests and theologians, now it trains MIC personnel and researchers. . . . The difference is that whereas the Church promised an eternal future, the MIC promises nothing.

By 1967, resistance against the draft had begun to take a variety of forms. Some young men went to Canada or Europe to escape the draft. Others sought deferment as conscientious objectors whose religious beliefs or belief in pacifism prevented them from engaging in war. The majority of draft resisters engaged in active protests, including burning their draft cards or returning their cards to the Selective Service System headquarters in Washington, D.C. On the weekend of October 20, 1967, an organization called the National Mobilization Committee to End the War in Vietnam (MOBE) sponsored a march by fifty thousand people on the Pentagon in Washington, D.C.

A crowd gathered in front of the five-sided building that houses the headquarters of the armed services; representatives of anti-war and anti-draft groups from across the country had come with bundles of draft cards which they put in a briefcase. Then Dr. Benjamin Spock, the well-known baby doctor (who some people said was responsible for much of what happened in the 1960s because he had counseled the mothers of the sixties youth to feed their babies on demand, thus setting up in the babies' minds unrealistic expectations about their ability to control their environment), the Reverend William Sloane Coffin, chaplain of Yale University, and a group of other well-known men took the briefcase to the Attorney General's office. They were refused admittance, and some of the marchers attempted to storm the Pentagon. More than six hundred people were arrested, including Spock and Coffin, who were charged with conspiring to "sponsor and support a nationwide program of resistance" to the draft. Though convicted of these charges in 1968, they saw their convictions reversed by a U.S. Court of Appeals the following year.

Spock and Coffin were but two of the many famous people who spoke out against and actively protested U.S. involvement in Vietnam. They included many black leaders, among them Dr. Martin Luther King, Jr., noted actors, including Jane Fonda and Shirley MacLaine, both of whom visited North Vietnam at the invitation of a Vietnamese women's organization, and folksingers Pete Seeger and Joan Baez.

JOAN BAEZ

Joan Baez was not just against the Vietnam War, she was against all war. She also opposed the use of guns. With her long hair, her guitar, and her championship of leftist causes, she was to some the epitome of the hippie. But she was against the use of drugs and so did not really fit the mold.

Born in Staten Island, New York, in January 1941, to an Irish mother and a Mexican father, Baez grew up in a Quaker home and thus learned the principles of nonviolence early. She needed the strength of those principles after her family moved to Redlands, California, where the Anglo kids looked down on her because she was part Mexican and the Mexican kids didn't like her because she couldn't speak Spanish. Her father, a college teacher, accepted a teaching job in Palo Alto, California, and she attended high school there. He then went to teach at Harvard, and Joan enrolled at Boston University. She did not want to attend college, however; she wanted to play her guitar and sing. She performed first in coffeehouses in Boston and Cambridge, then went to the Newport Folk Festival in the summer of 1959, where she made a vivid impression, though she sang only two songs. Strongly influenced by the older folksinger Pete Seeger, Baez's music appealed to the youth of the time, and soon afterward she began receiving invitations to perform and contract offers from record companies. She signed with Vanguard, which released her first album, *Joan Baez,* in 1960.

Her popularity as a singer grew through the years, especially among groups who applauded her political activism. She participated in the Free Speech Movement at Berkeley, in the 1963 civil rights march on Washington, in the Selma-to-Montgomery march for voting rights, and in a variety of pacifist and anti–Vietnam War crusades. She also refused to pay the sixty percent of her income taxes that she believed was used for military purposes; instead, she placed that amount in a special bank account each year and the government then "attached" it. In 1967, she was arrested for participating in an anti-draft protest and served forty-five days in jail in Oakland, California. Her husband, David Harris, whom she married in 1968, spent three years in jail in Arizona for failing to register for the draft. In 1966, she opened an Institute for the Study of Non-Violence in her home in Carmel, California. A writer for *The New Yorker* magazine visited her there and wrote an article quoting her on nonviolence and the work of her institute. That article is excerpted on the following pages.

NON-VIOLENT SOLDIER

What I'm all about is that I'm a non-violent soldier. That's to be distinguished a little from being a pacifist. It's not just withdrawing and growing your own vegetables and not paying taxes. It means doing more than being nice to birds and small animals. I dislike the word "goal," but I suppose that's what we have here—we want to let out the news that the time has come when killing in the outside world is no more proper than killing within the national boundaries. Not that absolutely everybody agrees yet that even killing within the nation is no longer acceptable.

There's still that cultural inertia left over from nearly three hundred years when it was the thing for us to carry guns, since there was always the chance we might have to shoot a neighbor. Today, there's certainly enough proof around that violence can't be appropriate anywhere, but people want to hang on to that old feeling. You know—"it's a sunny day. Let's go kill something." When the world was proved round, that news was evidently just as hard to accept. In spite of the disadvantages of a flat world—monsters at the edge, sailboats falling off—people hated giving it up. Right now, people hate to give up weapons. We've changed the War Department's name to the Defense Department, but weapons are still made for killing, and boys are still trained to run bayonets through people, and the word "murder" still doesn't seem to ring a bell. I don't mean to say that there may not always be barroom brawls and things like that—though among the Hopi and Zuñi [Pueblo Indian groups of the Southwest], if you slug someone, it's regarded as poor form and you're out of it—but brawling is on a different plane from organized mass killing. And non-violence is—well, totally misunderstood. It's not avoiding violence. It's the opposite of running. It means confronting violence and having to come up with something more intelligent in response. Perhaps the only response that can possibly be effective today is refusing to cooperate, and going to jail. But we don't go into tactics and techniques here. Dr. Martin Luther King's movement has problems because its emphasis is all on tactics. At the University of California, the kids' trouble was that they only had a technique; if the cops came in, they knew they were supposed to drop to the floor. However, if you're rooted in the understanding that the Ku Klux Klansman and the Negro garbageman are both your brothers, then there's a chance you'll know the right thing to do . . .

There are certain pitfalls. There's a Fort Ord [a U.S. Army post on Monterey Bay above Carmel] boy who comes here with the schizo idea that he's non-violent because he takes a supercilious view of the Army and can ridicule his job as a soldier.

And I've been corresponding with a boy in Vietnam who thinks he's eased his conscience because he managed to exchange his gun for a camera, and now he writes about the bizarre beauty of war. It's so easy to kid yourself. Like believing that an Army ambulance driver's first duty isn't to get banged-up soldiers back to their guns, as soon as possible. Not that one mustn't care for the hurt and dying—but for *all* the hurt and dying, on all sides. We don't always notice what we're doing . . .

After the United States withdrew from Vietnam in the early 1970s, the anti-war movement waned, as did popular interest in pacifism. Musical tastes changed as well, and Baez's type of guitar-strumming folksinging went out of fashion, replaced by country and western music and acid rock. Baez changed neither her politics nor her music. As a singer, she remained popular in Europe and Latin America, performing often on both continents. In the United States, she appeared most frequently on college campuses and usually with other folksingers from the 1960s. In the 1980s, a revival of interest in the folk music of the sixties brought her renewed popularity, but she preferred not to sing her old songs. She dreamed instead of writing a folk song that would have the same effect on eighties youngsters as Bob Dylan's songs had on the young people of her generation.

Politically, she remained committed to nonviolence and in the middle 1980s was optimistic that by the end of the decade the many different peace and human rights groups would get together again, as they had twenty years earlier. As she told David Hinckley of the *New York Daily News* in August 1984, "Right now we're in a period of searching. In the '60s the war, awful as it was, brought everyone together. There are just as many concerned people today, but they're in separate groups and we need to manufacture a catalyst. The [nuclear] freeze movement works for many of them, but I'm not sure it can take us the full distance. To oppose blowing up the world is fine; but does that mean conventional armies and wars are okay? I don't think so."

With each passing year, more and more American bombs were dropped on North Vietnam, more and more young Americans were killed, and more and more people back home joined the protest movement against the war, or at least began to feel that it was wrong. Meanwhile, however, those who favored U.S. involvement in Vietnam became hardened in their opinions and regarded anyone who was against the war as either terribly misguided or a Communist. Soldiers who enlisted in the military or allowed themselves to be drafted began to feel that the folks at home were not behind them, and this contributed to severe problems of morale in the military. Parents of those soldiers accused draft resisters and protesters of being unpatriotic. The tension at home between "hawks" and "doves" and particularly between Americans in law enforcement (the police, the FBI, the National Guard) and Americans who challenged the law through their protests was so severe that there was talk of a new civil war.

President Lyndon B. Johnson, who had done so much to secure civil rights legislation and initiate anti-poverty programs, became highly unpopular. Those who were against the war disliked him because he would not pull American troops out of Vietnam. Those who supported the war were against him because they felt he should make an all-out effort to win the war. A large number of Americans, whatever their views on the war, blamed his administration for the unrest at home. He was so unpopular, in fact, that on March 31, 1968, he announced that he would not seek reelection as president in November. In the same speech, he said that he had ordered a cutback in the bombing of North Vietnam and was arranging the initiation of peace talks in Paris in an effort to end the war.

The Anti-War Movement responded joyfully. With Johnson out of the running, those who were against the war saw an opportunity to elect a president who would decisively end U.S. involvement in Vietnam. Many peace activists supported Minnesota senator Eugene McCarthy for the Democratic presidential nomination because he was running on a peace platform. Others supported the candidacy of Robert F. Kennedy, senator from New York and the brother of slain President John F. Kennedy. The third major Democratic candidate was Vice President Hubert Humphrey, who had been obliged to support the general war policy of Johnson, the man under whom he had served. The three men represented a spectrum of ideas about the war, with McCarthy being the most "dovish," Humphrey being the most "hawkish," and Kennedy falling somewhere in between. That balance was upset in June 1968, when Robert Kennedy was assassinated. The majority of Democratic Party regulars who had supported him now shifted their allegiance to Humphrey. Peace activists were afraid that McCarthy would have no chance at the Democratic presidential convention in Chicago in August. They made plans to go to Chicago to make their voices heard.

A variety of activist groups became involved in the preparations for the demonstrations in Chicago. The major organization involved was the National Mobilization Committee to End the War in Vietnam (MOBE). Headed by David Dellinger, editor of *Liberation* magazine, its leaders also included Tom Hayden, former president of Students for a Democratic Society (SDS). Joining MOBE in planning demonstrations in Chicago were such other groups as the Yippies (Youth International Party), Youth Against War and Fascism, the Vietnam Peace Parade Committee, the Communist Party, and several religious and legal organizations.

With such a variety of groups involved, it is not surprising that the efforts to plan coordinated protests at Chicago were completely unsuccessful. Even the Yippies could not decide among themselves whether the live pig that they planned to release at Chicago Civic Center Place during the convention should be little and cute, or big and ugly (not just the Yippies but members of most radical movements of the 1960s referred to law-enforcement officers as "pigs," and the release of a live pig was calculated to enrage the Chicago police).

Nor is it surprising that the protests got out of hand. Many of the radical groups sought confrontation with the police, and both the federal government and the government of the city of Chicago had decided to come down hard on demonstrations and dissenters. Depending on one's point of view, the bloody confrontations that took place on the streets of Chicago during the 1968 Democratic convention were either a "police riot" or a "radicals riot." There was civil disorder and violence, the worst in the United States since the bloody confrontations between civil rights protesters and southern police. Well over a thousand people were injured, more than six hundred arrested. Seven months later, in March 1969, a federal grand jury in Chicago indicted eight people on charges of conspiracy to incite: David Dellinger and Tom Hayden of MOBE, Jerry Rubin and Abbie Hoffman of the Yuppies, Bobby Seale of the Black Panthers, Rennie Davis, head of the Center for Radical Research, Lee Weiner, a sociology teacher at Northwestern University, and John Froines, a chemistry professor at the University of Oregon. The last two, while not important members of any radical organization, had helped plan the Chicago demonstration. Later, the case of Seale was separated from that of the others, and the Chicago Eight became the Chicago Seven.

The trial of the Chicago Eight, and then Seven, was a historic event, not the least because it became a media circus. All of the defendants, plus two of their attorneys, were ruled in contempt of court for courtroom outbursts and given jail sentences by Judge Julius Hoffman. A jury convicted five of the seven for conspiracy. Later, all the contempt sentences were ruled invalid, and the convictions on riot charges were upset on appeal.

The trial was fully covered by the media, which was largely sympathetic to the defendants, and many Americans with liberal leanings became aware for the first time of tactics employed by

The media circus of the Chicago Eight trial begins, as (FROM LEFT TO RIGHT) Jerry Rubin, David T. Dellinger, and Abbie Hoffman hold a press conference in New York City before their indictments.

the government and by law-enforcement agencies to stanch protest. At the same time, many Americans with conservative leanings became even more convinced that anti-government protests were un-American. The polarization of Americans that began over the war in Vietnam became even more pronounced.

Meanwhile, at the Chicago convention, Vice President Humphrey secured the Democratic presidential nomination over Senator Eugene McCarthy, plunging the anti-war protesters into despair once again. In the November 1968 presidential election, Republican Richard Nixon beat Democrat Hubert Humphrey by a small margin and seemed ready to pursue a war strategy not much different from Johnson's. Some in the Anti-War Movement gave up; others vowed renewed and more violent protests. The radical group the Weathermen began to make homemade bombs for use against selected targets in the military-industrial complex. Still others neither escalated nor de-escalated their protest activities, but simply went on as before.

U.S. involvement in Vietnam, and the movement against it, continued as the sixties were coming to an end. In 1969, some 750,000 people marched on Washington, D.C., to demand an end to the war. The new decade ushered in not only an escalation of the war, with the commencement of U.S. bombings in neighboring Cambodia, but an escalation of the tensions between campus protesters and law-enforcement officers, heightened by the killing of the students at Kent State during the campus protests against the bombing. By 1971, the Anti-War Movement had ceased to be primarily a youth movement; at a mass rally that year in Washington, D.C., for three hours' worth of speeches not a single speaker against the war was *under* thirty. The following year, a group of congressmen and senators assembled outside the Capitol to emphasize their frustration at not being able to do anything *inside* the halls of Congress to prevent the activation of mines in the harbors of North Vietnam.

Finally, in 1973, real progress began to be made at the Paris peace talks, and President Nixon ordered the gradual withdrawal of U.S. forces from Vietnam. The last units left Saigon, capital of South Vietnam, in 1975.

The Anti-War Movement subsided, but the bitterness over Vietnam remained for more than a decade (and still has yet to end completely). In the 1980s, college courses began to include material on the war in recent-history curricula. Vietnam veterans began to be celebrated and a Vietnam War Memorial was erected in Washington, D.C. Public patriotism, which had suffered severely because of the national conflict over Vietnam, is back in style today. Most young men do not resent having to register with the Selective Service System when they reach the age of eighteen and in fact regard the act as a kind of rite of passage into adulthood (although, since the United States is not engaged in any major military conflict, their chances of having to serve in the military are slim).

The Peace Movement continues today, primarily in the form of anti-nuclear protests and protests against nuclear power plants. Whenever the United States engages in military action abroad, however, the peace activists make themselves heard. There were protests against the U.S. invasion of Grenada in 1983, and in recent years there have been protests against the U.S. role in El Salvador and Nicaragua and the U.S. bombing of the headquarters of General Muammar El-Qaddafi in Tripoli, Libya. It is safe to assume that as long as there is war, and as long as there is the possibility of nuclear disaster, there will always be a Peace Movement.

CHAPTER SEVEN

THE LATER SIXTIES

The early sixties were a time when young people, and not a few of their elders, were beginning to feel alienated from their government and the other institutions of their society. By the later sixties, this alienation was full-blown and seemed to affect nearly every aspect of American life.

The assassination of President John F. Kennedy in 1963 was a terrible blow to the country, but it was only the first of three murders of major leaders that rocked the nation. In April 1968, Martin Luther King, Jr., was assassinated. In June that same year, Senator Robert F. Kennedy, brother of the slain president, was himself assassinated as he campaigned in Los Angeles for the Democratic presidential nomination. To many Americans, it truly seemed as if the country had gone haywire and that murderers were stalking the best and the brightest of our leaders. All three slain men had been heroes to Americans who described themselves as liberal, and these Americans became especially alienated from the government and law-enforcement agencies such as the Federal Bureau of Investigation. While no one has ever been able to make a convincing connection among the three assassins—Lee Harvey Oswald, who killed President Kennedy, James Earl Ray, who killed Dr. King, and Sirhan Sirhan, who killed Senator Kennedy—to this day there are those who believe that the assassinations were part of some kind of conspiracy to eliminate the leaders who might have done the most to change American society. Similar suspicions remain about the assassination of Malcolm X in 1965.

By the later sixties, the more radical elements in both the Civil Rights and the Peace Movements had gained the upper hand. Among many young blacks, instead of "We Shall Overcome," the call was for "Black Power!" After the violence of the Selma-to-Montgomery march, and the riots in Watts and other urban ghettos outside the South, the tactics of nonviolence seemed out of date. They were replaced by a call to arms. Other racial minorities were making their numbers felt, and for them nonviolence was still a viable tactic. In California, a Mexican-American named Cesar Chavez had formed a union of migrant farm workers, the National Farm Workers Association, earlier in the decade; by 1966 he had attracted many supporters among civil rights workers and peace activists and had undertaken the largest farm workers strike in the history of California, targeting the major vineyards in the state. That March, with the help of sympathizers across the nation who boycotted California grapes, he won the first real contract for migrant workers in the the history of the American labor movement.

Meanwhile, U.S. involvement in the Vietnam conflict had escalated. Instead of polite teach-ins about the war in Vietnam there were violent protests and marches in which the North Vietnamese flag was prominently displayed. President Lyndon B. Johnson, who did more than any other president in U.S. history to get strong civil rights and anti-poverty legislation passed, fell from popularity because of his pursuit of a U.S. victory in Vietnam. Some of his most vehement critics were artists and intellectuals, and as a result members of these groups were no longer as welcome at, or as willing to appear at, the White House as they had been during the Kennedy administration. Now, the talk among radicals was of police as "pigs" who "busted heads," and the underground press circulated step-by-step instructions on how to make bombs. And indeed, bombs were made and buildings burned by such radical groups as the Weathermen.

While some students were protesting their universities' cooperation with industry in making life-threatening chemicals such as napalm, others were becoming caught up in the new technologies. Students were signing up in droves to take courses in computer studies, though having a home computer was beyond the wildest imaginings of most of them. They also marveled at the first human heart transplant (performed in 1967 by South African Dr. Christiaan Barnard) and at America's first manned spaceflights, culminating in Neil Armstrong's walk on the moon in 1969.

The excitement of technology led artists to create Op Art, which featured optical illusions. Paintings and posters showed spirals which seemed to go on forever and used theories of color contrast to play tricks on the eyes. The New Drug Culture helped to spur psychedelic art, whose most famous practitioner, Peter Max, was also strongly influenced by Eastern religions. In September 1966, *Life* magazine produced a whole issue on psychedelic art. Few college students considered their dormitory rooms properly decorated unless they displayed mobiles, psychedelic posters, and weird lighting effects. Incense sticks, which first became popular because of the interest in Eastern religions, were soon in use for creating light shows in darkened rooms.

The most popular music was now acid rock and anything with a lot of electronic synthesizers was considered fashionable—even Bob Dylan had gone electric. In 1967, the first psychedelic albums were released, such as *Are You Experienced?* (Jimi Hendrix), *Surrealistic Pillow* (Jefferson Airplane), *The Doors* (Jim Morrison and the Doors), and *Disraeli Gears* (Cream). Even the

Beatles went pyschedelic that year with *Sgt. Pepper's Lonely Hearts Club Band.*

In fiction, space exploration brought science fiction into the mainstream with such popular books as Michael Crichton's *The Andromeda Strain.* Kurt Vonnegut, Jr., used the excitement and fear of the new technology for social commentary and satire in his popular novels such as *Slaughterhouse Five* (1969). There was also continuing interest in spies and conspiracies, reflecting that strange phenomenon of the early sixties, the Cold War, as well as concern over the assassinations of the two Kennedys and of Martin Luther King, Jr. The interest in Eastern religions led to the reprinting of Hermann Hesse's novels *Siddhartha* and *Steppenwolf.*

But there was greater interest in nonfiction than in fiction, mostly because so much that was happening in the sixties was "stranger than fiction." There were books on the assassination of President Kennedy, among them William Manchester's *The Death of a President* (1967), on Vietnam, including Norman Mailer's *Why Are We in Vietnam?* (1967), and on the black experience, including *The Confessions of Nat Turner* by William Styron (1967). The new interest in Eastern religion led to the reprinting of Kahlil Gibran's books from the 1920s, the most popular of which was *The Prophet.*

The 1966 *Human Sexual Response* by William Masters and Virginia Johnson reflected the greater openness about sex that marked the decade. By the later 1960s, a full-blown sexual revolution was in progress, supported in part by the Pill and by the general sense of rebellion against established customs. Hippies and Yippies preached "free love" and started communes where people of all ages lived together and shared their possessions, their food, and their bodies. The musical *Hair* reflected this sexual revolution. It opened off-Broadway in 1967 and on Broadway in 1968. It celebrated not only long hair, but also drugs, free love, interracial sex, and anti-war and anti-establishment *everything.* In 1969, *Oh! Calcutta!,* a musical revue that featured nude performers, played to sold-out audiences. The number of couples who chose to live together without getting married increased.

Sit-ins and teach-ins on the part of political groups in the early sixties gave way to love-ins and be-ins and happenings on the part of nonpolitical hippies. Two of the largest happenings were the "World's First Human Be-In" in San Francisco's Golden Gate Park in January 1967 and the "Flower Power Love-In" in New York's Central Park in the spring of that same year. Over ten thousand young people, many dressed in exotic hippie costumes and wearing face and body paint, gathered in these two cities for a day of music, dancing, drugs, and celebration. Many hippies stayed on in the cities for the be-ins at Haight-Ashbury's "Summer of Love" and in Greenwich Village.

Hollywood continued to issue mildly anti-establishment films, and one of the most popular was *The Graduate,* starring Dustin Hoffman, about a young college graduate who is confused about the choices open to him, but is determined not to follow the advice of his parents' friends to seek a career in "plastics." Films such as *2001: A Space Odyssey* (1968) reflected the interest in outer space, as well as the new drug culture, with its psychedelic special effects. Films such as *Easy Rider* (1969) and *The Trip* (1967) reflected the drug culture more directly. By the end of the decade, a few black films were being aimed at the mass audience, including Gordon Parks's simple and sensitive *The Learning Tree* (1969) and Robert Downey's *Putney Swope* (also 1969), the first black film to poke fun at black America.

Television continued to be a conservative medium, aimed primarily at selling advertisers' products. Color televisions were in many homes by the late 1960s, and they were the perfect vehicles for pitching products—as well as for programs like "Star Trek." By the late 1960s, the people on television were also more "colorful," as the medium responded to the Civil Rights and Black Power Movements with shows that were about or included black people—such as "Julia" starring Diahann Carroll and "I Spy" starring Bill Cosby and Robert Culp. Television continued to bring history-as-it-happens into American living rooms with live coverage of the assassinations of Dr. Martin Luther King, Jr., and Senator Robert F. Kennedy, not to mention war footage from Vietnam and warlike footage from the streets of Watts during the riots there, and of Chicago during the 1968 Democratic convention. By the later 1960s, even television was broadcasting happenings, with shows like "Laugh-In," which made fun of, among other things, politics, sex, and drugs. Television tried to reflect popular interests and tastes without unduly offending anyone, and sometimes this led to odd combinations for winning shows. One of the strangest was "The Mod Squad," which tried to attract a wide range of viewers by appealing to blacks, women, hippies, and devotees of police stories with its cast of hippies—white man, white woman, black man—who worked as undercover cops.

By the later 1960s, the short mop-head style made popular by the Beatles seemed downright conservative compared with the shoulder-length hair and ponytails favored by white radicals and hippies and the huge Afros worn by many Black Pride advocates. The Broadway musical *Hair* summed up the feelings on the subject in a joyous hymn to the new hairstyles, and the statement of individualism those styles made.

By this time, fashion in clothing, as well as hair, had become strongly political. Blacks wore daishikis to express their cultural nationalism. Hippies wore love beads, headbands, peace symbols, and bell-bottom pants or long skirts. Some wore clothing made from American flags as a rebellion against "my country, right or wrong" patriotism. Everybody wore blue jeans without caring what designer's name was on the back pocket; free-form patch jobs, however, were "in." In most colleges, dress codes had been relaxed to the point of nonexistence, and similar freedoms of dress were percolating down to the high schools.

Even a new style of language had arisen from the counterculture and drug culture: "groovy" and "right on," getting "stoned," "tuning in" and "dropping out," "bad trips" and "crash pads." A host of new slogans were popularized, chanted at rallies, or worn on buttons: the Yippie "Question Authority" and the Peace Movement's "Hey, hey, LBJ, how many kids have you killed today?" and the simple "Peace," with the hand raised in the old World War II "V" for Victory sign.

By the later 1960s, even people who were not involved in politics were taking advantage of the new freedoms of individual style that had been made possible. These people who had avoided political movements earlier in the decade were becoming increasingly involved in activism, especially in the Anti–Vietnam War and Peace Movements. That was true especially of the activist priests who are discussed in the next chapter. At the same time, some people who had been active earlier in the decade were beginning to "turn off" and "drop out" of the mainstream movements, becoming more inner-directed through Eastern religions as well as through the use of drugs. The movements of the late sixties were characterized by both extreme activism and extreme passivity.

CHAPTER EIGHT

THE NEW RELIGIOUS MOVEMENT

In addition to all the other turmoils, the 1960s saw a revolution in religion. Much of the upheaval came in response to what was going on in secular society—the Civil Rights Movement, the Peace Movement—and in response to new liberal lifestyles, and a changing spiritual awareness brought about by the "Peace and Love" Movement, "Flower Power," and a restructuring of the family unit spurred on by the popularity of communes. By 1962 it was obvious that there was a growing "secularization" of life in America: Church and temple membership was down and people's lives no longer centered so much around their religious communities. Great advances in science had called into question many basic religious beliefs, such as the belief in Creation as set forth in the Bible, or the belief that man was earthbound and that the universe "out there" belonged to God (when man began to explore space in the 1960s, people saw that the world did not end because of this unprecedented encroachment). Probably the most shocking concept advanced in the 1960s was the notorious "God is Dead" idea. The 1960s also saw a greater awareness, at least on the part of citizens of an affluent country such as the United States, of other cultures. Because of jet travel and mass communication, such as television and radio, newspapers and magazines, the world had truly grown smaller. Because of the bomb with its threat of mass annihilation, people and nations with very divergent views had to learn to live with one another.

A revolution in the Catholic Church began with the Second Vatican Council, which Pope John XXIII convened in October 1962. It was the function of the Vatican Councils to address the reality of a changing world. Vatican I had been convened nearly a century earlier, in 1869, to deal with the bewildering effects of an ever-widening industrial revolution. Vatican II addressed the effects of the technological and scientific revolution on the Catholic Church. For the first time, observers from Protestant and Greek Orthodox churches (traditionally regarded by the Catholic Church as heretical) were invited to attend and were consulted during debates. The sixteen decrees handed down by Vatican II were no less revolutionary. They provided for masses to be said in the national languages of parishioners instead of in Latin, gave more power to bishops (in effect, decentralizing the power of Rome), committed the Church to work with other Christian faiths, and expressed the Church's position on peace and war, world poverty, industrialism, and social and economic justice.

They also condemned anti-Semitism and launched a major attempt to rectify the ancient anti-Jewish record of the Church. This movement was applauded by Jews, who enjoyed in the United States, particularly in the early 1960s, a period when there was little overt anti-Semitism. Jews were active in the Direct Action Civil Rights Movement. In the later 1960s, however, the Black Power Movement seemed to turn against Jews, and Jews, in turn, began to fear that the economic and social gains of blacks would be won at Jewish expense. Jews were also active in the Campus and Peace Movements, and as the sixties wore on, there were problems within Jewish communities as urban working- and lower-middle-class Jews complained that middle- and upper-class Jews cared more about intellectual causes than about less fortunate Jews. The focus of American Jewish interests changed in 1967, when Israel attacked Jordan, Syria, and Egypt and the Six-Day War ensued. American Jews rallied to Israel's cause and there was not only an increase in Jewish American aid to Israel but also increased immigration to Israel on the part of American Jews. Among the middle-class and intellectual young Jews who stayed behind, however, there was no reason not to combine an increased commitment to Israel with a continued commitment to fighting social and political injustice in the United States. For most, being Jewish did not preclude being activist.

It was different for American Catholics, especially Catholic priests. For them, the results of Vatican II were crucial; either the decrees meant that they would have to change their traditional ways of ministering to their parishioners and interpreting Catholic doctrine, or the decrees meant that they were finally free to relax some of the more rigid aspects of Church teachings. For Daniel and Philip Berrigan, the results of Vatican II were a step in the right direction, but were hardly cause for rejoicing. They doubted that the Church, like the American system, really had the ability to change in any fundamental way.

DANIEL AND PHILIP BERRIGAN

The Berrigan brothers, both of whom were priests (Daniel was a Jesuit, Philip a Josephite), had already decided that the Church had become stodgy and ingrown and was shunning its responsibilities to the world's poor. Philip, the younger brother, came to this realization first, but Daniel was not far behind. In the latter half of the 1960s, the names of the two brothers were linked together in a number of political and religious controversies.

Both spent time in the early sixties working in black ghettos. Philip worked closely with CORE, SNCC, and other civil rights organizations. Participation in the Anti-War Movement and fighting the draft seemed a natural next step. In October 1967, he and three other men went to the Customs House in Baltimore, Maryland, and in an act of civil disobedience poured animal blood on the Selective Service files kept there. All four were arrested and on April 1, 1968, brought to trial on felony charges, for which they were convicted. On May 17, while awaiting sentencing, Philip Berrigan, accompanied by another member of the "Baltimore Four," two nuns, his brother, Daniel, and four other churchmen, went to Catonsville, Maryland, and burned draft records there using homemade napalm. The following June, the State of Maryland brought suit against the "Catonsville Nine" on the same charges which the Baltimore Four had faced.

Both Daniel and Philip Berrigan are writers. Daniel is a poet as well as a prose writer. The following is the introduction he wrote for Philip's 1970 book, *Prison Journals of a Priest Revolutionary.*

THE BREAKING OF MEN AND THE BREAKING OF BREAD: AN INTRODUCTION

On April 1, 1968, the trial of the "Baltimore Four" opened in the federal court of that city. David Eberhardt, Tom Lewis, Jim Mengel, and Phil Berrigan went on trial for pouring of blood on draft files in the Customs House in October of the previous year.

Three days prior to the opening of the trial, the government dropped the most serious of its charges, that of conspiracy. There remained three felony charges: hindering Selective Service operations, disrupting them, and destroying Selective Service records.

The night before the trial opened, President Johnson ordered his bombers home; no more forays over North Viet Nam. I remember how we received the news—as men who were accustomed only to bad news, suddenly and unexpectedly granted a breakthrough. It was as though we had surfaced with bursting lungs after a long and dangerous submersion. Indeed, the hope we were going on was a precarious resource. We seemed to be thrashing about, functioning without organs and limbs, our hearts almost ceasing to beat.

Then suddenly, a strange onset, a new emotion, so long absent from our lives so as to seem almost a myth. The President had stopped the bombing. Could Americans make it after all, racist and bellicose as we were?

Alas, alas. Johnson stalked off, a sullen marauder, recouping his losses as best he might. Kennedy died, McCarthy faded, Nixon came on; last year's Halloween was this year's political charade. The war goes on. For all we know at present writing, the incumbent and his palace court might bequeath the Viet Nam war, a mad national treasure, to a presidential successor in 1972, he to the next in line, and so on. For all we know, for all our scanning of the owlish eyes of Kissinger [Secretary of State] or the iron scowl of Mitchell [Attorney General], our leaders might see a new thing coming; a war in which the vets of 1965–69 will someday, from wheelchairs, send off their grandsons to bleed and let blood, for the sake of some fictive "finest national hour," under the aegis of some Asian bullyboy, thereafter to be hailed as "one of the two or three finest statesmen of the world."

And what of the impact of the war upon the Church? Officially speaking, in the Catholic instance, the sacred power has quite simply followed the secular, its sedulous ape. Bishops have blessed the war, in word and in silence. They have supplied chaplains to the military as usual and have kept their eyes studiously averted from related questions—ROTC on Catholic campuses, military installations, diocesan investments.

And yet, in a quite astonishing way, the war has shaken the

Church. Indeed, for the first time in the history of the American church, warfare has emerged as a question worthy of attention. A number of priests are in trouble on this deadly serious and secular issue. Consciences are shaken, the law of the land is being broken.

The good old definition of church renewal (everything in its place, children seen and not heard, virtue its own reward, a stitch in time, a bird in the hand, render unto Caesar) is shattered. The hope for strong, open, affectionate relationships between bishops and communities is dissipated. The war has deepened and widened the chasm; the bishops spoke too late and acted not at all. So the war, along with questions like birth control, the survival of school systems, speech and its unfreedoms, control of properties and income, has made less and less credible official claims to superior wisdom and access to the divine will . . .

The trial of the Baltimore Four is over, the sentence has been passed. Six years for Philip Berrigan and Tom Lewis, the chief protagonists. Catonsville followed, raining fire upon the files, a new instrument of destruction. Punishment also descended with all deliberate speed—concurrent sentences for Philip and Tom, 2½- and 3-year sentences for the others.

And the war went on, a Marat-Sade [Jean-Paul Marat, a leader of the radicals in the French Revolution of the 1790s, and the Marquis de Sade, a nobleman with strange sexual tendencies who supported the French Revolution] Johnson-Nixon mad-house farce. There was no letup; we, and others like us, were in for it; a long, long push up Sisyphus Hill [in a Greek myth, a man named Sisyphus is doomed to spend eternity in Hades pushing a rock up a hill, only to see it fall back down every time].

And yet, something else has happened. In Catonsville, more hands than ours have stretched out, to block the brute gravity of that boulder. The Boston Two, the Milwaukee Fourteen, the D. C. Nine, the Pasadena Three, the Silver Springs Three, the Chicago Fifteen, the Women Against Daddy Warbucks, the New

York Eight, the Boston Eight, the East Coast Conspiracy to Save Lives (the Philadelphia Eleven). Thus goes the current score; Mr. Nixon and his advisers and generals seem determined to extend it. Let the decision be theirs.

If there is one feature common to all the draft-file attacks, it is that they were invariably planned, and in major part executed, by Catholics. The fact is all the more remarkable, in the face of the official stance of the Church; in face also of the dissolution of the Left, broken by the repeated blows of national policy and factional despair. The Catholic community, that sturdy and well-fashioned hawk's nest, has suffered an invasion of doves; against all expectations, against nature and (they say) grace, a cross-breeding has followed.

Indeed, the Four of the Customs House—Mengel, Eberhardt, Lewis and Berrigan—got something going. Their hands reached deeply into the spring of existence, cleared away the debris and filth, and set the pure waters running again. Some of us drank there, and took heart once more.

Maybe there was something about this Catholic tradition after all! We used to joke about it, in jail or out, reading our New Testament, breaking the Eucharist, battling to keep our perspective and good humor, trying with all our might to do something quite simple—to keep from going insane. Can it be that in this year, in this age of man, sanity requires so close a struggle? Is sanity so rare a resource on the American scene? Silone [an Italian Socialist] said once: It is difficult, but it is necessary, above all, to know who is insane and who is not.

Here are a few criteria:

It is madness to squander the world's resources on lethal military toys, while social misery and despair rise around a chorus of the damned.

It is madness to create the illusion of political or social change, all the while standing firm for spurious normalcy.

It is madness to renege on one's word, by activity which plays out the game one pretended to replace.

It is madness to ignore, with special savagery and determination, the viable and impassioned activities in our midst . . .

During World War II, I was tucked away in a seminary in the Maryland hills. We followed the war with maps and radios, a safe alternative. War raised no questions among us, it had no place in the sacred curriculum; we rejoiced and sorrowed and carried flags and paraded, even after Hiroshima [the Japanese city where the United States first exploded an atom bomb]. It was the worst conceivable method of transforming boys into men. Immunity from the grievous facts of modern war was part of an arrangement designed to keep us "pure" of bloodshed. In fact, the system did something else; it made us opt for complicity in an activity it purported to free us from. The source of our immunity was bad history; inevitably, it rendered us impure.

But we were to learn the truth later; and even then, only a few of us learned it at all.

Philip fought in World War II. He was a soldier's soldier, decorated and commissioned in the European theater.

One prospective juror at his trial was an old lady; her son was a chaplain in the armed forces. The judge asked, "Would you be capable of coming to an unbiased conclusion in this case?" She answered, "I would, with the help of God."

It became clearer, as the jurors were questioned, how nearly impossible it was to come upon an American who was not, in some tragic and real way, through relatives or friends or emotional bias, involved in the war game. Wars—World I, World II, Korean, Vietnamese, Cold, Hot—the choices were rich, a technological feast.

After his ordination, Philip spent several years in ghetto parishes and schools in Washington, New Orleans, and Baltimore. He was undergoing a kind of boot-camp training, the creation of a dedicated activist. From the beginning, he stood with the urban poor. He rejected the traditional, isolated stance of the Church in black communities. He was also incurably secular: he saw the Church as one resource, bringing to bear on the squalid facts of racism the light of the Gospel, the presence of inventive courage and hope. He worked with CORE, SNCC, the Urban League, the forms of Catholic action then in vogue. He took Freedom Rides, did manual work of all kinds, begged money and gave it away, struggled for scholarships for black students . . .

[In the Baltimore ghetto] he set about organizing in the inner city. Housing was the main issue locally; so was the war, for the poor were the first victims of the roundup. In all the troubled days that followed, I remember how the poor people stood with him and with his friends.

The Vatican Council found him only mildly interested.

And I think now, in the light of all we have endured since, how correct his detachment was; no illusions made for no disillusion. Both he and I were cooled, I think, by our sense of the pervasive cultural illness of the American Church, its illusion about moral superiority, its massive victimization by racism, by cold- and hot-war fervor, by anticommunism. We suspected that the Council would offer only a limited kind of help. Those who were acting on the assumption of instant change from Rome were bound, someday, and soon, to be put down hard . . .

I sat in court; my brother was a defendant; it was a new scene for priests. And I thought of the delicious logic which had brought him to such a place. The war would continue, other priests would be drawn into trouble. But Philip was the first. As far as we can discover, he was the first priest to be tried for a political crime, to be convicted and imprisoned . . .

I sat in the courtroom, still a spectator. And I thought how inconceivable it was that Philip should have been spared. For he is free, lucid, and fearless. He is a public man who chooses his issues, one or two at a time, one or two in a lifetime. He would say that if the issue is the right one, one issue is enough. It will lead one to all the others.

But what of our brothers, the American Catholic community? Who will lead them, and in what direction? For most of them,

Reverend Philip Berrigan (CENTER) and his brother Father Daniel Berrigan (RIGHT), already facing criminal charges, burn draft records in Catonsville, Maryland.

the war years have been a kind of Dantesque twilight [the reference is to Dante's *Inferno,* a book about a tour through hell]. Nothing is clear. Phantoms and demons mingle, men and trees, no great evil, no great good. Normalcy and numbers are the game. Catholics fit into the cultural landscape so neatly that Kennedy or Johnson or Nixon could fairly count on us for a Sunday blessing in a typical, filthy week of war.

Philip is something else. And this is why Philip stood in that courtroom, stood again with the Nine at Catonsville. It is why he stood with us for a third time, equally angry, equally helpless, for a travesty conducted on duplicate charges by the state of Maryland in June of 1969. Three trials, a few resisting men, a war that wheels around us, coherent as a solar system, implacable as the gods of violence, long gone in madness.

I finish these notes in the autumn of 1969. "Men had hoped," writes [Bertolt] Brecht, "that someday there might be bread to eat. Now they hope that someday there may be stones to eat." Stones for bread; it is the reversal of the old biblical temptation. Everything we used to call hope is gone.

But this may be exactly the moment we were hoping for, in spite of all. For despair is not a proper word to apply to this man Philip, or to his friends. Indeed, it is a time of the breaking of men. And yet one hears, in such lives, in such hands, in a courtroom where justice is corrupted and the innocent stand in ordeal, the sound of the breaking of bread.

As Daniel Berrigan related, Philip Berrigan was sentenced to six years in prison. At first, he was denied bail on appeal. He spent time in the federal correctional institutions at Lewisburg and Allenwood, Pennsylvania. Seven months later, he was released on bail pending appeal. The following June (1969), he stood trial again, with other members of the Catonsville Nine.

Both Berrigans were to be imprisoned at Danbury Federal

Prison in Connecticut, but Daniel chose to resist that sentence. He became a fugitive for four months, embarrassing authorities by appearing via various media to protest the war. Captured on Block Island, off Rhode Island, he joined his brother at Danbury, where he served eighteen months of his three-year sentence and was released on parole in 1971.

That year, 1971, both Berrigans were nominated for the Nobel Peace Prize by U.S. anti-war groups, and the nomination was accepted by the Norwegian Parliament. (However, Mayor Willy Brandt of West Germany won the prize that year.)

While in prison, Philip Berrigan corresponded in secret with Sister Elizabeth McAlister, who shared his radical views. He also worked with his fellow convicts. During the time he was incarcerated at Lewisburg, one of the convicts he "recruited" to the cause was Boyd Douglas, a convicted arsonist, forger, and perjurer who also happened to be a paid FBI informant. Douglas tipped the FBI off about the letters being smuggled in and out. He also informed the FBI that Berrigan, McAlister, and others were planning to kidnap Secretary of State Henry Kissinger and to blow up heating ducts in the Pentagon. Berrigan, McAlister, and six other church men and women were tried in the fall of 1971 at Harrisburg, Pennsylvania, on conspiracy charges. The chief witness against the "Harrisburg Eight" was Boyd Douglas. Although the government was able to prove that the kidnapping and the blowing up of Pentagon heating ducts had been discussed, they were unable to prove that such crimes had actually been planned. The Eight were acquitted of the charges.

In the spring of 1973, Philip Berrigan and Sister Elizabeth McAlister announced that they had considered themselves married, by mutual agreement, for four years. Then they had a formal ceremony. After the announcement of their marriage, Sister Elizabeth accepted a dispensation of her vows, but Berrigan refused to seek any formal permission from the Church. He was later "defrocked," or denied his membership in the priesthood.

Berrigan and McAlister, who retained her maiden name, have

continued to be active in various civil rights and peace causes. In 1980, they helped form a group called the Ploughshares, whose purpose was to damage the weapons of war. In September 1980, they and six others, who came to be known collectively as the "Ploughshares Eight," were arrested for breaking into a factory in Pennsylvania and damaging missiles. Philip and three of the others received jail sentences, and at this writing he is still fighting his conviction. In 1986, he was arrested in another Ploughshares action in Baltimore. In the preceding twenty-three years he had been arrested more than thirty times and had spent more than five years in prison. His wife served two years in prison and was released in 1986. The couple have three children; the youngest is four years old.

Daniel Berrigan also continued his activism, though on a less radical level. In 1979, he was sharing an apartment with four other Jesuit priests on Manhattan's Upper West Side, working part-time in a hospital with dying patients and also teaching courses in black prison literature at a local college. Later in that same year, he and fourteen others were arrested in connection with a demonstration at Riverside Research Institute; the charges were later dismissed.

In November 1986, as an eight-month, coast-to-coast March for Peace ended in Baltimore, both Philip and Daniel Berrigan were there to greet the marchers.

In the Peace Movement, the Berrigans, by virtue of their membership in the Catholic priesthood, called attention to the deep resentment against the Vietnam War and the draft on the part of the people they represented. In the New Religious Movement, they hastened what might be called the declericalization of the Church: Many Catholics began to hold priests and those in religious orders in less awe, and priests and nuns began to turn toward activism in the secular society. The Berrigans also forced more people to think critically about the Church's role in political and social issues.

FATHER JAMES GROPPI

As Daniel Berrigan pointed out, while many of the radical protests against the war in Vietnam and the draft were conceived and executed by Catholic nuns and priests, many other Church people confined their activism to the parishes where they lived and worked. Many in parishes that were predominantly black and poor were drawn into the Civil Rights Movement. Father James Groppi of Milwaukee was among them. Born in that city in 1930, he was ordained a priest in the Roman Catholic Church and by 1963 was assistant pastor of St. Boniface Church, located in Milwaukee's black ghetto.

Groppi was an advisor to the NAACP's local youth council, and he marched in Mississippi in 1964 and in Selma, Alabama, in 1965. In 1967, he led one hundred days of marches and protests in Milwaukee for open housing and incurred the criticism of both city officials and his Church superiors, who issued statements of nonsupport of his activities. Having resisted arrest during the marches, he was tried in February 1968, convicted and sentenced to six months in jail; but the sentence was stayed and after paying a $500 fine he was placed on probation for two years.

The following year he appeared as a guest on the radio call-in program "Night Call" to talk about his civil rights work. Following are excerpts from that program.

THE NEW CIVIL RIGHTS—
SECULAR AND RELIGIOUS
FATHER JAMES GROPPI OF MILWAUKEE

Dell Shields, host: At a time when many of the black militants are asking to do their own thing and rejecting, in many instances, white leadership and . . . cooperation from whites, how is it that you have managed to remain out in front?

Groppi: Well, I think this has a lot to do with the news media. I am a priest in a parish which is predominantly black and in attendance the neighborhood is entirely black, the school is all black, and I am concerned about the needs of the people in my parish, and the needs of these people are what determined my actions. I haven't had time to worry about leadership. I am involved because I am a human being and I'm involved because of the struggle for human justice. I don't think a man can be true to his calling and not exert all of his energy and all of his influence toward wiping out racism in this country and the oppression of blacks by whites, because I think this is the basis of all the problems in our community. I feel this is relevant Christianity, being involved in the needs of our people. This is what determines my actions. I haven't time to think about other things, leadership or whatever you call it. I am a pastor, I am involved. What results from that I cannot help. What I am saying is, people choose their own leaders. I don't need to know whether or not a person can say that I speak for black people. There are many leaders here in the black community, and people will follow them and listen to them if they want.

Shields: Are you satisfied with the progress the churches are making in the area of social justice?

Groppi: Certainly not. We had a horrible incident here in Milwaukee just a few months ago where a teacher in a white school [put] up a picture of Dr. [Martin Luther] King. The Christian mothers in that parish saw the picture and complained about it to the pastor; and the pastor made her take down the picture and then fired her from the school. The pastor is still the pastor of that parish. I think that the church is still stunted in its silence and it hasn't done what it should do in the areas of social justice. We have always had dedicated individuals within the church who have committed themselves totally and wonderfully to the black man's struggle towards equality, but this has always been a minority. We need a hierarchy of the church to come out and speak strongly. I think it is time for the church to get out of the bedroom conflict [the controversy over birth control] and get into the marketplace where it belongs. We spent all this time talking about sex and not enough time talking about social justice.

Caller from New Orleans, Louisiana: The first Civil Rights Bill is a joke because the first amendment of the original Constitution guarantees us freedom of religion. God demands separation of the races; therefore under the First Amendment of the Constitution I remain in segregation as long as we have a regular Constitution. The RC [Roman Catholic] Church, the pope, and all the clergy combined cannot produce any church doctrine on integration. They lie to the people when they say integration is the Christian way of life. . . . Can [you] be man enough to refute my statement from the Holy Scriptures and/or church doctrine?

Groppi: You haven't stated anything from the sacred scriptures that said that God is a segregationist. I think if you looked to the life of Christ that Christ often associated with people who were ostracized, particularly the Samaritans, and he himself was Jewish, of a minority group.

Caller: Oh, Father Groppi, don't be silly. Of course Christ was not a Jew. He was a Judean and an Israelite and there is nowhere in the scriptures that he was a Jew. From the beginning of the Bible to the end is separation of the races. Now stop lying to the people and quote scriptures, not your own ideas.

Groppi: Lady, you are sick; you are a white supremacist, and you are a bigot. Now I fail to see how any person who is a white supremacist and bigot can go to church on Sunday and say he believes in God.

Caller: I am a Catholic excommunicant, and I don't go to church.

Groppi: Well, I don't think you should go to church. That is the one good act you have performed that you don't go to church. You ought to stay out.

Caller from Dallas, Texas: I wanted to ask Father Groppi if I'm mistaken in my view that the church should be the pillar of the community. As a black Catholic, we seem to have had a problem in our parish where we have a priest who doesn't really care about the parish or the parishioners. We have made several requests, indirectly and directly, to either talk with the priest and have him understand our problem or have him removed. Each time we have always gotten the same thing and a different priest . . . and I just don't understand our diocese here. It seems as if we as Negroes are nothing, apparently, to our bishop, as far as his needs and wants are concerned. . . . If you can't find any type of spiritual guidance through your church and you can't talk to your priest about your problems and he tells you he doesn't have time, then where are you to go?

Groppi: I understand what you mean. Are you criticizing the priest because of lack of commitment to black people? Fine, real good. I think it is the real problem with the church that it has always chosen to be noninvolved and that through its silence it speaks. . . . You see, the problem with white racist priests and clergymen is that they are the product of white ghettos, of a racist cultural background, and they don't understand the problems of the people who live in poverty, they don't understand the racist system in which we live, they don't understand that they also have been affected by racism. It is a tragedy, but many of our priests are racists and many of our sisters are affected by the racist cultures in which they live. I think what you ought to do there is, you organize the black parishioners there and you get together with Father and you put it to him . . . you tell him like it is. I don't think there should be any question whatsoever as to how the church stands about the oppression of black people by white America, and I think he has got to commit himself strongly. And if you feel that he is prejudiced, you ought to tell him, well please leave us alone and go out into white America and we don't need any priest in our community who doesn't like black people. And if the priest himself does not ask for a transfer, I would suggest that you get the black parishioners from your parish and you go and see the bishop and you demand his removal. If the bishop isn't going to remove him, then you go for further direct action.

On September 29, 1969, Father Groppi led a takeover of the state assembly chambers in Madison, Wisconsin, to protest cuts in the state's welfare budget. He was sentenced to a six-month jail term on October 17, on the grounds that his actions had violated the terms of his probation; but ten days later Supreme Court Justice Thurgood Marshall ordered that he was entitled to freedom on bail.

By 1970, Groppi had been jailed at least a dozen times in connection with his civil rights activities. He said that he considered going to jail for the cause a "holy act."

He left St. Boniface on June 1, 1970, and was reassigned to St. Michael's, a racially mixed parish in Milwaukee. Six years later, he married Margaret Rozga and left the priesthood, though he remained active in parish work as a member of the pastoral team of St. Michael's. In the early 1980s, he was driving a bus for a living.

THE REVEREND ALBERT B. CLEAGE, JR.

Cleage was a black minister in the United Church of Christ, a Protestant sect, who decided early on that he could not help his parishioners within the framework of the established church system. The main problem, as he saw it, was not so much that the Church was tradition-bound and rigid as that it was basically a white institution. Rather like the black cultural nationalist Ron Karenga, Cleage decided that a new black theology was needed, one that addressed itself to the needs of the black revolution. Unlike Karenga, Cleage did not feel he needed to go outside established Christianity to find black roots.

Born in 1912, the son of Detroit's first black physician, Cleage felt called to the ministry as a youngster. He was educated at the liberal institutions of Oberlin College and the University of California at Los Angeles, then returned to Detroit to serve as pastor to both black and racially mixed congregations and to work for integration. As the black population of Detroit increased before and during World War II, so did the poverty and unemployment in black communities. And so did tensions between blacks and whites. Cleage, influenced in part by the ideas of Malcolm X, came to believe that most whites had little inclination to work toward bettering racial relations and that the black community would do well to cease relying on whites and concentrate on helping itself. Gradually, he came to feel that a positive separatism was the best policy for blacks to pursue. How could blacks feel pride in their blackness while worshiping a white Christ?

Cleage studied the geography and history of the Holy Land and read whatever he could about countries that had patron saints who were portrayed as black Madonnas holding black Christs, such as Poland, Austria, Portugal, and Costa Rica. He developed a consistent black theology that blended Christianity and black nationalism, and in 1968 he published a book of sermons titled *The Black Messiah*. In his introduction to the book, he explains his purpose in developing a separate theology for black people.

THE BLACK MESSIAH: INTRODUCTION

For nearly 500 years the illusion that Jesus was white dominated the world only because white Europeans dominated the world. Now, with the emergence of the nationalist movements of the world's colored majority, the historic truth is finally beginning to emerge—that Jesus was the non-white leader of a non-white people struggling for national liberation against the rule of a white nation, Rome. The intermingling of the races in Africa and the Mediterranean area is an established fact. The Nation Israel was a mixture of Chaldeans, Egyptians, Midianites, Ethiopians, Kushites, Babylonians and other dark peoples, all of whom were already mixed with the black people of Central Africa.

That white Americans continue to insist upon a white Christ in the face of all historical evidence to the contrary and despite the hundreds of shrines to Black Madonnas all over the world, is the crowning demonstration of their white supremacist conviction that all things good and valuable must be white. On the other hand, until black Christians are ready to challenge this lie, they have not freed themselves from their spiritual bondage to the white man nor established in their own minds their right to first-class citizenship in Christ's kingdom on earth. Black people cannot build dignity on their knees worshipping a white Christ. We must put down this white Jesus which the white man gave us in slavery and which has been tearing us to pieces.

Black Americans need to know that the historic Jesus was a leader who went about among the people of Israel, seeking to root out the individualism and the identification with their oppressor which had corrupted them, and to give them faith in their own power to rebuild the Nation. This was the real Jesus whose life is most accurately reported in the first three Gospels of the New Testament. On the other hand, there is the spiritualized Jesus, reconstructed many years later by the Apostle Paul who never knew Jesus and who modified his teachings to conform to the pagan philosophies of the white gentiles. Considering himself an apostle to the gentiles, Paul preached individual salvation and life after death. We, as black Christians suffering oppression in a white man's land, do not need the individualistic and otherworldly doctrines of Paul and the white man. We need to recapture the faith in our power as a *people* and the concept of Nation, which are the foundation of the Old

Testament and the prophets, and upon which Jesus built all of his teachings 2,000 years ago.

Jesus was a revolutionary black leader, a Zealot, seeking to lead a Black Nation to freedom . . .

Basic to our struggle and the revitalization of the Black Church is the simple fact that we are building a totally new self-image. Our rediscovery of the Black Messiah is part of our rediscovery of ourselves. We could not worship a Black Jesus until we had thrown off the shackles of self-hate. We could not follow a Black Messiah in the tasks of building a Black Nation until we had found the courage to look back beyond the slave block and the slave ship without shame.

In recent years the contradiction inherent in the worship of a white Christ by black people oppressed by whites has become increasingly acute. In the Negro Renaissance after World War I the anguish of this contradiction was voiced by poet Countee Cullen in his famous lines:

. . . My conversion came high-priced;
I belong to Jesus Christ, . . .
Lamb of God, although I speak
With my mouth thus, in my heart
Do I play a double part . . .
Wishing he I served were black . . . ?

The widespread repudiation by many black Americans of a white Christ has added to the attractiveness of the Black Muslim movement. But many more black Americans, race conscious enough to reject a white Christ, have been reluctant to embrace Islam in view of the role played by the Arabs in fostering and carrying on the slave trade in Africa. The result has been the self-exclusion of most black militants from any religious affiliations whatsoever.

The only black leader in this country to meet this problem head-on was Marcus Garvey who organized the African Orthodox Church with a black hierarchy, including a Black God, a Black Jesus, a Black Madonna, and black angels. Forty years ago black Americans apparently were not yet ready for Garvey's religious ideas, although to this day, in every major city, individual Garveyites continue to circulate portraits of a Black Jesus. In Africa, however, Garvey's religious ideas played a key role in founding the African Independent Churches which in many countries acted as the center of the liberation movement . . .

The Black Church in America has served as the heart and center of the life of black communities everywhere, but, for the most part, without a consciousness of its responsibility and potential power to give a lost people a sense of earthly purpose and direction. During the Black Revolt following the 1954 Supreme Court desegregation decision, the Southern Black Church found that involvement in the struggle of black people for freedom was inescapable. Without a theology to support its actions (actions almost in contradiction to its otherworldly preachings), it provided spokesmen and served as a meeting place and source of emotional inspiration. In the North, where the black man's problems at one time seemed less pressing, the Black Church has failed miserably to relate itself to the seething ghetto rebellions and therefore has practically cut itself off from vast segments of the black community. The Northern Church has been black on the outside only, borrowing its theology, its orientation and its social ideology largely from the white Church and the white power structure.

The present crisis, involving as it does the black man's struggle for survival in America, demands the resurrection of a Black Church with its own Black Messiah. Only this kind of Black Christian Church can serve as the unifying center for the totality of the black man's life and struggle. Only this kind of Black Christian Church can force each individual black man to decide where he will stand—united with his own people and laboring and sacrificing in the spirit of the Black Messiah, or individualistically seeking his own advancement and maintaining his slave identification with the white oppressor.

To spread his new theology, Cleage founded the Black Christian Nationalist Movement "to rebuild the disunited Black Nation just as Jesus did two thousand years ago." On Easter Sunday, 1967, he unveiled a huge oil painting titled *The Black Madonna* at his Central United Church of Christ in Detroit. In late January 1968, the thousand-member church was officially renamed the Shrine of the Black Madonna.

By the end of the 1960s, there had been a great upheaval in the Western churches, both Catholic and Protestant, and to a lesser extent in Judaism. Some serious religious students had turned to God for answers and, finding no response, they pronounced God dead. One of the most short-lived movements of the decade was the God-Is-Dead Movement.

That movement did have a basis in tradition, however. In the United States, the question as to whether God existed had been asked by theologians in the nineteenth century and again in the 1920s when the "twilight of Christianity" was predicted. In the late 1960s, the basic meaning of the slogan was that modern people lived as if God had nothing to do with their daily lives and was therefore as good as dead.

The immediate reaction by some was expressed in a bumper sticker that read MY GOD'S NOT DEAD—SORRY ABOUT YOURS. By the mid-1970s, there was a full-scale Christian revival, beginning with the Jesus Freaks, Jews for Jesus, and the Born-Again Christian Movement.

Others may have turned away from the Judeo-Christian concept of God, but they did not turn away from faith altogether.

Instead, they looked to Eastern religions, which seemed to offer a radically different alternative. Where the Western religions were struggling to become more relevant, to "solve" human problems, to turn *outward,* Eastern religions like Buddhism, Hinduism, and Taoism stressed a turning *inward.* The religions of Asia stress the reaching of a higher level of consciousness through self-transformation. They employ meditation techniques and physical and psychological exercises such as fasting and chanting. They emphasize the need for a guru, or master. Whereas in Western religions people strive for happiness through the satisfaction of desire, in many Eastern religions the emphasis is on not striving at all, in fact to eliminate all desires.

Western interest in Eastern religions coincided with a movement among psychologists who believe that psychology had the potential not just for curing the sick but for improving humankind. This movement, which began in the 1940s and 1950s and came to be called the Human-Potential Movement, stressed a belief in the perfectibility of human nature. Thus, it had little in common with Western religion, which is based on the idea that man is sinful and can be saved only by believing in God.

That the Human-Potential Movement might have quite a bit in common with Eastern religions was first proposed by a British-born philosopher who lived in the United States, Alan Watts. In 1961, he published an article titled "Psychotherapy East and West," in which he proposed that Buddhism was more a kind of psychotherapy than it was either a philosophy or a religion, at least as those two ideas were currently understood in the West.

Human-Potential Movement psychologists took his ideas to heart and began traveling to India and visiting Buddhist monasteries and ashrams. They began to incorporate elements of Buddhism in their therapies. Naturally, the middle-class Westerners who went into therapy also became interested in Buddhism, and by the late 1960s, there was a virtual invasion of

India by Westerners—backpacking hippies, rock stars, photographers, designers, and so on, all seeking the magic that seemed to be found in Buddhism. Meanwhile, Indian gurus, or masters, began to find great popularity in Western countries such as France and England and the United States. In the 1960s, the most celebrated of these gurus was the Maharishi Mahesh Yogi.

THE MAHARISHI MAHESH YOGI

In his youth in India, the Maharishi Mahesh Yogi was a student of and a close personal aide to Guru Dev, spiritual leader of Northern India for thirteen years. Five years after Dev's death in 1953, the Maharishi undertook a ten-year period of missionary work in the West. His aim was to get ten percent, or at the very least one percent, of the world's population to practice transcendental meditation, claiming that it would be enough to neutralize the power of war for thousands of years. He defined transcendental meditation as turning one's attention inward to the source of thought, which expands the conscious mind and brings it into contact with one's creative intelligence; it brings about a deep and basic connection with the universe and makes inner conflicts disappear. He believed that war, poverty, injustice, and crime would cease to exist if enough people practiced transcendental meditation.

In the West, in a decade when many people were concerned about war and injustice, and many young people felt a deep commitment to change the world, the Maharishi's message was extremely popular.

Most of his published teachings, like those of other Eastern religious leaders, appeared in the form of dialogues, with the Maharishi giving answers to an anonymous questioner. Following is one of his dialogues about the goal of transcendental meditation.

The Maharishi Mahesh Yogi, the most celebrated guru of Eastern philosophy, lectures on Transcendental Meditation to students at Harvard Law School.

THE STATE OF ENLIGHTENMENT

"The goal of the Transcendental Meditation Technique is the state of enlightenment," Maharishi says . . . "This means we experience that inner calmness, that quiet state of least excitation, even when we are dynamically busy."

But activity and quietness seem to be opposites. Isn't it necessary to sit and close the eyes in order to enjoy the peaceful effects of the TM Technique?

"It's only in the beginning days of meditation that one has to meditate in order to experience that silent, quiet level of the mind, that state of pure consciousness. As we continue to alternate the experience of meditation with daily activity, the value of that pure consciousness is infused into the mind. The pure level of consciousness becomes stabilized in our awareness. And when that pure level—the state of least excitation—is a living reality even during daily activity, this is the state of enlightenment. This is life free from suffering, life when every thought and action is spontaneously correct."

But how is it possible for the mind to experience two different states at the same time?

"This is the question. How can the mind be both active and silent? How can we have the state of least excitation in the midst of all activity? What we find is that it is the natural ability of the nervous system to live one hundred per cent of the inner value of life, and one hundred per cent of the outer value. It is only stresses and strains which restrict this normal functioning of the nervous system."

Then it would be necessary to dissolve stress in order to experience the state of enlightenment.

"Yes. And it brings very practical value to life. Even if we forget about 'enlightenment' for a moment—maybe that state seems to be inconceivable—still it is our daily experience that the whole value of life is very little if we are tired, if we are stressed. If we think of a morning when we have not rested well in the night, then we feel so groggy and everything just collapses into dullness and inertia. The *world* is the same as on the other days, but our appreciation of the world is so much less. And with the Transcendental Meditation Technique we have a natural and effective means to dissolve even deeply rooted fatigue and stress. This is the way to unfold full value of life. Even in the first days of meditation we find that our eyes seem to be a little more open, our mind seems a bit more clear. Our feeling towards our friends seems to be more harmonious. And then, as the practice is continued every day, a time will come when we will start living life free from *all* stresses. We cleanse the awareness of all stresses and strains, leaving the conscious mind completely free in its pure value."

Does this mean that evolution toward enlightenment is automatic as stresses are released?

"Yes. When all stresses are gone, the whole appreciation of life is so much greater. Then the value of every perception, every thought, every action, every feeling will be supported by the full value of that pure awareness. This is enlightenment. It is like the ability to maintain contact with a bank even while out in the marketplace."

This would be the experience of the state of pure consciousness at the same time as daily activity. But it's still not clear how the mind is capable of maintaining this pure state in a permanent manner outside of the meditation period.

"What we find is that this ability depends on the condition of the body and nervous system. We have said the mind and body work together. This is true in every state of consciousness. When the body is tired, for instance, the mind doesn't function very effectively. The metabolic rate changes, the brain wave patterns change, and due to that the mind experiences dullness and inconsistency, and then the sleep state of consciousness. Or, if there is another specific type of physiology—brain waves are different, the metabolic rate is different—then we experience dreaming, the dream state of consciousness. And with another type of physiology, a different type of physical activity, the waking state comes up. Waking, sleeping, dreaming—all these three states of consciousness have corresponding styles of physiological activity. The mind and body always work together. Like that, the Transcendental Meditation Technique produces its own style of physiology. Due to that particular style of activity in the body, the mind experiences the state of least excitation, a fourth state of consciouness."

This is referring to the research on the Transcendental Meditation Technique showing very low metabolic rate, orderly brain waves, and so on?

"Yes. Blood chemistry changes, blood pressure changes—the body and nervous systems are functioning in a particular manner and due to that, consciousness has that value of restful alertness, of least activity, of pure consciousness."

During meditation, then, the body is operating in a certain way, and this correlates to the pure state of consciousness—a fourth state. But the question is still how to experience that level of silence at the same time as activity?

"What happens is that during Transcendental Meditation Technique, the mind experiences the fourth state of consciousness. That experience takes the nervous system to a particular style of functioning. As we repeat our meditation, this inspires the nervous system to function in that new style more and more. It's the nature of life. Something is more fulfilling and life goes for it."

The nervous system gets used to functioning in this way?

"It gets into that habit. This is how the experience of pure consciousness is infused into the conscious thinking level of the mind. It's like the principle of dying a cloth. We take a white cloth, dip it in yellow color and then put it in the sun. In the sun the color fades away, but it doesn't fade away completely. Dip it back in the color, put it back in the sun, and more of the color remains. Just like that, we meditate morning and evening, dipping the mind in that pure awareness and then exposing it to action. In action, the value of pure awareness fades, but it doesn't fade away completely. Meditation and action—this is the procedure which stabilizes that pure awareness. This gradual and systematic culturing of the physical nervous system creates a physiological situation in which the two states of consciousness exist together simultaneously. And once it's done, it's done forever. Once the cloth is colorfast, it doesn't fade."

And then the nervous system maintains the ability to contact the state of least excitation even while functioning in the waking state of consciousness?

"Or in the sleep state. Or in the dream state. And in this is eternal freedom for every human being, like having the full wealth of the bank in your pocket at all times. There are changing values on the surface of the mind and then there is that non-changing steady state of the mind deep inside. And this is not just in fanciful thinking, but in the transformation of the physiology to maintain that pure state of consciousness in a permanent manner. And the research shows that with the Transcendental Meditation Technique, progress begins in this direction right from the first day of meditation. All the studies are there to indicate that a man develops inner stability and at the same time increases in his ability to adapt to the environment. The nervous system becomes more stable even under stressful stimuli. What we notice from this is that we seem to have our feet more on the ground. We are finding stability. We are finding more contentment within ourselves. We are experiencing the growth of that pure level of consciousness."

And all that is necessary to experience this growth is to meditate?

"What is important is the *alternation* of the Transcendental Meditation Technique with daily activity. Rest and activity—this is the way to grow in enlightenment—to live free from suffering, to live life in bliss consciousness. Now with this knowledge there is no reason why every man cannot enjoy life at full potential, why he cannot experience unshakeable peace and joy in the midst of great successful, dynamic activity."

The Maharishi's message appealed to the young people of the 1960s. Based in California, the center of the Human-Potential Movement, the Maharishi had become a media celebrity by the middle of the decade, and the celebrities' guru as well, counting among his followers the Beatles, the Rolling Stones, and Mia Farrow. From the end of 1967 through 1968, he was the subject of cover stories in *Time, Life, Newsweek, The New York Times Magazine,* and other major publications. He was a guest on "The Tonight Show" with Johnny Carson. As a result of all this attention, many of his critics branded him a publicity-seeker. If he sought only the spotlight, however, it is unlikely that he would have returned to India, which he did at the end of 1968, which marked the end of his ten-year mission to the West. Though he and his message had received wide publicity, he had not managed to get even one percent of the people in the West to engage in transcendental meditation. He now occupies a respected position as a religious leader in India and attracts a substantial number of students from the West, but he had little impact on Western thought.

Other gurus and religious leaders have taken his place. In fact, it can be said that the Eastern religions have been taken into the so-called great American melting pot. Today, the Reverend Sun Myung Moon, despite his problems with the government tax authorities, influences the lives of many young Americans. The Hare Krishna sect has a loyal following. The Baghwan Shree Rajneesh presided over an entire town in Oregon, called Rajneeshpuram, until, facing illegal immigration charges, he was forced to leave America in 1986. Internal conflicts caused the followers he left behind to disperse.

Those who actually belong to such Eastern religious sects

represent a small proportion of the population. But some of the concepts, such as meditation, have been adopted for nonreligious purposes. Dr. Timothy Leary, who will be discussed at greater length in the next chapter, went through a deep involvement in Eastern religions himself. He suggested that the "new religiosity" that began in the 1960s "was part of our wonderful aristocratic American consumerism, the insatiable American televoid brain demanding new sensations, new surprises, new heroes, new reality scripts."

Whatever effects the Eastern religions had on Americans in the 1960s, they did not present any real threat to established Western religions. Indeed, it may be argued that the very upheaval of the 1960s breathed new life into religion in general, and may have helped plant the seeds for the Born-Again Christian Movement of the 1970s and 1980s. By the late 1960s, there had arisen in California, specifically in the Haight-Ashbury district of San Francisco, a movement of "Jesus Freaks," primarily young drug addicts who were desperately seeking a way out of their misery. They had fallen victim to another movement of the 1960s, the New Drug Culture.

CHAPTER NINE

THE NEW DRUG CULTURE

The New Drug Culture was the opposite of the activist political movements of the 1960s. In some ways, it might be viewed as the forerunner of the 1970s "Me Decade," during which people turned inward and ceased to care about what was going on in the world around them. The first proponents of the New Drug Culture considered drug use a political act, and espoused the use of drugs while at the same time engaging in political activities. But the majority of their followers didn't seem to have the ability to use drugs as a political tool. They simply became addicted.

Drug use in America has a long history and did not originate in the 1960s. Soldiers returned from World War I addicted to morphine, which had been used to treat their injuries. Coca-Cola, when first introduced, contained cocaine. Sigmund Freud, the founder of modern psychology, used and prescribed cocaine. Opium arrived with the first Asian immigants, and laudanum, an alcoholic solution of opium, was widely used up through the end of the nineteenth century to treat a variety of disorders. Many literary and artistic personalities, among them Samuel Taylor Coleridge and Edgar Allan Poe, were addicted to opium.

By 1925, increasing use of opium and marijuana, which had been introduced from Latin America, prompted an international opium convention, which placed controls on the international trade in both substances. The 1930s saw the first federal laws against the use of marijuana. Once the use of these drugs was made illegal, organized crime found a market for them, although at that time it was not nearly as lucrative as the business in illegal liquor had been during Prohibition. With the repeal of Prohibition in 1931, the underworld could no longer make millions of dollars in the illegal liquor business and began to deal in illegal drugs, along with prostitution, gambling, and extortion. Their largest markets for drugs were in poor areas, where people in despair found temporary relief in a shot of heroin or a marijuana reefer. Drugs were in widespread use in the ghettos long before the 1960s, as well as in centers of bohemianism such as Greenwich Village in New York City. In places like Greenwich Village, it was not so much despair as a desire for new experiences that prompted drug use. But bohemians became just as quickly addicted as unemployed ghetto dwellers.

Meanwhile, advances in chemistry made possible the manufacture in laboratories of synthetic marijuana and other mind-altering drugs. The U.S. military experimented with such drugs on its own soldiers in the 1950s, and in recent years the military has been the target of legal suits filed by soldiers who charge that their personalities were altered and their abilities impaired by these experiments. Civilian psychologists were also fascinated by the possibilities of using mind-altering drugs in the treatment of various mental disorders, not to mention alcoholism and other diseases.

These psychologists probably contributed to the attitude among many sixties young people that drugs such as marijuana and LSD (a synthetic drug) were fashionable. The tradition among bohemian intellectuals of using drugs was also a contributing factor. And, since drugs were illegal, using them also represented a rebellion against established authority. A combination of these and other factors contributed to make the 1960s a period of widespread drug use among middle-class young people.

For a lot of them, Dr. Timothy Leary became a kind of guru of the drug culture.

DR. TIMOTHY LEARY

Leary was born in Springfield, Massachusetts, in 1920, the son of a pious Roman Catholic mother and a hard-drinking father. He grew up bright and rowdy and was expelled from high school, silenced at West Point [forbidden to speak or be spoken to by his fellow cadets], and expelled from the University of Alabama. Eventually, at the age of thirty, he received a Ph.D. in psychology from the University of California at Berkeley. A pioneer in "interpersonal diagnosis of personality," he was especially interested in behavior modification, that is, changing the way a person behaves in the course of psychotherapy. Over the next ten years he became well known and respected in the field, and in 1960, he was hired in the Department of Psychology at Harvard University.

The summer of that same year, Leary visited Cuernavaca, Mexico, where he met an anthropologist from the University of Mexico. Mexicans have a long tradition of eating certain mushrooms and mescal to induce altered states while participating in their religious ceremonies. At the urging of his anthropologist friend, Leary ate a sacred mushroom and went through an experience that changed his life. He later said that in four hours he learned more about the mind, the brain, and its structures than he had in all his previous years of study.

Two years later, Leary tried LSD for the first time. Lysergic acid diethylamide is a synthetic drug, a hallucinogenic. It had an effect on Leary similar to that of the sacred mushrooms. Leary

Dr. Timothy Leary, the guru of the drug culture, preaches his message of "Turn on, tune in, and drop out" before a crowd of thousands of hippies gathered in San Francisco's Golden Gate Park.

believed that the human being actually develops several "minds," or neural circuits, over the course of a lifetime and that these minds could be selectively turned on and off. He began to experiment with drug-induced brain-change with prisoners and institutionalized mental patients. Achieving great praise for his results, he expanded the range of his experiments, treating students and some very famous people as well. For a couple of years Leary ran what *Newsweek* called "a star-studded psychedelic salon" that included author Aldous Huxley, poets Robert Lowell and Allen Ginsberg, jazz musician Charles Mingus, and actor Cary Grant. But the administrators at Harvard were getting nervous, especially over Leary's use of undergraduate students in his experiments. In May 1963, Leary was dismissed from Harvard, along with Richard Alpert, an assistant professor in clinical psychology who had also been involved in the experiments.

Leary undertook to defend himself by making a thorough study of the use of psychedelic plants in religious history. This study brought him into contact with the Eastern religions of Hinduism, Buddhism, and Taoism, which greatly influenced him. Convinced that LSD—and his work with it—represented a true progression in the historical use of mind-altering substances, Leary decided to take LSD and his mind-altering theories "to the people." He moved to California and started the Castalia Foundation, a center for training in consciousness expansion, began to publish a scientific journal, and went on lecture tours. He also wrote many articles for radical publications. The following article appeared in 1966 in the *East Village Other,* an underground newspaper in New York. To the 1980s sensibility, Leary's use of new pronouns like "SHe" and "hir" might at first seem to indicate an early sensitivity to the incipient Women's Movement. But he uses them only when describing a person who has "turned on" and achieved the divine state of consciousness that is above such considerations as gender differences.

YOU ARE A GOD, ACT LIKE ONE

The experienced psychedelic adept can move consciousness from one level to another. But then the experience must be communicated, harmonized with the greater flow. The "turned on" person realizes that SHe is not an isolated, separate social ego, but rather one transient energy process hooked up with the energy dance around hir.

The "turned on" person realizes that every action is a reflection of where SHe is at. The "turned on" person knows hir world is created by hir consciousness—existing only because SHe has arranged hir sensory and neural cameras to shoot these particular scenes. Hir movements, dress, grooming, room, house, the neighborhood in which SHe lives, are exact external replicas of hir state of consciousness. If the outside environment doesn't harmonize with hir state of mind, SHe knows that SHe must move gracefully to get in tune.

"Tune in" means arrange your environment so that it reflects your state of consciousness, to harness your internal energy to the flow around you. If you understand this most practical, liberating message, you are free to live a life of beauty.

Your State of Consciousness Is Reflected in Your Environment

Let us consider a sad illumination. The Manhattan office worker moves through a clutter of factory-made, anonymous furniture to a plastic, impersonal kitchen, to breakfast on canned, packaged anonymous food-fuel; dresses himself in anonymous-city-dweller costume, travels through dark tunnels of sooty metal and gray concrete to a dark metal room, foul with polluted air. All day he deals with symbols that have no relevance to his divine possibilities. This person is surrounded by the dreary, impersonal, assembly-line, mass-produced, anonymous environment of an automated robot, which perfectly mirror his "turned off" awareness.

When this person "turns on," SHe sees at once the horror of hir surroundings. If SHe "tunes in," SHe begins to change hir movements and hir surroundings so that they become more in harmony with hir internal beauty. If everyone in Manhattan were to "turn on" and "tune in," grass would grow on First Avenue and tieless, shoeless divinities would dance or rollerskate down the carless streets. Ecological consciousness would emerge within 25 years. Fish would swim in a clear-blue Hudson.

Every action of a human being reflects his state of consciousness. Therefore, every person is an artist who communicates his experience. Most people are not "tuned in" consciously. They experience only in terms of static, tired symbols. Therefore, their actions and surroundings are dead, robot art.

After you "turn on," you must "tune in": start changing your dress, your home, to reflect the grandeur and glory of your vision. But this process must be harmonious and graceful. No abrupt, destructive, rebellious actions, please! Start "tuning in" through your body movements. Walk, talk, eat, drink like a joyous, forest-dwelling god.

Next, change your dwelling place. If you have to live in the city for the time being, arrange your apartment so that it becomes a shrine. Your room should reflect a timeless, eternal beauty. Every object should make immediate sense to the sense organs of a visitor from the 6th century B.C. to the 20th century.

When you have made your body a sacred temple and your apartment a navigational, seduction cabin in a 20th-century time-ship you are ready to change your broader social commitments. Do not "drop out" until you have "tuned in." Do not "turn on" unless you know how to "tune in," or you will get "hung up!" Every "bad trip" is caused by the failure to "tune in." Here's why . . .

When you "tune in" you open up neural receptors. Cannabis [marijuana] flicks on sensory receptors, hashish [the most potent grade of cannabis] somatic receptors, LSD cellular and molecular receptors. These forceful energies cannot be harnessed to a hive-ego game board. You cannot hook up 100 million years of sensory-somatic revelation in your puny, trivial-personality chessboard. You cannot access 2 billion years of evolutionary revelation to your petty social program. This is why marijuana and LSD, if used in a closed system, will, sooner or later, freak you out.

Of over 5,000 persons who have begun the yoga of LSD with me, the large majority could not harness their reactivated energies to a more harmonious game. You cannot take LSD once a week and stay rigidly rooted in a low-level ego game. You have to grow with the flow, or you will stop taking LSD. To continue to use LSD, you must generate around you an ever-widening ring of "tune in" actions. You must hook up your inner power to a life of expanding intelligence.

Exercises

1.) Go home and look at yourself in the mirror. Start changing your dress, your behavior, so that you float like a god, not shuffle like a robot.
2.) Look around your home. What kind of dead robot lives here? Start throwing out everything that is not "tuned in" to your highest vision.
3.) Make your body a temple, your home a shrine.
4.) You are a God, live like one!

By the time that article appeared, LSD had come under the restrictions of the Drug Control Use Act of 1965. Leary had testified against this proposed law, which essentially outlawed LSD, but was unsuccessful in persuading Congress not to pass it. In 1967, results of laboratory studies linking LSD to genetic damage began to appear in scientific literature. Neither the 1965 law nor the medical reports stopped Leary and others from using LSD or other drugs.

Leary's determination to stay "tuned in" and "turned on" brought him into contact with a variety of other sixties stars and movements. In 1970 he ran for the governorship of California and got John Lennon to write the song "Come Together" for his campaign. Jailed for possession of a small amount of marijuana in 1970, he managed to escape from prison with the help of the Weathermen, and ended up in exile in Algiers with Eldridge Cleaver. U.S. authorities finally caught up with him in Afghanistan. Over the next thirteen years he was jailed forty times, mostly for drug possession, and served forty-four months altogether.

In the early 1980s, Leary reemerged as a kind of grand old man of the good old days. He published a book in 1982 called *Changing My Mind, Among Others.* The following year his *Flashbacks* was published. Both were about his heyday, the 1960s. In April 1983, he and Richard Alpert, the man who had been dismissed from Harvard with him twenty years earlier, returned to Harvard at the invitation of students there. Leary gave a lecture on his experiences with drugs and the mind. Crowds of students had to be turned away from the lecture hall. Meanwhile, Leary had gone on the college lecture circuit with an unlikely debating partner, G. Gordon Liddy, the mastermind of the Watergate break-in of 1972. Before his involvement in the Nixon administration, Liddy was assistant district attorney in Dutchess County, New York, and had prosecuted Leary for illegal possession of narcotics in 1966. They were called the "odd couple." A filmed documentary of their public debates was titled, appropriately, *Return Engagement.*

Drug use is a terrible problem in the United States today. Drugs are killers, and it is not the intention here to make light of the drug problem. Drugs ruined lives in the 1960s—and far more poor black lives than middle-class white ones. But Leary and Jerry Rubin, the chief spokesmen for the New Drug Culture of the 1960s, had a sense of humor. One might argue that they laughed because they had drug-scrambled brains. But it might also be said that they had a keen sense of the power of the media; they knew that humor was, and is, more salable than somberness. Timothy Leary actually consulted Professor Marshall McLuhan, who in the sixties was the most famous and devoted student of the media. Jerry Rubin, on the other hand, seems to have needed no coaching.

JERRY RUBIN AND THE YIPPIES

Jerry Rubin was born into a middle-class, hard-working family. His father was a labor organizer and a child of the Depression who wanted to give his children the things that he had not been able to have. Jerry got a car of his own at the age of sixteen. He attended a prestigious high school. He went to Oberlin College for a year, then transferred to the University of Cincinnati. While at Cincinnati he was sports reporter for the *Cincinnati Post* and *Times-Star*. After graduation from the University of Cincinnati, he spent a year and a half in Israel. Then he went to California and enrolled in the graduate program at Berkeley. There, he was radicalized.

He participated in the Free Speech Movement. He dodged the draft. He ran for the office of mayor of Berkeley. In the fall of 1967 he moved to New York and became project director of the anti-war March on the Pentagon. By 1968, he and his friend Abbie Hoffman had founded the Yippies, which stands for the Youth International Party.

The Yippies were hippies, but—well, crazier. They were New Left radicals, but crazier. Theirs was a no-holds-barred approach that challenged just about every custom of society. When called to appear before the House UnAmerican Activities Committee in Washington, D.C., Rubin showed up wearing a Santa Claus suit. For other committee hearings he dressed as a bare-chested, armed guerrilla and a Revolutionary War soldier. The Yippies worked closely with other radical groups. Rubin was Eldridge Cleaver's vice presidential choice on the Peace and Freedom Party ticket in 1968. Rubin and Hoffman were members of the Chicago Seven, and were tried for disrupting the 1968 Democratic convention in Chicago. But Rubin and the Yippies came off as less serious than other radicals of the time. The very nickname, Yippies, was more humorous then evocative of any political stance, at least in the traditional sense of the word *political.* Their "program" was more reactive than active. Their major purpose was to celebrate youth and anti-establishmentarianism. This is not to say that Rubin and his fellow Yippies did not have serious ideas and causes, but in the main they chose to express their views in playful terms. In the late 1960s, Rubin compiled a book called *DO IT!* in which he expressed his feelings on a wide range of subjects. Here is what he had to say about the controversy over marijuana.

KEEP POT LEGAL

Marijuana makes each person God.

Get high and you want to turn on the world. It's never "my dope"—it's always "our dope." Everything for everybody. The Communist drug.

Pot transforms environments. All the barriers we build to protect ourselves from each other disappear.

Grass travels around the room like a continually moving kiss. Smoke grass in the morning. Stay high all day.

The eight-hour day is the enemy.

When you're high on pot you enjoy only one thing—the moment. A minute feels like an hour; an hour can be a minute. "Damn it, I missed that appointment." All appointments and schedules, times and deadlines disappear. Man can do what he wants whenever he wants to do it.

Marijuana is the street theater of the mind.

Marijuana is destroying the schools. Education is conditioning. Pot deconditions. School makes us cynics. Pot makes us dreamers.

Education polarizes our brains into subjects, categories, divisions, concepts. Pot scrambles your brains and presents everything as one perfect mess.

We fall off chairs roaring with laughter when we hear our professors, teachers, experts—the people we're supposed to learn from—discussing us, our culture, grass. We feel like those primitive African tribes must have felt when Margaret Mead [a famous anthropologist] came popping in with her pencil and paper.

Hearing someone who has not smoked grass talk about it is like hearing a nun talk about sex.

The only expert is the person who does it.

The family that smokes together stays together.

Pot is a magic drug because it can transcend the generation gap. Everyone should try to turn on his parents. Marijuana enables the old to become young again; it breaks down defenses parents have about their past.

But it is the rare parent who will even try it. Parents talk about marijuana the way their parents talked about masturbation. How many thousands of kids have been sent to mental hospitals by their parents because they smoke pot? Schools aren't effective enough as prisons: Once inside a mental hospital there's no way out.

Professors are afraid to go to parties with students because they may be handed a joint. And joints are illegal. If joints are illegal, they might get busted. If they get busted, they lose their jobs. The logic of fear. People who fear have nothing to teach us.

In 1968, marijuana became rampant in the army. In 1969 low morale, even civil disobedience, became rampant in the army.

Why does grass inspire the Viet Kong and kill the fighting spirit of the American GI? Any pot-smoker can understand it: Marijuana is a truth serum. The Viet Kong are defending their parents, children and homes—their deaths are noble and heroic. The Amerikans are fighting for nothing you can see, feel, touch or believe in. Their deaths are futile and wasted. "Why die on Hamburger Hill?" asks the pot-smoking Amerikan soldier, as he points his gun at the head of the captain who ordered him to take a hill that only the Viet Kong want.

If the Pentagon tries to stop pot in the army, she'll end up destroying her army in the process. But if the army brass leaves grass-smokers alone, army bases will soon be as turned on and uncontrollable as college campuses.

What's going to happen when all those Amerikan GI's come home? "What do you mean, we're old enough to fight and die but not old enough to smoke?"

The New Left said: I protest.
The hippies said: I am . . .

Make pot legal, and society will fall apart.
Keep it illegal, and soon there will be revolution.

Rubin was one of the five members of the Chicago Seven who were convicted of crossing state lines to incite riot. In November 1972, however, the convictions were overturned by an appeals court on the grounds that the judge in the trial had been prejudiced against the defendants and had committed legal errors. The overturning of his conviction seemed to bring about a change of attitude in Rubin toward the society he had often severely criticized. He ceased his political activity and turned to introspection and group therapy. He moved to Manhattan's eminently straight Upper East Side, got a job on Wall Street, and in 1976 published *Growing (Up) at Thirty-Seven,* in which he admitted that he had indeed gone to Chicago to disrupt the 1968 Democratic convention and the normal life of the city. The government's case in the trial of the Chicago Seven was, wrote Rubin, "right in theory, wrong in specifics." In 1984, in the course of an interview for *People* magazine, he declared that a Yuppie (young urban professional) was just a grown-up Yippie. This put him in direct opposition to his former fellow Yippie Abbie Hoffman. Hoffman attended a Woodstock reunion in a T-shirt that read YIPPIE, SI, YUPPIE, NO. In September 1984, the two began a tour of the country debating the issue "Yippies vs. Yuppies."

WILLIAM BURROUGHS

Whether taken as an act of political defiance, as with Jerry Rubin, or as a way into the glamorous world of Timothy Leary, drugs became very popular with many middle-class youngsters in the 1960s. The drugs themselves, especially the hallucinogens, caused users to feel tremendously powerful and highly creative. It was not unusual for a college professor to receive a student paper with the proud postscript: "I wrote this paper while on LSD." The popularization of the drug greatly disturbed writer William Burroughs. He'd been a drug addict for fifteen years before successfully kicking the habit, and he knew the seamy underside of drug addiction. He identified with the middle-class kids who thought they were doing the "in" thing and had no idea of the consequences.

Burroughs, born in 1914 in St. Louis, Missouri, grew up in comfortable circumstances and graduated from Harvard in 1936. Unsure of exactly what he wanted to do, he took additional courses at Harvard for a time, then held a variety of jobs, including reporter, advertising writer, private detective, bartender, and pest exterminator. During World War II he served in the Army. He became addicted to drugs in New York in 1944 and moved with his wife to Mexico, where he experimented with peyote, cannabis, and other hallucinogens. There, he shot his wife in a tragic accident. After that, he wandered through the jungles of South America, continuing his experiments with drugs.

Burroughs published his first novel, under the pen name William Lee, in 1953. It was called *Junk: Confessions of an Unredeemed Drug Addict* and it brought him great popularity among the Beat generation of writers such as Allen Ginsberg and Jack Kerouac. But for Burroughs, drug addiction became a kind of hell, and in the late 1950s he sought treatment in London. Cured, he published under his own name *Naked Lunch,* a satire on the bizarre world of drugs, where all users are victims.

The excerpts on the next pages are from an article Burroughs wrote for the *Village Voice* in 1967. The fact that the *Voice* published such an article indicates that even the radical press (of which the *Voice* was a part in the 1960s) was not as wholeheartedly pro-drugs as might have been assumed. Burroughs is an experimental writer, so the excerpts that follow don't have much punctuation; but it is fairly easy to understand what he is saying once you begin to read.

ACADEMY 23: A DECONDITIONING

The drug problem is camouflage like all problems wouldn't be there if things had been handled right in the beginning considering a model drug problem in the United States where the addict is a criminal by legal definition and the proliferation of state laws making it a felony illegally to sell possess or be addicted to opiates, marijuana, barbiturates, benzedrine, LSD, and new drugs are constantly added to the list. A continual outcry in the press creates interest and curiosity people wanting to try these drugs so more users more outcry more laws more young people in jail. Until even senators ask themselves plaintively

"Do we really want to put a good percentage of our young people in jail?" "Is this our only answer to the narcotics problem?"

The American Narcotics Department [there was no such department; Burroughs used it as an umbrella term for the various government agencies concerned with drug law enforcement] says frankly yes the drug user is a criminal and should be treated as such jail best Rx for addicts expert says the laws must reflect society's disapproval of the addict possessing a reefer cigarette in the state of Texas you will see fifteen years of society's disapproval reflected from decent church going eyes. Any serious attempt to actually enforce this welter of state and federal laws should entail a computerized invasion of privacy a total police terror a police machine that would pull the entire population into its orbit of violators, police, custody, courts, defense, probation, and parole. Just tell the machine to enforce all laws by whatever means and the machine will sweep us to the disaster of a computerized police state . . .

Now the press gives LSD the build-up it's new it's exciting anybody who is anybody in literature and the arts has logged a trip and jolly dull reading too the pop stars are using it it's dangerous it's glamorous it's the thing to do so all the young people hear about it and want to try it that's what youth wants is adventure remember the needle beer in Sid's speakeasy over on Olive Street drunk before you put the glass down well a few illegal beers in Sid's speak was an adventure for Eddie and Bill back in the 1920s only the cops didn't put us in jail just told us to go home those dear dead days now we have a drug problem after shoving a sugar cube [laced with LSD] in every open mouth the press is now screaming to stamp out this evil jumped from a sixth floor window hacked his mother-in-law to death more laws more criminals more young people in jail more pot dogs sniffing through flats and country houses nuzzling young people in coffee bars we now have a "drug problem" that is to say the problem of a number of drugs now in common use varying considerably in destructive action. Pep pills and all variation of the benzedrine formulae present no valid excuse for continued existence. After an overdose of these drugs the user undergoes excruciating depressions, when high "meth heads" may become compulsive talkers who stalk the streets in search of victims when experienced friends have bolted their doors. His mouth is dry his hair is mussed his eyes are wild he's gotta talk to somebody. The whole spectrum of benzedrine intoxication is deplorable. Since these drugs have slight medical indication that could not be covered by a safer stimulant like caffeine why not close the whole ugly scene once and for all by stopping the manufacture of benzedrine or any variation of the formula?

Cannabis is certainly the safest of the hallucinogenic drugs in common use large number of people in African and Near Eastern countries smoking it all their lives without apparent ill effects. As to its legalization in Western countries I do not have an opinion. If English doctors are empowered to prescribe heroin and cocaine it seems reasonable that they should be empowered to prescribe cannabis.

The strong hallucinogenic drugs: LSD, mescaline, psylocybin, dim-N, bannisteria caapi do present more serious dangers than their evangelical partisans would care to admit. States of panic are not infrequent and death has resulted from a safe dose of LSD. . . . Setting aside the factor of tolerance there is considerable variation in reaction to these drugs from one individual to another a safe dose for one tripper could be dangerous for another. The prolonged use of LSD may give rise in some cases to a crazed unwholesome benevolence the old tripster smiling into your face sees all your thoughts loving and accepting you inside out. Admittedly these drugs can be dangerous and they can give rise to deplorable states of mind. To bring the use of these drugs in perspective I would suggest that academies be established where young people will learn to get really high . . . high as the Zen master is high when his arrow hits a target in the dark—high as the Karate master is high when he smashes a brick with his fist . . . high . . . weightless . . . in space.

This is the space age. Time to look beyond this run down radioactive cop rotten planet. Time to look beyond this animal body. Remember anything that can be done chemically can be done in other ways. You don't need drugs to get high but drugs do serve as a useful short cut at certain stages of training. The students would receive a basic course of training in the non-chemical disciplines of Yoga, Karate, prolonged sense withdrawal, stroboscopic lights, the constant use of tape recorders to break down verbal association lines. Techniques now being used for control of thought could be used instead for liberation . . .

The initial training in non-chemical methods of expanding awareness would last at least two years. During this period the student would be requested to refrain from all drugs including alcohol since bodily health is essential to minimize mental disturbance. After basic training the student would be prepared for drug trips to reach areas difficult to explore by other means in the present state of our knowledge. The program proposed is essentially a disintoxication from inner fear and inner control a liberation of thought and energy to prepare a new generation for the adventure of space. With such possibilities open to them I doubt if many young people would want the destructive drugs. Remember junk keeps you right here in junky flesh on this earth where Boot's [a chain of British drugstores] is open all night. You can't make space in an aqualung of junk. The problem of those already addicted remains. Addicts need medical treatment not jail and not prayers. I have spoken frequently of the apomorphine treatment as the quickest and most efficacious method of treating addicts. Variations and synthesis of the apo-morphine formula might well yield a miracle drug for disintoxication. The drug Lomotil which greatly reduces the need for opiates but is not in itself addicting might prove useful. With experimentation a painless cure would certainly emerge. What makes a cure stick is when the cured addict finds something better to do and realizes he could not do it on junk. Academies of this type described would give young people something better to do incidentally reducing the drug problem in importance.

Burroughs has said that drug addiction is counterproductive to writing, and his own literary career seems to bear this out. While an addict, he published only one book, although his correspondence with Allen Ginsberg in 1953 was published as a book titled *The Yage Letters* in 1963 (*yage* is the name given a native hallucinogenic plant by the Indians of South America; during his wanderings, Burroughs experimented with it). Since being cured of his addiction, he has written numerous novels and plays. Among his recent ventures is the production of interactive fiction computer programs in collaboration with Timothy Leary.

Drug addiction is not only counterproductive to writing, it is also counterproductive to political activity. By the middle of the 1960s, a lot of young people had followed Timothy Leary's advice to "turn on, tune in, and drop out." Known as hippies, they congregated in areas such as New York's East Village and San Francisco's Haight-Ashbury district and tried to create new societies where "Flower Power" and "Make Love, Not War" were the operative slogans. They wore long hair and beads, sandals and loose clothing. They spent most of their time either getting or taking drugs. The area in San Francisco around Haight and Ashbury Streets became a center for the "love generation." In the summer of 1967, thousands of young people made pilgrimages to the district to celebrate a "Summer of Love" in a place where, as a popular song put it, they would find "gentle people" who wore "flowers in their hair."

But life in the Haight-Ashbury was not as idyllic as its image suggested. A group called Communication Company, the news center of the San Francisco underground, published numerous pamphlets exposing the myths that clouded the reality of life in the Haight. The bulletin that is reprinted on the following pages was issued in August 1967, in the midst of the celebrated "Summer of Love," and was reprinted in a number of underground newspapers around the country.

HAIGHT/HATE?

Pretty little 16-year-old middle-class chick comes to the Haight to see what it's all about and gets picked up by a 17-year-old street dealer who spends all day shooting her full of speed again and again, then feeds her 3000 mikes and raffles her temporarily unemployed body for the biggest Haight Street gang bang since night before last.

The politics and ethics of ecstasy.

Rape is as common as bullshit on Haight Street.

The Love Generation never sleeps.

The Oracle [a local underground newspaper] continues to recruit for this summer's Human Shit-In, but the psychedelic plastic flower and god's eye merchants, shocked by the discovery that increased population doesn't necessarily guarantee increased profits at all, have invented the Council for a Summer of Love to keep us all from interfering with commerce.

Kids are starving on The Street. Minds and bodies are being maimed as we watch, a scale model of Vietnam. There are people—our people—dying hideous long deaths among us and the Council is planning alternative activities. Haight Street is ugly shitdeath and Alan Watts [the English-born philosopher who devoted his life to bringing Eastern philosophies to the young American masses and was called the chief guru of the counterculture] suggests more elegant attire.

The Oracle, I admit, *has* done something to ease life on Haight Street; it's hired street kids to peddle the paper. Having with

San Francisco's "Summer of Love" drew thousands of young people to the city's Haight-Ashbury district. ABOVE, with fall approaching, members of the movement celebrate the "Death of the Hippie" with a musical wake. BELOW, street people linger on the skid row that sprang up over the summer.

brilliant graphics and sophomoric prose urged millions of kids to Drop Out of school and jobs it now offers its dropouts menial jobs. That's hypocritical and shitty, but it's something. It means that a few dozen kids who can meet the Oracle's requirements can avert starvation whenever the Oracle comes out.

Groovy.

And why hasn't the man who *really* did it to us done something about the problem he has created? Why doesn't Doctor Timothy Leary help the Diggers [a group based in the district that tried to help with free meals, clothes, referrals]? He's now at work on yet another Psychedelic Circus at $3.50 a head, presumably to raise enough cash to keep himself out of jail, and there isn't even a rumor that he's contributed any of the fortune he made with the last circus toward alleviating the misery of the psychedelphia he created.

Tune in, turn on, drop dead? One wonders. Are Leary and Alpert and the Oracle all in the same greedy place? Does acid still have to be sold as hard as Madison Avenue still sells sex? What do these nice people mean by "Love"?

Are you aware that Haight Street is just as bad as the squares say it is? Have you heard of the killings we've had on Haight Street? Have you seen dozens of hippies watching passively while some burly square beats another hippy to a psychedelic red pulp? Have you walked down Haight Street at dawn and seen and talked with the survivors?

By the end of the 1960s, the so-called New Drug Culture was not much different from the old, ghetto-based variety, and in the 1970s, middle-class drug users began to turn away from the more dangerous drugs that had been popular in the 1960s: LSD because of too many bad trips and the real fear that it causes permanent brain damage, and heroin because of the well-publicized deaths of musical stars Janis Joplin and Jimi Hendrix. Marijuana continued to be popular and is one of the most widely used drugs today.

In the 1980s, cocaine is the "in" drug, preferred by many movie and musical stars and those who would "share" their glamour. The Yippies of the 1960s have been replaced by the Yuppies of the 1980s, for whom cocaine use is a status symbol, with no political implications. Drug use in the ghetto now includes not just heroin, but crack, a potent form of cocaine; there is some glamour attached to crack, but as always, drug use in the ghetto is mainly a statement of despair.

CHAPTER TEN

THE LEGACY OF THE SIXTIES

Some people blame nearly every scourge of modern society on the sixties, and in a way they are right. Some people credit the sixties with the best things about modern society, and in a way they are right, too. The sixties were a truly incredible decade, and a complex one, and they affected our lives in many ways.

In race relations, outright racism in areas such as housing, education, employment, and politics is now against the law. Of course, no one can legislate racism out of people's minds and hearts, and black Americans still have a long way to go before they achieve real equality. But they have the vote, and since the 1960s they have used that vote to elect representatives at every level of government. In 1984, the Reverend Jesse Jackson mounted a serious campaign for the Democratic presidential nomination, and while he did not win, he showed that black voting power is a force to be reckoned with in American presidential politics.

Among a large proportion of Americans, obvious racism is no

longer acceptable, and young black Americans can barely imagine what it was like to live in a time when they were legally barred from many public facilities or denied service just because of the color of their skin.

On the campus, students don't even question their right to demonstrate for causes in which they believe (or against causes with which they differ). Back in the 1960s, the question was whether or not students had a right to protest; now, the questions are about the tactics they use in their protests. At Kent State University a memorial to the four students killed by Ohio National Guardsmen in 1970 has been erected on the site where they died.

Minority studies and women's studies are part of the curriculums of most major colleges and universities. The relationships between the university and industry, and between the university and the government/military are much different, and most universities refuse to enter into private contracts with the government or the military without deeply questioning the ethics and morals of these contracts. Overall, the relationship between the student and the university has changed greatly. Some characterize that relationship as a lack of trust on the part of the students. Others suggest that any trust that used to exist was misplaced to begin with and that trust has no place in such a relationship.

Musical tastes have gone through any number of changes since the 1960s, but that decade established the activist kind of music that found its 1980s expression in "We Are the World," a song and album that were created specifically to raise money to feed the starving people in Africa. The sixties generation would have loved the idea of "We Are the World." But at the time the record industry was not sufficiently centralized, nor was recording technology sufficiently advanced, for such an event to take place.

There has been no Black Power Movement since the 1960s, but influences of the sixties version can be felt to this day. There is a greater knowledge of and respect for the African heritage in the larger society, and aspects of black culture are everywhere, from music to fashion to slang—with such phrases as "blow your mind," "bad-mouth," "take care of business," and "get on someone's case."

The Anti–Vietnam War Movement continued into the 1970s after President Nixon expanded the war into Cambodia. In May 1970, more than two hundred thousand protesters staged a huge March on Washington, and while it was an orderly demonstration it resulted in thirteen thousand arrests. Meanwhile, in Paris, representatives of the various sides in the war were talking about peace, and in early 1973 a treaty was at last signed that provided for the withdrawal of all American forces and the return of all American prisoners of war. In April 1975, as the last Americans pulled out of Vietnam, South Vietnam surrendered to the North.

The war left a bitter taste in the mouths of Americans. Some continued to believe that the United States could have won the war if it had not been for the anti-war protests; but most feel that the U.S. should never have become involved in the conflict to begin with. Since that time, Congress has passed laws aimed at preventing the president of the United States from engaging in secret war operations, although the Iran/Contra scandal of 1986–87 proved that such laws were not wholly successful.

The legacy of the Peace Movement can be seen in the active Anti-Nuclear Movement and the Ecology and Whole Earth Movements, all of which aim to preserve life. It can be seen, too, in the protests against U.S. involvement in the affairs of other nations, from Nicaragua to El Salvador. Also, since the 1960s there has been no compulsory draft; administrations since then have preferred a volunteer military.

In the area of religion, American Catholics continue to question some of the tenets handed down by Rome: They accept birth control, abortion, and homosexuality in far greater numbers than other Catholics around the world, and see no reason why they cannot still be good Catholics while refusing to accept *all* Catholic doctrines. The seventies and eighties have seen a huge revival of Christian fundamentalism, whose leaders, such as the Reverend Jerry Falwell, have used the power of their numbers to push political causes such as prayer in the schools and the Anti-Abortion Movement. The eighties may see the first presidential campaign by a fundamentalist leader, the Reverend Pat Robertson. Eastern religions continue to maintain a strong foothold among Americans, and practices such as transcendental meditation are quite widespread.

Drug use is still prevalent among all classes, and this is one of the negative legacies of the 1960s. While drug use may have been a political act for some twenty years ago, it is now either an act of materialism and conformity or an act of despair. It is no longer an act of spirit. The Hippie and Yippie Movements subsided after the early seventies, although in 1984, in Modoc National Forest in California, some twenty-five thousand members of the counterculture held a reunion at which they used drugs openly and conducted an hour of silent prayer on a mountaintop.

During the 1960s and early 1970s, there was deep hatred of the hippies and other counterculture groups on the part of white working-class people. In May 1970, construction workers in New York City broke up an anti-war demonstration on Wall Street and clubbed every long-haired young man they could grab. Ironically, by the 1980s, "hard hats" have come to favor long hair themselves.

The sexual permissiveness of the sixties continued into the eighties, although the herpes and AIDS epidemics have resulted in greater sexual conservatism. Homosexuality became more open and more accepted in the seventies, and this trend is seen as a result of the new sexuality of the sixties.

While the seeds of the Women's Movement were planted in the sixties, the period of greatest activism came later. Using tactics from the sixties movement, women won gains in education and employment, although they failed to get the necessary number of state votes to add an Equal Rights Amendment to the U.S. Constitution. Several states, however, have enacted equal rights bills. In 1984, Geraldine Ferraro, congresswoman from New York, became the first female vice presidential candidate of a major party when Democrat Walter Mondale chose her as his running mate.

The legacy of the sixties will be felt for many years to come. Many of those who were activists in the decade feel nostalgia for a time when questions of what was right and what was wrong seemed so simple. Many who are too young to have participated wish that they, too, could have lived through such a spirited time when it really seemed possible to change the world. What they perhaps do not realize is that they, too, have been affected by the sixites.

What the sixties did, above all else, was to make it possible for people to ask questions—about their lives, their values, their society—and to challenge the things they did not like. For the sixties generation, and the generations since, it is a given that nobody can tell them what to do.

BIBLIOGRAPHY

Archer, Jules. *The Incredible Sixties* (New York: Harcourt Brace Jovanovich, 1986)

Berrigan, Philip. *Prison Journals of a Priest Revolutionary*, compiled and edited by Vincent McGee (New York: Holt, Rinehart & Winston, 1970)

Bogle, Donald. *Toms, Coons, Mulattoes, Mammies, & Bucks* (New York: The Viking Press, 1973)

Clarke, John Henrik, ed. *Malcolm X: The Man and His Times* (New York: Collier Books, 1969)

Cleage, The Reverend Albert B. *The Black Messiah* (Fairway, Kansas: Andrews & McMeel, 1968)

Dorman, Michael. *Confrontation: Politics and Protest* (New York: Delacorte Press, 1974)

Farmer, James. *Lay Bare the Heart* (New York: Arbor House, 1985)

Forman, James. *The Making of Black Revolutionaries* (New York: The Macmillan Company, 1972)

Garabedian, John H., and Orde Coombs. *Eastern Religions in the Electric Age* (New York: Grosset & Dunlap, 1969)

Gettleman, Marvin E., ed. *Viet Nam: History, Documents, and Opinions on a Major World Crisis* (New York: Fawcett Publications, 1965)

Goldwin, Robert A., ed. *100 Years of Emancipation* (Chicago: Rand McNally & Co., 1964)

Haskins, James. *Diana Ross: Star Surpreme* (New York: Viking Penguin, 1985)

———*The Life and Death of Martin Luther King, Jr.* (New York: Lothrop, Lee & Shepard, 1977)

———*Profiles in Black Power* (Garden City, N.Y.: Doubleday & Company, 1972)

———*Resistance: Profiles in Nonviolence* (Garden City, N.Y.: Doubleday & Company, 1970)

———*The War and the Protest: Vietnam* (Garden City, N.Y.: Doubleday & Company, 1971)

Hayden, Tom. *Trial* (New York: Holt, Rinehart & Winston, 1970)

Hine, Thomas. *Populuxe* (New York: Alfred A. Knopf, 1986)

Hirshey, Geri. *Nowhere to Run: The Story of Soul Music* (New York: Times Books, 1984)

King, Martin Luther, Jr. *Why We Can't Wait* (New York: Harper & Row, 1963)

Kornbluth, Jesse, ed. *Notes from the New Underground* (New York: The Viking Press, 1968)

Leary, Timothy. *Changing My Mind, Among Others* (Englewood Cliffs, N.J.: Prentice-Hall, 1982)

Oates, Bob, Jr. *Celebrating the Dawn: Maharishi Mahesh Yogi and the TM Technique* (New York: Putnam, 1976)

Oglesby, Carl, ed. *The New Left Reader* (New York: Grove Press, 1969)

Peck, Abe. *Uncovering the Sixties: The Life and Times of the Underground Press* (New York: Pantheon Books, 1986)

Rubin, Jerry. *DO IT!* (New York: Simon & Schuster, 1970)

Schlesinger, Arthur M., Jr. *The Cycles of American History* (Boston: Houghton Mifflin Co., 1986)

Spitz, Robert Stephen. *Barefoot in Babylon: The Creation of the Woodstock Music Festival, 1969* (New York: The Viking Press, 1979)

Weiner, Rex, and Deanne Stillman. *Woodstock Census: The Nationwide Survey of the Sixties Generation* (New York: The Viking Press, 1979)

Wheeler, John. *Touched with Fire: The Future of the Vietnam Generation* (New York: Franklin Watts, 1984)

Williams, Juan, ed. *Eyes on the Prize: America's Civil Rights Years, 1954–1965* (New York: The Viking Press, 1987)

Wolfe, Tom. *Radical Chic & Mau-Mauing the Flack Catchers* (New York: Farrar, Straus & Giroux, 1970)

Also consulted were the sound recording *Cronkite: The Way It Was: The Sixties,* produced by Walter Cronkite and Fred W. Friendly, and articles from *The Encyclopedia Judaica, Foreign Affairs, Life* magazine, *Newsweek, The New York Times, The New Yorker, Time* magazine, *U.S. News & World Report,* and *The Village Voice.*

INDEX